Restitution

Trans-Canada Killer Series Book 3

J E Friend

ISBN 978-1-9991192-6-3

Publisher: Dark Cellar Publications, <u>darkcellarpublications@yahoo.com</u>

Author: J. E. Friend

<u>www.jefriend.ca</u>

Cover Designer: A. E. Hellstorm at Flying Elk Photography

http://www.flying-elk-photography.com/about-book-covers

Cover photograph: J. E. Friend

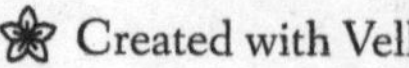 Created with Vellum

For my children, Darren, Tanya and Cynthia. Who have always brought me joy and filled my life with love.

1

The whiny burr of machines drifted through Maggie's subconsciousness, dragging her from a drug induced slumber. A blinding brightness glowed from the overhead florescent lights, forcing her to squint through her already swollen eyes. The pain in her head threatened a wave of nausea as it pounded with a constant thrum. She raised her left hand to shield her eyes from the intense light that emanated, causing a prickling pain to radiate like hot rods imbedded into her emerald orbs. Her hand brushed against the gauze bandages wrapped around her head. Grit grated in her eyes, which caused her to blink before forcing them to open wider so she could observe her surroundings. Her right hand throbbed, she glanced down and noticed the IV line. Below it the swollen and bruised, split skin surrounding her knuckles. With care, Maggie turned her head to look up at the bags of fluid, attempting to focus on the smaller one, containing the medication, but her eyes watered, blurring her vision.

Struggling against the pain, visions of what had brought her here flashed through her mind. Her years hunting the man responsible for killing her father and forever changing her life left damaging threads

1

interwoven into the fabric of her being. The faces of all the deserving men she killed along the way blurred into one. Frank Carter's. Those were the dregs of society, lurking in the shadows just beyond the range of vision of those not affected by trauma and horror. But she saw them. There was always a telling sign to recognize, and she made sure they'd hurt no one again. The ultimate reward for her diligence was watching the man she hunted die. His screams for help as the flames flicked across his skin, was a balm to the torture of her soul.

Attempting to break free of the vengeful monster within herself, she rebuilt her life. And for a brief stint, found happiness with Liam. If she was being honest with herself, it was he who found her. It took time, but his persistence won out. For the first time in her life, since her father died, she felt an immense joy that radiated to the darkest corners of her soul pulsating through the beast, lurking in the cobwebs, pushing it back into the shadows.

The loneliness that became second nature dissipated as they became a family with a child on the way. In the blink of an eye, everything changed because of the Dark Enders. A case of mistaken identity, as the police called it, cost her everything. Her husband, her child, and the ability to have children.

Out of the tragedy, the monster re-emerged, and she made the members of the Dark Enders pay for their crimes. She'd dealt with Butch and Quinn personally, but the fallout of her decision would remain buried in her heart with an ache so deep she no longer believed in happiness. Noelle died because of her recklessness and Maggie's failure to protect her. The images of her broken body haunted her as a reminder that she was the one responsible. It was time to re-evaluate her choices.

'*Another hospital and another hospital bed,*' Maggie thought and winced, shifting painfully on the bed. '*This time, at least, I know why*

I'm here.' Her lips partially curled into a painful grin, knowing that she'd gone against two criminals in one day and somehow survived. She'd been lucky and knew it. If the homeless man hadn't intervened after her battle with Quinn, who knows where she'd be? If she survived, it's likely she'd find herself handcuffed to another hospital bed with an officer guarding her. How would she explain that to Colby? Audrey's quick thinking saved her. She came when Maggie called, took her to a hospital away from the downtown core and Quinn's body, then covered for her.

Maggie inhaled through her mouth, struggling against the ache in her chest as she shifted on the bed, gasping in pain. Everything hurt. She didn't know how bad her injuries were, but this time she knew why. Somehow Quinn found out she killed Butch and he beat her, allowing his anger to overwhelm him. Her ability to defend herself, took him off guard, but she fought and lived. A smile played at the corner of her mouth; she was sure by now Quinn was laying in the morgue.

'One less criminal on the street.' She thought with malice, praying she'd left nothing behind to link her to his murder. If she did, hopefully the homeless man who saved her, found it and stashed it out of sight, like he'd done with her knife.

A movement by the door startled her, and she turned her head to watch as Audrey slipped into the room, carrying two cups of coffee. The aroma drifted to Maggie's clogged nostrils, and she sighed. The doctor may not have ordered the caffeine, but it was just what she needed. She struggled to sit up, but in the end, relented and used the remote control to lift the head of her bed, grimacing as the movement shifted her damaged body into an upright position.

"Oh, thank God, Maggie. I was beginning to think you'd never regain consciousness. It's good to see you're awake. How are you feeling?" Audrey asked as she passed Maggie one of the two cups of coffee and laid a palm against her cheek.

"How long this time?" Maggie croaked. Her voice was hoarse from the damage to her windpipe where Quinn strangled her.

"How long what?" Audrey asked, a puzzled look darting in her eyes.

"How long have I been here?"

Audrey sank into a nearby chair. The telltale signs of stress radiated from her face. Her voice hitched when she spoke. "I brought you in last night. You were a mess, still are, for that matter. You won't be winning any beauty contests in the near future."

Maggie winced. "Have I ever? How bad is it?"

Audrey hesitated before pulling a mirror from her purse and passing it to Maggie. Maggie held up the mirror. As she caught her reflection, her jaw slackened at her reflected image.

A deep shade of eggplant surrounded both eyes. The swelling over one forced it closed, the other hooded with puffy flesh. Now she understood why she'd had difficulty opening them. Gauze packed each nostril, explaining the dryness in her mouth. Now she remembered hearing the crunching sound when Quinn punched her in the face. She lowered the mirror to look at the bruising along her jawline and around her neck. The unmistakable marks of strangulation branded her neck like an angry tattoo.

"I guess it could be worse." Maggie said, rasping. "I don't seem to have anything broken."

"You're wrong. You have several fractured ribs and a tear in your spleen the doctors had to repair. But you're lucky. If it was any bigger, they would have removed it. There is also some internal bruising, but I'm sure the doctor will explain everything when he comes in to see you." Audrey choked the words out and fretted with a speck of Maggie's blood on the cuff of her sleeve.

Maggie lowered the blankets and lifted the hospital gown to see the damage. She sighed when she saw the small bandages over her incisions and realized the doctor did the repair laparoscopically. Her shattered glass tattoo remained intact, but almost her entire midsection bloomed with mottled bruises. Maggie trailed her fingers over the colourful surface and winced at the tenderness beneath her touch.

She brought her hand up to her head to feel the bandages. Her fingers prodded the tender spot, feeling the sharp stitches poking through the gauze. She looked up at Audrey and watched her shaking her head.

"How many stitches?" Maggie asked.

"Does it matter? You had a gash to your scalp, and a concussion. Maggie, if you don't stop your vendetta, you're going to die," Audrey gasped. A small tear escaped from the corner of her eye and trickled down her cheek. "I can't watch you die!"

2

After the doctor came in to update them on Maggie's status, Audrey returned to the house to shower and gather some things to make Maggie more comfortable. The doctor estimated that Maggie needed to remain in the hospital for observation for a few more days. Before she left, Audrey paused, stroked Maggie's cheek, and begged her to get some sleep.

Maggie stared at the empty room and reached for her cell phone. The pay-as-you-go she'd used with Quinn lay shattered along the highway after she tossed it out the car window on their way to the hospital. She looked at the screen and saw all the missed calls and texts from Colby. A frown creased her brow. She needed to respond to him before he worried, but first, she needed a plausible explanation for why she was in the hospital. He couldn't know the truth.

Being a cop, Colby could check the hospital records, and discover she came in after being attacked. There was no sense in hiding that from him, but it had to be a situation where she defended herself, or she'd have a hard time explaining the split knuckles and bruises to her right hand. *'An attempted mugging!'* Maggie thought with excitement, *'it was the perfect explanation.'* She'd tell him someone grabbed her, and she defended herself, and that a good Samaritan intervened. If she explained she was on her way to meet Audrey when it happened and Audrey took her to the hospital, he might believe her.

Maggie contemplated what wording she'd use when telling Colby, then hit the call back button. Beads of sweat dotted her brow and her heart pounded in her chest when she heard his voice.

"Hello Maggie."

Colby left the station soon after he got off the phone with Maggie and now sat in the corner of the darkened hospital room, staring at the sleeping form of the woman he was falling in love with. When he first arrived at the hospital, he stayed out of sight until her friend left for the night. He didn't want to deal with her or her questions. Only then, when Maggie was alone, did he enter the room.

His step faltered when he caught sight of her. Even though she explained about the mugging and trying to defend herself, and he knew what her chart said, nothing prepared him for the visual extent of her injuries. Colby's stomach clenched along with his fist at his outrage that someone had hurt her. But the bruises still didn't hide her beauty.

He sighed, trying to make himself comfortable as he stretched his long legs out in front of him, crossed his arms and contemplated the situation he was in. He struggled to make sense of everything that had happened over the last year, since the Dark Enders killed Liam Murphy. Falling for his widow wasn't in the plan and was probably a mistake, but sometimes these things were out of everyone's control.

Colby glanced back up at the petite woman on the bed across the room. It seemed she was at the centre of everything that had transpired since the shooting, but the dark questions shadowing his thoughts were unbelievable. *'She's a journalist, for Pete's sake. She couldn't weigh more than 110 pounds. There was no way she could be involved with Quinn and Butch's murders.'* He knew she'd revel in the knowledge of their deaths, because of their involvement in Liam's murder, but he doubted she was strong enough to fight off Quinn, or kill Butch. The evidence suggested that Quinn was in a brutal fight before he died. It could only be a coincidence that her attack happened on the same night.

When she returned his calls and told him she was in the hospital, he disregarded the surveillance photo his partner showed him of the red-headed motorcycle rider. There was no way it was Maggie.

While he waited for Audrey to leave, he spoke with the attending physician, and confirmed that her injuries were consistent with a mugging. Her beating was severe and her recovery would take time. It was lucky Audrey found her. If Audrey wasn't there, Maggie would have died.

One thing bothered him as he examined her bruises. He couldn't help but think the attack appeared personal. She was stubborn, but would she have fought off a mugger? Tried to hold on to her purse until the mugger became more and more violent? Something wasn't adding up. All he had were more questions, but they could wait until she recovered.

The call to Colby was more difficult than Maggie imagined. She heard the suspicion in his voice when he answered. He should have sounded concerned after all the missed calls, and when she explained what happened, she wasn't sure he believed her. After ensuring she was ok, he shifted gears, went right into cop mode and fired off a round of questions.

It didn't surprise her when, later that day, an officer arrived to take her statement. A part of her felt disappointed Colby didn't come himself. Nausea rolled through her, clenching at her stomach, and she wondered if Colby believed her.

Her body shook when she woke up the second morning to find him sitting in the chair across the room, watching her. She croaked his name and noticed he winced at the raspy sound in her voice.

"You look like shit." He said in greeting.

"I feel worse than I look." She retorted.

"This is getting to be a habit."

"Excuse me? What is?" She snapped.

"Finding you in a hospital room."

She sighed. His expression was of concern, but there was a hint of anger in his tone. She couldn't whitewash this. His expression revealed that he knew the full extent of her injuries.

He stood up and approached the bed, placed a bouquet of mixed flowers on the tray along with a handmade get-well card from Evelyn before kissing her forehead and tucking her hair behind her ear.

Her eyes welled with tears as she reached out and let her finger trail along the card.

"How is Evelyn?"

"She's fine. Right now, she is with my mother. She was very upset to learn you were in the hospital. I had to promise she could visit when you got home. You'll have to let us come over because I don't break my promises to her."

Maggie smiled weakly. "Of course, you both can come for a visit. I don't want you breaking your promise. Although it will have to be soon after I get home, because I'm going back to Cobden to be with my family for an extended visit. If this experience has shown me anything, it's that I need to put some distance between myself and this city for a while. My aunt and uncle are worried about me and I promised them I'd go back with Audrey as soon as I'm well enough to travel."

Colby's head snapped up and his eyes narrowed. "You're leaving?

I thought we were starting something here. If I knew you were going to up and leave, I would never have let you get close to Evelyn." His words came out harsher than he'd expected.

"I'm not leaving forever." She snapped, flinching from the pain of raising her voice. "My job is here. My home is here. I just need to get away and spend some time with my family while I recuperate. If you can't understand that, it's a good thing I found out now before I got too attached." Her chest rose and fell with each laboured breath, and tears of frustration seeped out and trickled down her cheeks.

Colby reached over, rubbed his thumb along her cheek, catching her tears, and took her hand. She jerked her hand back but winced at the pain the movement caused her.

"I'm sorry Maggie. I didn't come here to fight. It's just that the last time a woman I cared about was in a hospital, she didn't come home."

Maggie's eyes shifted up to his face and saw the pain there. Through fresh tears she whispered, "I'm sorry," and intertwined her fingers in his.

3

A week following her battle with Quinn, the hospital released Maggie. Throughout her time there, Audrey remained at her side, only going home to sleep. She hovered with constant worry and fused over Maggie like a mother hen. It was Audrey who brought Maggie home after they released her.

The first thing Maggie did when she got home was to take a long hot shower, then she stood in front of the full-length mirror in her room and examined the bruises in various stages of healing which mottled her skin. If she took too deep a breath, she still gasped in pain from her multiple fractured ribs, but Maggie knew no matter how bad she felt, it could have been worse. She got lucky, and now both Quinn and Butch were dead. It was time to rethink what she wanted out of life and how to move forward. Maggie knew if she allowed her anger to get the better of her again, she may not survive. The anguished look on Audrey's face when she said, "I can't watch you die!" still haunted her.

Audrey's comment forced Maggie to think about her aunt and uncle and how her death would affect them. When they heard she was in the hospital again, they both wanted to hop on the next flight. The only way she could put them off was by allowing them to speak with Audrey, who reassured them Maggie wasn't that bad, and then she had to promise to come back with Audrey after she left the hospital and felt ready to travel, a promise she regretted making, but one she would keep.

She slipped into a pair of pyjamas and padded out to the living room, where she found Audrey pacing. She looked up at Maggie, her expression filled with concern. Audrey had something on her mind and was struggling with how to proceed.

Maggie plopped down onto the chair by the window, wincing at the sudden jarring to her body, and watched Audrey, who had settled her pacing and had now chosen to sit on the sofa across the room. She looked up at Maggie but still didn't say what was on her mind.

"Ok! Enough of this! Why don't you just tell me what's going on?" Maggie demanded.

"All right, I will! But you won't like it."

Maggie couldn't help herself and rolled her eyes like a petulant child and crossed her arms across her chest.

"Maggie, you have to stop your vendetta. Those most responsible for Liam's murder are dead. You've seen to that. If that man hadn't helped you in the alleyway, it's possible you would have died, too."

At the mention of the man in the alley, Maggie made a mental note to find him and thank him again, but continued to listen to Audrey.

"There has been so much bloodshed already. First in your hunt for Frank Carter and now this. Innocent people have lost their lives. Do you think Noelle thought she'd die helping you?"

Maggie's eyes narrowed. That was a low blow. Her heart still ached for Noelle. She'd become the closest friend Maggie had ever had, even though they were an unlikely pair. But both had gumption. It wasn't her intention for Noelle to get hurt, let alone die, and Audrey knew that. She turned her head to look out of the window.

"You can't stick your head in the sand and ignore me, Maggie!"

Maggie's body tensed as the anger rose to the surface. She jumped up and closed the distance between them in a few quick steps. Her chest heaved as she looked down at Audrey, who crossed her legs and stared up at her.

"Noelle's death wasn't my fault!" Maggie yelled. "She knew it was a dangerous situation. I told her not to go back, and she did." Tears threatened to spill from her eyes as she continued. "She was the only innocent person who died. Everyone else got what they deserved." Maggie's chest rose and fell in rapid succession, her fists balled up at her sides as she glared at Audrey, daring her to contradict what she knew to be true.

Audrey stood up and wrapped her arms around Maggie, who struggled with resistance before accepting the embrace as a strangled sob escaped her lips and the tears flowed. Audrey knew this was the first step to Maggie's healing and acceptance. They had a long road ahead and much to do, but now she could help her come to terms with everything that transpired over the last year.

4

A few days later, Maggie sat on the sofa waiting for Colby and Evelyn to visit, fidgeting with the plate of cookies she'd made on the coffee table. She picked up her phone to check the time again before tossing it back down in exasperation.

"Maggie, you're working yourself up over nothing. Colby said they'd be here and they will."

"I can't believe how nervous I am. It's not like it's a date or anything, but I can't help wondering if I was someone else, where this could lead. I really like him."

"Maggie, it's been over a year since Liam died. You're still young. He'd want you to find happiness and so do I. Take a chance on love. You deserve it."

The doorbell chimed, and Maggie jumped. She turned to Audrey. "Do I look ok?"

Audrey nodded, and a smile spread across Maggie's face as she went to answer the door. As soon as she opened it, Evelyn flew into her arms. Maggie winced, but wrapped her arms around the child and inhaled the sweet scent herbal of her shampoo.

"Careful Evelyn. Maggie just got home from the Hospital." Colby warned as he leaned in to embrace her.

"I missed you." Evelyn said before eyeing the plate of cookies on the coffee table and releasing her hold on Maggie.

"I missed you too, Evelyn. I'm sorry that I haven't been around. Why don't you have one of the cookies I made?"

Evelyn turned to her father for permission and, at his nod, grabbed a cookie, biting into it with gusto. "Mmm, yummy!"

"Hi Audrey, nice seeing you again," Colby greeted as he took a seat on the sofa, pulling Evelyn onto his lap while she munched away on one of Maggie's homemade chocolate chip cookies.

"Hi Colby, nice to see you, and you too, Evelyn. If you'll excuse me, I have some things to take care of," Audrey said as she left the room.

Maggie settled on the other end of the sofa, her hands folded in her lap, and struggled to find the words she was looking for. Before she could, Colby cut in.

"How are you feeling, Maggie?"

"Not too bad, all things considered." She replied, giving Colby a small smile.

'Why was this so awkward?' She wondered. *'Whenever we've met before, we've never once had a problem talking.'* Then it hit her. *'He feels the same way about me as I feel about him. That's why this is so awkward.'*

Maggie leaned back and forced herself to relax, hoping it would help Colby relax as well. She swallowed several times before proceeding with the news about her trip to Ontario.

"I told you I'm going back to Cobden to visit with my aunt and uncle, but did I say that I will stay until after Christmas?" Maggie asked.

She watched the look of surprise flicker in his eyes. "I'm not sure how long I'll stay after that, though. The plan is for Audrey and I to drive back together in my car, so I can take her home, and then have it available to drive home. I need to spend some time with my family."

"You won't be here for Christmas? Did I do something wrong?" Evelyn asked, before bursting into tears.

Maggie scooped Evelyn up and held her. "Evelyn, sweetie, you did nothing wrong. I have a family in Cobden and I need to heal. I just came home from the hospital and need my family."

"Can't daddy take care of you?"

Maggie caught Colby's eyes over Evelyn's head.

"Honey, daddy has to work. I can't take care of Maggie. And Audrey has to go home. It'll be ok! Maggie's coming back." Colby kissed the top of Evelyn's head, his eyes never leaving Maggie's.

"Oh yes, Evelyn, I'm coming back. My home is here."

Maggie felt a wave of relief wash over her when Audrey stepped back into the room and asked Evelyn if she'd like to do some colouring in the kitchen. It was obvious Audrey realized the conversation would be easier if Evelyn wasn't in the room. Evelyn nodded, slid out of Maggie's grasp, hesitated in front of the cookies until Colby gave her permission to have another and joined Audrey in the other room.

When they were alone, Colby chuckled, "I hope you won't stay away too long; you still owe me a dinner."

"If you don't mind my bruises, we can have that dinner before I go."

Colby hesitated. "Are you serious? You've always insisted on Evelyn being present. What's changed? Why now?"

That wasn't the response she expected. Maybe she'd overestimated his feelings for her. Her stomach rolled and clenched. "Um, if you don't want to have dinner with me, that's okay, I understand."

Colby ran his hand through his hair. "Maggie, I very much want to have dinner with you. I just wondered what changed your mind? Aren't you planning on coming back? Is this a goodbye dinner?"

Maggie reached out and clasped Colby's hand. "I'll be back. This is where my life is. I just need to think about a few things. And as for why now? I think my attack is proof that one needs to live in the here and now. Something I should have already realized after Liam's murder. Life is short, Colby, and I like you."

A smile swept across his face as he reached his other hand out, let his fingers wind into her hair, pulled her to him, and captured her lips with his.

5

Maggie tried on several dresses as she fussed over what to wear on her date with Colby. A couple of days ago, she and Audrey argued, because Audrey thought the date should wait until Maggie returned and knew what her plan was. However she couldn't fault Maggie's excitement at the prospect of normalcy. Maggie stepped out into the living room wearing yet another dress, and Audrey sighed.

"Maggie, go back and put on the first dress you tried on. You know it's the right one, that's why you chose it. If you get dressed, you can start on your makeup. It's going to take a bit of work to cover those bruises, and if you wear the silk scarf that matches the dress, you can hide the worst ones around your neck. You don't want people giving Colby sideways glances thinking he's the cause."

"Damn! I didn't even think about that. Maybe I should call and cancel?" Maggie sagged onto the edge of the couch.

Audrey laughed. "I doubt he'd let you at this point. He knows we're leaving in a few days and he's found a babysitter for Evelyn plus made reservations. Pull yourself together. This was your idea."

"I don't know why I'm so nervous."

"I do."

Maggie turned and looked at Audrey, waiting for her to explain.

"First, when was the last time you went on a date? Even with Liam, he just kept pursuing you until he wore you down. You already know, Colby. He's solid. But you also know your own history. Therefore his being a cop is scary." Audrey took a sip of her tea. "The long and short of it is he likes you and you like him. You already know my feelings about why you should have waited, but it's too late now. Why not take a chance and have some fun? After everything you've been through, you deserve it."

"Do you really think so? I'm conflicted. He's a cop and I'm a killer. But I can change, we both know that. And I like him." Maggie paused and looked down at the dress she was wearing and replied, "The first one? You're right! It's the one! I better get a move on if I'm going to be ready on time."

Twenty minutes later, Maggie joined Audrey in the living room to wait for Colby. Audrey looked up as Maggie entered and smiled.

"You look beautiful, Maggie. I can barely see the bruises and the multi-hued silk scarf hides the ones around your neck. Colby is going to be speechless." Audrey said, patting the seat beside her, indicating Maggie should join her. "What time is he coming?"

Maggie sat down and checked her phone. "He'll be here in half an hour."

"Perfect! We have time for a small glass of wine before he arrives. It will help you relax!"

Forty minutes later, Maggie was sitting in the front seat of Colby's car as he drove to the restaurant. She stole a side glance at him and admired that he'd chosen to wear blue jeans, a collared shirt and a sports jacket. She took a deep breath and inhaled the aroma of his cologne and a smile crept to her lips, knowing he'd made as much of an effort in preparing for their date as she had.

When they arrived at the restaurant, Colby took her hand and led her inside. The restaurant offered a relaxed atmosphere, so they could take their time and enjoy a pleasant meal together with simple conversation. It wasn't until after dinner, when Colby suggested he'd like to go back to his place for a night cap, that the fluttering butterflies of uncertainty spread through her stomach. She knew Evelyn was at Colby's moms for the night, but she wasn't ready for the next step and wondered if that was what he was alluding to. Noticing her hesitation, he was quick to cut in.

"Maggie, it's not what you're thinking. I just want a quiet place where we can talk, without interruptions. I'd suggest your place, but Audrey is there. If you're uncomfortable, we can go somewhere else or park the car and sit and talk."

"I'm being silly. I trust you. If I can't trust a cop, we're in trouble." She teased as they left the restaurant.

Maggie settled into the seat beside Colby as he drove to his home. If she was being honest with herself, it wasn't him she was worried about. She knew that if she said no, he'd stop. The problem was with her. She wasn't sure she could say no. The last person she'd slept with was Quinn, and that was by necessity, not choice. Maggie wanted to erase the memory of his touch from her body, but wouldn't use Colby to do so. If she slept with Colby, it would be because they were in a relationship. Something she wasn't sure they could have until she figured out what was next on her agenda.

Maggie was deep in thought when Colby pulled up in front of a small bungalow in a modest neighbourhood. Maggie's first thought was, '*I wonder if he bought it when he and Stephanie first got married?*' She could tell that there was plenty of room for two and Maggie was certain she'd find a tidy, fenced yard in the back, set up with a playhouse and other toys essential for a young child.

Maggie remained in her seat and waited while Colby came around to her side of the vehicle and opened the door. She smiled up at him when he offered her his hand to help her out, and wondered how many curtains in the nearby homes parted, as neighbours peered out to see who was with the good looking, eligible widower.

Colby placed his hand on her lower back as he guided her to the front door. At the feel of his touch, Maggie shivered as the warmth of contentment enveloped her body. She smiled up at him and at that moment knew that if she was a different person, he could make her happy. Then she sighed, as the reality hit her. She was a killer, and he was a cop. Tonight, she'd enjoy the happiness she felt. Tomorrow, she'd distance herself as she prepared to head to Ontario. Time away would allow her to think.

6

Maggie made herself comfortable at one end of the sofa in Colby's living room and looked around, and noticed how tidy everything was. She wondered if he cleaned it himself or if he had help? With an active kindergarten aged child, keeping it clean must be a constant battle. She could hear Colby rattling around in the kitchen and called out that she needed to use the washroom.

"It's at the end of the hall." Colby replied, "Red or white wine?"

"Red please." Maggie responded as she made her way down the hall. She paused at the door to Evelyn's room, noting the varying shades of purple throughout. The room had toys strewn about, but someone had made the bed and left an open story book on the bedside table. The sight warmed her. Colby allowed Evelyn to express herself and didn't insist on a spotless bedroom.

At the end of the hall, she saw the bathroom and to the right was his bedroom, as tidy as the living room, and to the left was Colby's office. She noticed some files on the desk and couldn't help herself. She looked back down the hall to see where he was, then slipped inside.

On the desk, she found an open file for a murder from a few months ago. She remembered seeing it in her news feed. Beside the file was the picture of their prime suspect and the notation, 'Not Enough Evidence'. The familiar sensation of rage prickled up her spine, and Maggie pulled her phone from her pocket and took a few pictures of the contents. Then she went to the washroom before Colby came in search of her.

When she returned to the living room, she found Colby on the sofa with two glasses of red on the coffee table. She smiled at him, allowing her hair to drop across her shoulder before settling down beside him.

"You have a lovely home." Maggie said, taking the glass Colby offered her.

"Thank you, I've changed nothing since Stephanie passed." Colby hesitated before continuing, "That doesn't bother you, does it?"

"What?"

"That my wife decorated the house and I've left it the same way."

Maggie chuckled. "I'd be more surprised if you changed it. Stephanie only died a few years ago and Liam has only been dead for just over a year. I've changed nothing inside my house either. Everything is how it was. To be honest, I haven't even been able to pack up his clothes."

Colby took her hand in his. "It took me two years to pack up Stephanie's clothing to donate. Grief has no timeline. But speaking of Liam, I thought I should give you an update."

Maggie tensed.

"I'm not able to provide proof, but I believe the person who ordered the hit which killed Liam is dead."

Maggie released the breath she was unaware she'd held. "What makes you say that?"

"If you recall, I told you we thought Liam was in the wrong place at the wrong time and wasn't the target of the hit, and that his death resulted from a case of mistaken identity. The intended target turned up dead a few days later. Now, both the president and vice president of the other gang, we think, ordered the hit, are dead. It happened the same day as your assault."

Maggie's eyes flickered up to his. Was that an accusation? A question or a hidden threat? She braced herself before asking what was on her mind.

"Does that mean there is no way to prove who killed him?"

"It's unfortunate, but even though we are ninety percent certain who was behind the hit, we can't prove anything. People clam up or go missing when gangs are involved. Sometimes we get lucky and have irrefutable evidence that leads to an arrest and a conviction, but not always."

"Does that happen often? Where you know who's guilty but can't prove it?"

"More times than I care to admit." Colby sighed.

A wave of relief passed through her, realizing he didn't suspect her of Butch or Quinn's murders. Wanting to change the subject, Maggie interjected, "Murder talk is depressing. I walked past what I assume is Evelyn's room, and I like it. It looks well lived in."

Colby leaned back and laughed. "That's one way to put it. It's her bedroom and playroom rolled into one. Once a month I help her put everything away, but other than when we clean her room, it always looks like that. But I insist she make her bed."

They sat together chatting while sipping their wine, taking their time to get to know one and another, without outside influences. Colby held Maggie's hand in his while they talked, rubbing his thumb along the back of it, sending shivers up her arm.

As the night wore on, Colby leaned into Maggie, captured the back of her head in his free hand and pulled her into a kiss. She responded, allowing her hand to play with the thick hair at the nape of his neck. Maggie felt her resolve weakening just as Colby broke the spell and sat back.

"I'd love to ask you to spend the night, but I know it's too early in our relationship for that. I just wanted to give you a taste of what's to come." He said to her with a wink. "I guess I'd better get you home. I'm sure Audrey is waiting up to see how things went. She acts like a mother hen."

Maggie felt the heat rise to her cheeks. He didn't know how close he was to the truth. Audrey sat her down and warned her about playing with fire when Maggie first suggested the date and said she'd wait up.

"I'm sure you're right. She is the closest thing I have to a grandmother."

With reluctance, they both stood to leave. Maggie put the wine glasses on the counter and Colby took her by the hand as they headed back out to his car.

7

The next morning, as Maggie left her bedroom, a smile played on her lips. A new sense of resolve washed over her after her dinner with Colby.

Audrey glanced up as Maggie entered the kitchen. "I'm guessing by that smile somebody had a good night."

"Yes, somebody did." Maggie replied as she poured herself a cup of coffee.

"Are you going to tell me about it?"

"Yes, but not now. Now I'm going to call my aunt and tell her we're coming home. I think we should leave tomorrow, as long as I can get us a room at the Quality Inn in Grey Rock for the night."

"Finally! I still have clients who need me, you know. Somehow, video chats make things a little impersonal, and I'm sure Ash and Blue miss me, although I know your aunt is taking wonderful care of them."

"You didn't have to stay so long, but I'm glad you did. I don't think you have to worry about Ash and Blue, knowing aunt Julie, she's gone out, bought toys, and special treats. It wouldn't surprise me if she's letting them sleep in her bed."

"Oh no, they won't enjoy being kicked out of my bed then!" Audrey frowned before continuing. "Why the sudden change in plans? Does it have anything to do with last night?"

"Yes, and no. Let me make my phone calls and I'll fill you in."

Maggie left Audrey in the kitchen and took her coffee out to the living to make the calls. The first one she made was to the hotel to book a room, then to her aunt, whose excitement drifted across the line with a warm whoopee! Then she made a call to her editor requesting an extended leave of absence. She explained she could still write from her aunts, but wouldn't be able to do any investigative reporting. The last call Maggie made was to Colby thanking him for an enjoyable evening and to let him know what her plans were.

With her calls completed, Maggie told Audrey about her night and why they were leaving so soon, omitting telling Audrey about the pictures she took of the file from Colby's desk.

They didn't linger over their coffees. They had a lot to accomplish before leaving: packing, storing things, and clearing out the fridge. It was going to be a busy day. Aside from packing, Maggie also needed to pick up her car and motorcycle from the condo and bring them home. Luckily, Audrey could drive her back and forth in Liam's SUV to make things easier.

Maggie knew the condo would need clearing out at some point. There were things in both bedrooms that needed to be sorted, but it could wait until she returned. At least Noelle's belongings were boxed up. With everything that transpired over the last month, she didn't get around to donating Noelle's clothing before her confrontation with Quinn.

During her stay in the hospital, Audrey arranged for Noelle's body to be cremated at Maggie's request, but now Noelle's remains were in a box in the front hall closet of the condo, where they'd stay until she decided what to do with them. The thought of Noelle's body waiting to be claimed, and knowing there was no one to do it, tore at her heart. Maggie felt grateful that Audrey agreed and took care of that for her. Noelle deserved more than a pauper's grave. But in the meantime, she needed to get some distance and clarity first. Then she'd know what to do with her ashes.

After one trip to the condo, the bike was back in the garage. Audrey dropped Maggie at the building to pick up her car and returned to the house to finish packing. Maggie went up the elevator instead of going to the parking garage, unable to fight the feeling that compelled her to go up to the unit. She entered, hesitating in front of the hall closet, touching the door with her fingertips. She'd check on its contents in a minute. The air smelt musty after being closed up for a few weeks. She went to the balcony and opened the door to air it out. When she opened the door to the room Noelle occupied, her breath hitched. A tear escaped, which she brushed away with the back of her hand, then she stepped out and re-closed the door. She couldn't deal with it now. It hurt too much.

Next, Maggie went to the fridge. She knew she'd left some food inside, which needed to be tossed before it became a science experiment. There wasn't much in there, so everything went into a kitchen catcher, which she dropped down the garbage chute. She took a rag to wipe out the inside of the fridge and put a box of baking soda on a shelf to absorb odour.

Maggie knew it was time to leave, but the sight of the closed door in the hall left her rooted in place. She sighed, and with leaden feet, made her way to the closet. Maggie took a deep breath and swung open the door. The closet was empty except for some hangers and the cardboard box in the centre of the top shelf. Maggie trailed her fingers over the surface.

"I'm so sorry Noelle. I never meant for you to get hurt, let alone die." A small sob escaped her lips. "I'll be back. Then I'll take you to your final resting place. You were a wonderful friend. I'm sorry I wasn't a better one."

Maggie pulled her shoulders back and closed the door, took one last look around the apartment, and left.

They were both exhausted when supper time came around, and ordered a pizza, preferring a quiet evening at home. Maggie opened a bottle of chianti after supper and they settled in front of the television to watch a movie, each lost in their own thoughts.

A blue sky dotted with fluffy cotton clouds greeted them when they woke up to hit the road. They planned to stop in Amherst or Moncton for lunch and continue on to the hotel in Edmundston. Although Maggie was still recovering from her injuries, she insisted on driving, which led to another heated debate. But Maggie pointed out she was the professional driver and promised to switch out if it became too much. What Maggie didn't tell Audrey was that part of her reasoning for wanting to drive, was she couldn't give up control of the wheel. Secretly, she was sure Audrey already knew that.

The golden yellow orb of the sun, glistened through the sky as they continued down the highway. The road was clear and dry and the soft sound of jazz drifted from the radio as they chatted while the landscape zipped by.

It was past dinner time when they checked into the Quality Inn. As they headed to their room on the second floor, Maggie rolled her shoulders to release the tension that had built up from driving. Her body ached, and she'd need some of the Tylenol 3s the doctor prescribed before heading to bed. A hot shower would also ease the aches and pains. They'd travelled the best part of their journey today. Tomorrow they'd battle with the Quebec traffic before arriving in Cobden.

Once they settled and showered, they went to the restaurant inside the casino for dinner instead of picking one of the fast-food places nearby. They were lucky the restaurant wasn't busy, and they enjoyed a delicious meal. Audrey picked the maple salmon and Maggie the corned beef on rye. After dinner, they lingered over a glass of wine before heading to the room for a good night's sleep.

8

Colby sat hunched over his desk and opened the files from Quinn and Butches murders. Something about their deaths didn't feel right, and it had nothing to do with the surveillance photo of the red-headed motorcycle rider. These acts were up close and personal, not from a distance the way a hit was. Could it be the work of a disgruntled club member looking for power? Colby made a few notes. One thing he couldn't help but notice was that things had gotten quiet since both the President and the VP of the Dark Enders died. He wondered if it was a coincidence or if there was something else behind it.

He pulled up the grainy street cam photograph of the rider leaving the area of Butch's murder. The hair was so similar to Maggie's, but it couldn't be her, could it? She'd been kilometres away waiting to meet up with Audrey, who'd confirmed this. Then she ended up in the hospital after being mugged. There wasn't a scenario he could come up with where she could overpower, kill Butch, and then get away.

If the photograph on the bike was of her, there must be a plausible explanation for it, and it wasn't to murder Butch Barker. He realized she had plenty of reasons to want him dead, but her killing him didn't add up. No matter how he looked at it, Colby couldn't imagine her battling with Butch and surviving. He was sure the similarities between her and the rider in the picture were just a coincidence.

Colby closed the file folders and pushed them aside. Both were still active, but he believed the murders were the work of the High Rollers, and at some point, soon, the war between the two gangs would continue.

He knew the Dark Enders would gather ranks once they elected a new President and VP and go after the High Rollers, and the body count would stack up again. There wasn't anything he could do to prevent it. He only hoped there weren't any more innocent victims.

Colby looked around the room and pushed back his chair. He tapped his pen on his desk and wondered where Maggie was now when his phone alerted him to a text.

> Hey. I thought I'd let you know I arrived safely at my aunt's. Give Evelyn a big hug for me.

> Thanks for letting me know. Only a hug for Evelyn? What about me?

> Lol. Ok, you too. I'm needed in the kitchen; my uncle's coming home and we are having a celebratory supper. Chat later xo.

> Enjoy. Xo

Colby couldn't help but smile. She sent XO's and let him know she was ok. Maybe he was winning her over, and when she returned, they could see where things were going.

"Tate!" a voice boomed across the squad room; Colby flipped his phone over before responding.

"Yes, sir?"

"Grab the files on the Dark Ender murders and join me in my office."

Colby scooped up the files and followed the captain. He had a gut feeling the captain was going to tell him to put the case aside and work on some more recent developments in another case.

Colby sighed, sitting down in the chair across from the captain's desk as he shut the door. Sometimes the legal restrictions of the job were frustrating, otherwise Quinn and Butch would be behind bars for the murder of Liam Murphy, instead of laying in the morgue. But then again, if they could apprehend perpetrators based on their knowledge rather than concrete evidence, Liam Murphy would still be alive because Quinn and Butch would have been in custody a long time ago.

9

Maggie awoke to find herself in her childhood bedroom for the first time in six years and felt disoriented. It took her a few minutes to remember why she was here. The decor had changed multiple times over the years, but the furniture remained the same. The room was small and only accommodated a dresser and the single bed, which was nestled under the dormer window. She didn't need a bigger bed. A larger one only accentuated the loss of Liam's presence.

Maggie sighed. There was something comforting about coming home. It's possible that if she came back after Liam's murder, she wouldn't have killed again. But if she didn't seek her revenge, then Liam's murderers would have gotten away with their crime. The constant reminder from the police that there wasn't enough evidence to make an arrest grated on her.

Now that both Quinn and Butch were dead, she could heal. Not just from her recent physical injuries, but from her emotional ones as well. The ones that left scars on her soul, hidden from the naked eye. So much had happened in the last year, and she realized she hadn't taken the time to process it. She'd gone from a married woman expecting a child to a barren widow in the blink of an eye.

Maggie slid out from beneath the covers as a tear blurred her vision. She wouldn't allow herself to wallow in her sorrow. Her incisions were healing well, and although it still hurt to breathe, she was improving. The purple hued raccoon eyes from her broken nose had faded to varying shades of green and yellow. Maggie paused and looked in the mirror over the dresser, and realized how lucky she was. Whoever set her nose did a good job, and the slight bump she felt beneath the swelling wouldn't be too noticeable.

She ran a brush through her hair, pulled it back into a ponytail, and went downstairs to the kitchen for some of her aunt's coffee. She smelled the aroma drifting upstairs, beckoning her. Her bare feet padded on the well-worn wooden steps as she snuck down the back stairwell, which exited right into the kitchen.

The kitchen was empty, with a note on the table letting Maggie know her aunt was already at work in the shop. After her coffee, she'd head over and take her mind off everything by helping around the garage. She figured some hard work would clear her head. There was a lot to think about.

"Good morning sleepyhead." Julie called out from the pit as Maggie entered the building.

Maggie laughed, "I've been up for a while, I just needed some coffee to kick start my day. It's been a rough year."

The other mechanics paused at the greeting but were quick to turn back to their work. Maggie felt the tension in the air. Her aunt said little to her when she arrived the night before, but Maggie could tell there was something on her aunt's mind, and the mechanics felt it, too.

Maggie flinched when she heard the curse and clatter of tools before Julie climbed out of the pit.

"Maggie. I was going to wait until your uncle got home, but I can't. It's weighing too much on me."

"Just spit it out."

"Okay, I will. It seems since Liam's murder, you've had a death wish. You can't tell me that Audrey's sudden trip to visit you was without cause. I can only assume something happened to you, and she went to help. Even the mugging seems suspicious to me. I don't doubt someone attacked you, but Audrey being close enough to rescue you and take you to the hospital is far-fetched."

Her aunt's words stung. Maggie turned to leave, but Julie grabbed her by the arm and swung her back around.

"Don't walk away from me! We can do this now or wait for your uncle. But trust me, we both feel the same way. We need to be certain you're not involved in anything dangerous, or the next time something happens to you may be the last!" Julie's fist curled up into a small ball, her chest heaved and she wiped her eyes with the back of her hand, smearing a streak of grease across her face.

Maggie sighed. The last thing she wanted to do was upset her aunt. She moved forward and wrapped her arms around her, pulling her close. It was the same thing Audrey had said to her in the hospital. She felt Julie resist her embrace before succumbing to it.

"I promise I'm not into anything dangerous." Maggie replied, whitewashing the truth. "I'll explain everything tonight. What I need is to do some work, something physical to alleviate the stress I've been under. Let me get into a pair of coveralls and give you a hand."

Julie pushed Maggie back to look into her eyes before giving a quick nod.

"If you feel up to it, okay. There's a pair of your old coveralls in the back. I can't let you do anything that requires a licensed mechanic, but there is plenty of work you can do. Go check with the boys. I'm sure one of them has something for you to work on." Julie replied as she climbed back into the pit. "And we *are* going to talk about this later."

Maggie nodded, mumbling under her breath as she went to the back room to get the coveralls. Julie had a few pairs made for her for when she was younger and working in the garage. Because of her petite frame, it was challenging to find ready-made coveralls that would fit. When she was trucking, she kept a pair in her truck for when she worked on her rig. Growing up in the shop taught her a lot about truck mechanics, something that was invaluable to her when she was an owner/operator, and a skill that helped in other areas of her life as well.

When she donned the coveralls and was ready for work, Maggie approached Jack, one of the senior members of Julie's team, to see where he wanted her and got to work, relishing in the distraction the work provided.

10

Maggie left the shop ahead of her aunt to grab a shower and prepare supper. Her body ached from working in the pits all day, but it felt good to be useful again. While working, she'd figured out an excuse for Audrey flying out to her aide and gave Audrey a call to collaborate. She knew when her uncle returned, they'd have a family dinner and include Audrey, then either her aunt or uncle would bring it up, so their stories had to match.

"Something smells good." Julie called out as she entered the house. "Give me a few minutes to wash up and we can eat."

The savoury aroma of the meatloaf, mashed potatoes and mixed vegetables, Maggie made filled the air. There was so much, there'd be enough for leftovers the next night, too. The following night, Uncle Bobbie would be home and they'd have their family's celebratory dinner.

While Julie showered, Maggie set the table and opened a bottle of wine. Julie was more of a whiskey girl, but still appreciated a delicious glass of wine. It was a long time since they'd shared one.

When she heard the shower shut off, Maggie poured the wine and doled the food out. She was just placing the plates on the table when Julie entered.

"Ah Maggie, this looks great." She said as she settled herself down at the table. Tapping the glass, she asked, "Wine? Are we celebrating something?"

Maggie smiled. "It's been a long time since I've been back and the last time I saw you, things were different. I just thought it would be nice, especially while it's just us girls."

Julie raised her glass in a salute and took a sip. "You picked a nice one. But don't think wine changes anything. I still want answers."

"Aunt Julie, I wouldn't think a little wine and some good cooking would change your mind." Maggie feigned looking shocked. "But can we talk about everything after we eat?"

Julie nodded. "Although, I think you're getting ahead of yourself about this being 'good', I haven't tried it yet." She teased.

After supper, they washed the dishes, then retired to the living room. There was still some wine left, so Maggie topped up their glasses as they made themselves comfortable.

"Okay girl, spill."

"I will, but please can you fill in uncle Bobby for me? I don't want to rehash this again when he gets home."

Julie nodded and motioned for Maggie to continue while she took a sip of her wine.

"As you know, I was struggling after Liam died. The injustice of what happened to us haunted me. I tried to get back to work, but I couldn't concentrate. I started talking to Audrey again. She helped me get focused and work out my feelings." Maggie paused and took a sip of her wine. "Then one day I went for a ride. I'll have you know; it took a lot for me to get back on the bike and when I did, I thought it was the first step in healing. If you remember, I found riding calming."

Julie reached out and took Maggie's hand.

"Anyway, this one day I was out on a ride and a group of Dark Enders rode by. I knew about them from the police report, and I lost it and started following them."

"Maggie! You didn't?"

Maggie hung her head and peered up at Julie behind a curtain of burnished curls. Julie reached out and tucked Maggie's hair behind her ear as she nodded.

"Aunt Julie, I'm sorry, but I was in a terrible place. I didn't tell Audrey, not at first, so don't be mad at her. But the day she flew out was the day I told her and I made her promise not to tell you." Maggie was trying to keep the story of events as close to accurate as possible. "I followed some of the gang members to a warehouse. Something went wrong and a gun fight ensued. I ran for cover, but a bullet grazed my left arm."

Julie grabbed Maggie's arm and shoved her sleeve up, exposing the puckered, angry scar. Julie opened her mouth to speak, and Maggie held up her hand. "Please let me finish, then I'll answer all of your questions."

Maggie rolled her sleeve back down, covering the scar. "I didn't want to go to the Hospital because I'd have to explain how I got a bullet wound and what I was doing there. I didn't want to deal with the attention. The hospital would call the police and if the Dark Enders found out I was there, they'd consider me a threat. So, I called Audrey. I just wanted to see if I needed medical attention. She said it needed stitches and when I explained what happened, she hopped on the first available flight. She stitched me up and stayed to help me work through my anger. You knew she was coming out to see me, now you know why."

"I see." Julie sighed. "Maggie, are you okay now? And I don't mean physically!"

"Not quite, but I'm getting there. The mugging was a fluke, and yes, Audrey was meeting me. She helped me to the car and drove me to the hospital. You know the rest. Audrey persuaded me to come home and get some clarity after the hospital released me. So here I am."

Julie pulled Maggie to her and wrapped her arms around her. "You're safe here Maggie. Stay as long as you need to."

11

Maggie slipped out of the house into the crisp fall air and headed over to Audrey's. There was something calming about Audrey's cottage nestled deep in the woods by the lake. She parked under an umbrella of saffron to burnt umber leaves that canopied the laneway. Her footsteps rustled in the fallen leaves that blanketed the ground when she stepped out of the car.

As she walked, she pulled her jacket collar up close to her neck against the chill in the air. She looked up and saw the smoke coming from Audrey's chimney and realized there was a fire going. With her hands shoved deep into her pockets for warmth, she approached the cottage, eager to warm herself in front of the waiting fire.

Maggie raised her hand to knock, but before she could, the door swung open and Audrey motioned her inside, and quickly closed the door. Maggie removed her shoes, hung her coat on the rack before settling down with Audrey in front of the fire, her hands raised to the flames.

"You can feel fall in the air now, even peeking towards winter. Can I offer you a coffee or tea?"

"Sure, whichever's easiest. I love fall, the warm burst of colours as the leaves change, the slight nip in the air. It's my favourite time of the year. But it also reminds me I have to figure out what's next in my life."

"Hold that thought. I'll put the kettle on for tea."

The heat from the fire eased the chill from her bones, and Maggie relaxed, allowing her body to sag into the sofa. She still hadn't decided what was next for her, where she'd settle, if she'd stay, or would she go back on the road. But today wasn't about what her plans were, it was about finding the families of the remaining hair clips on the ribbon she found in Frank Carter's truck.

After a few minutes of bustling around in the kitchen, Audrey emerged with a tea tray, complete with biscuits. She placed the tray on the coffee table and motioned to Maggie to help herself before going to a drawer in the sideboard to retrieve the pouch where she stored the hair clips and research. She placed it on the table and poured them each a mug of tea.

"Have you decided what you want to do?" Audrey asked, nibbling a cookie.

"No, not yet. But I'll have to figure things out soon. Aunt Julie is gunning for me to stay. But you and I both know I can't do that. Something will happen and I won't be able to help myself."

"There are ways of coping, Maggie. We've discussed this. But you have plenty of time to decide."

"I want a plan in place by Christmas. In the new year, I'll need to head home and deal with everything. Noelle's ashes, Colby, the house and condo, plus I need to get back to some semblance of normal. I just can't keep hiding away from it all. But I promised my aunt I'd stay for Christmas. Of course, you'll join us. They consider you family."

Audrey's smile radiated with warmth as she reached out and patted Maggie's hand. "I wouldn't miss it."

"Okay, enough about my plans. Where are we with the hair clips?"

Audrey opened the pouch and pulled out the remaining clips.

There were three left. All faded and frayed. Maggie couldn't help but feel saddened at the sight of them. She knew they were the oldest ones. Little girls long forgotten by the law, but not their families, and they were also the hardest to find. These children's lives ended before social media was mainstream and their families would be the most difficult to track down.

"As you can see, we have three more families to locate. So far, my search has come up empty. It's too bad we can't enlist Colby's help. It could make a difference, but I know there would be too many questions if we did."

Maggie sighed. Colby would be the perfect person to have in their corner, but Audrey was right, there would be questions. Questions she couldn't answer.

"Maybe it's time to get drastic."

"What do you mean, Maggie?"

"Let's create a Facebook page for survivors. We can set up a basic email account in which to do it, one we both can access. We can send out friend requests to the families we've already brought closure to. Include a picture of Sara's hair clip as a start. No one around here knows about it, so it won't come back on you. You and I both know we can't use a picture of mine because my aunt and uncle are too familiar with it. If either of them sees it, they'd connect us to the Facebook page. We could start the conversations with the fact that someone returned the clip, but we don't know who. It could help. If we're lucky, someone out there whose family member went missing or died and knows about the hair clip connection may be on Facebook by now. That might help us find them."

"That just might work!" Audrey beamed at Maggie, grabbing her laptop.

"No!"

Audrey hesitated, "No?"

"We won't set it up or access it here. Not from your IP address and not on either of our devices, not if we can help it. Tomorrow we'll head to Ottawa and use the library there. It's not far, and we can have lunch while we're out. Take a picture of Sara's hair clip with your phone, and you can email it to the account we set up and upload it to the Facebook account. For the time being, we will have to access the accounts from public libraries. It won't protect us, but it will help."

"This just might work." Audrey replied, leaning back in her seat and sipping her tea. There was a lightness in her chest as she held her chin high.

12

First thing the next morning, Maggie and Audrey drove into Ottawa to the Public Library, picking the Beaverbrook branch because it was the closest. The library was busier than they expected, and they had to sign up and wait to use a computer. While they waited, Audrey wandered the shelves, and Maggie sent a few texts to Colby, as a way of passing time. Once they accessed the computer, it didn't take long for Maggie to set up an email and Facebook account.

Last night, Audrey wrote out what happened to Sara and emailed Maggie so she could upload it. They included a picture of Sara's two hair clips, the one she was wearing when the police found her and the one Maggie recovered from Frank Carter's truck. Next, they sent out some invitations to join the page to the families of his victim's. They set the account to private, so people could find it, but in order to join, they had to send in a request and answer a series of questions. Either Audrey or Maggie would review the answers before granting access.

Maggie also set up a fake profile from an old email so she could be a member of the group and still maintain her anonymity. She posted her own story, but not a picture of her hair clip. People needed to know someone survived. She hoped by doing so, they'd find more survivors. As a member, Maggie could check the activity on the account from anywhere. To access the admin side, for the time being, they'd use public libraries. Luckily, there were lots of libraries in Ottawa to choose from. Of course, one of them could access the account from the Cobden library as well.

Just before their allotted time on the computer was up, a notification came in. Someone accepted their friend request. They checked the profile and realized it was the mother of one of Carter's more recent victims. The mother sent a messenger message asking how they'd found her. Audrey let Maggie take over. Maggie, pretending to be Audrey, explained how someone kidnapped her daughter, assaulted and murdered her and that the killer took her barrette. She continued to explain that recently someone returned the barrette with a note and that prompted her to search for others. The woman's name came up in a search for missing children and thought she may benefit from the group.

There was a hesitation before the dots indicating she was replying appeared on the screen.

"I got a note too," the woman explained. "What did yours say?"

They'd prepared for this scenario and uploaded a photo of the card and waited while the text box remained stagnate.

Soon, a response came in. "How many of us do you think there are?"

Maggie typed, "If I had to hazard a guess? I'd say dozens."

They continued back and forth for a few more minutes until Maggie asked the woman to post her story. She explained it would help connect the victims of the monster who ruined their lives and they could help each other heal. If they were lucky, maybe they'd find out who sent the notes. There was something to be said for solidarity.

They waited until the mother posted her story before closing down their page and erasing the history from the computer. They were in good spirits when they left the library. Neither thought they'd have contact with a family so soon. Now they were optimistic that the Facebook page would help them find homes for the remaining hair clips.

It was lunchtime, so Maggie suggested they eat at Moxie's while they were in the area. The hostess led them to a booth, where they settled and ordered a glass of wine to toast to the successful launch of their Victims of Frank Carter's Facebook page. Of course, they didn't call it that. Instead, it was The Barrette Butcher. Audrey felt the page could help with healing, having members who'd gone through similar circumstances and giving them a safe place to discuss and share their experiences.

Maggie hadn't looked at it that way, but agreed. She'd felt a sense of peace when she posted her story. It wasn't complete. She didn't include her father's death in her post, because she didn't want her aunt or uncle to know she had her hair clip back and didn't tell them. Not that they'd find it. Both of her hair clips were now buried with her father. There were some things better left unsaid.

Before they left the restaurant, Maggie used her cell to check the status of the page. Several more families they'd sent requests to had accepted and posted their stories. Maggie took a moment to comment on each post before signing out.

"I think one of us will need to go to the library every few days and sign in as administrator. The site is already getting a lot of attention and we want to accept/weed out new friend requests. I think this is going to work." Maggie smiled at Audrey; confident they would finish the task they started over six years ago.

13

Christmas was just around the corner and with it, the need for Maggie to decide what her future entailed. After much contemplation, Maggie decided what her plan was. Over a long video conference with her editor, explaining to him what her idea was, and discussing the logistics of it, he was on board. Maggie hadn't told Audrey or her aunt and uncle yet. She'd tell them over Christmas. She crossed her fingers, but knew combining life on the road and writing was the right choice.

In the weeks leading up to Christmas, Maggie picked out and shipped a few packages off for Evelyn to unwrap. She chatted several times with Colby and promised to get together when she returned in the new year. She didn't include a gift for Colby in the packages she mailed for Evelyn; they weren't there yet, but buying for Evelyn gave her pleasure and felt right. If things were different, she'd be buying gifts for her own child, and the thought saddened her.

Colby asked her several times what her plans were, but other than telling him she'd be back in the new year, she chose not to elaborate. She didn't tell Colby, because it was a conversation better done face-to-face, and she needed to talk to her family first.

She sighed as she placed the last gift under the tree. A part of her wished she could be there Christmas morning to watch Evelyn open her gifts. '*Maybe next year,*' Maggie thought. The gifts she'd picked up for her uncle, aunt and Audrey lay under the tree, wrapped in colourful festive paper and bows. She only bought a few things for them, because they all agreed they needed nothing except to be together. Maggie knew this, but there was something exciting about waking up Christmas morning to find a parcel to unwrap, no matter how small.

Maggie felt nostalgic as she thought back to the last Christmas her father was alive. Her memory of that day, once vivid, now resembled the faded photographs of a by-gone era. Through pictures, she could recall the details. One thing she remembered was the mountain of wrapped gifts under the tree, which made the small pile in the living room pale in comparison.

Julie suggested Maggie decorate the house and tree, knowing how much she enjoyed the season. Not having to worry about decorating gave Julie more time in the shop so she could be off for Christmas. Now everything was ready, but there was still the baking to do. Maggie promised she'd take care of it, so she headed to the kitchen to begin. She pulled out her mother's worn recipe cards, thankful she had the forethought to pack them when she left home and searched for the ones she wanted. Christmas wouldn't be the same without her mother's chewy noel bars. Maggie combined the ingredients and put them in the oven before she started the shortbread.

By the time Julie came in from the shop, Maggie was still cleaning up the kitchen. The aroma of shortbread cookies permeated the air as the last batch cooled on the counter. On the table, Maggie had stacked several containers stuffed with a variety of baked goods.

"I see you've had a productive day." Julie said as she snatched a still warm cookie from the tray.

"Oh, drat!" Maggie exclaimed. "I didn't realize it was so late. I haven't prepared supper."

"We can always dine on cookies." Julie teased.

Maggie scowled. "I'm sorry aunt Julie, I said I'd cook while I was here, but the time got away from me."

"No worries, Mag. We can always order pizza. Let me call Milano Pizzeria and place an order. If you want, you can pick it up while I shower."

"Oh pizza, yum, it's been a while since I've had a pizza."

"Me too, problem solved."

After Julie retired for the night, Maggie picked up her phone and switched her Facebook account to the one she used to access the Barrette Butcher page. She began scrolling through the posts and came across one where the mother wasn't sure she was in the right spot. The person returning hair clips had yet to return her daughter's. She said that her daughter died almost forty years ago and the hair clip she wore was missing when the police found her, and the clip was never found.

Maggie hesitated before responding.

> I'm sorry for your loss. I think I'm the only survivor. If it's the same person who attacked me that killed your daughter, you belong here. Just because you haven't received the clip back doesn't mean you won't. I think whoever set up this page did it, so we could support each other.

Maggie was about to log off when she saw the three dots showing the woman was replying.

You survived? How? Can I ask what happened? What he did?

Sorry and can't relive it again. I posted my story on here before just scroll down and you'll find it.

I'd given up hope they would catch him. But based on what others are saying, he's dead. I hope he rots in hell.

Do you have a picture or description of your daughter's hair clip? I keep hoping that whoever was returning them joins this page, and it helps them bring closure to more families.

I don't have a picture, but it was mauve with yellow sunflowers, but I can post a description.

Maggie's heart pounded in her chest. She knew the clip was one of the three remaining on the ribbon. Maggie licked her lips, but her mouth remained dry. She saw the time was midnight. Was it too late to call Audrey? No, she'd want to know.

Why don't you edit your post? Describe the hair clip in it. That way, if someone is out there trying to find you, they can.

Do you think so? Even after all these years?

Yes, I do.

Ok, thanks. I'll do that right now.

As Maggie signed out from Facebook, her face split into a wide grin. Her eyes sparkled as she picked favourites and called Audrey. Her voice was groggy when she answered on the fourth ring.

"It worked Audrey."

"Maggie? Is that you? What worked?"

"Our Facebook page!"

"Maggie, what are you talking about?" Audrey asked, stifling a yawn.

"The Barrette Butcher Facebook page. We've found the family of the mauve clip with sunflowers."

"Are you sure?"

"Yes, I was just messaging with whom I assume was her mother. She wasn't sure if she belonged on the page because she hadn't received the hair clip back. I got her talking, and she described it. I knew right away we found another one, so I called you immediately."

"Oh Maggie, this is the best Christmas present ever."

"Tomorrow we'll go to the library in town and sign onto the page so you can see for yourself. Then we can check out her profile, find out where she's living and give her a happy Christmas."

14

Christmas morning was a blur of activity. Bobby arrived home two days prior and was currently drinking his coffee in the living room in his favourite chair by the tree. They'd chosen to wait until Audrey arrived before opening gifts. Julie was busy setting the table for supper, pulling out her grandmother's Christmas China to make the day more festive.

Meanwhile, Maggie was in the kitchen. The turkey was in the oven, the stuffing in a casserole dish. Maggie never stuffed it inside the turkey. She felt the stuffing became soggy when cooked inside the bird. Bobby would mash the potatoes later and they'd have a mixture of roasted vegetables to accompany the meal. Maggie was making a salad as a starter, and had a tray of snacks ready to pull out of the fridge when Audrey arrived.

Maggie just finished basting the turkey when she heard a knock at the door and uncle Bobby greeting Audrey. She closed the oven door, removed her apron, grabbed the tray and headed out to the living room to find Audrey placing some gifts under the tree. They embraced and Maggie whispered in Audrey's ear, "The mom has already posted about getting her daughter's barrette back."

Audrey beamed and whispered back. "That makes my day."

They sat snacking on the hors d'oeuvres while opening their gifts. Then, Maggie bustled back and forth to check the meal before calling everyone to the table. Now with their stomachs full, they retired to the living room for coffee and the sweet tray. There was a lull in the conversation and Maggie cut in to tell everyone her decision.

"I have some news." Maggie announced.

All three turned towards her. Audrey paused with a sweet to her lips before taking a bite. Both Bobby's and Julie's jaws sagged, a look of disappointed flashing in their eyes.

"What kind of news?" Audrey asked, watching the faces of Maggie's aunt and uncle.

"About what my plans are," Maggie replied, noticing Audrey relax, but saw that her aunt and uncle looked worried. "Don't worry, it's good news." She laughed.

"Okay girl, we're listening." Uncle Bobby interjected.

"I'm going to travel coast to coast and write a blog!"

From the looks of confusion on everyone's faces, Maggie knew she had to explain.

"Are you getting back into trucking?" Bobby asked.

"No. I've found a sprinter camper van for sale in Halifax. I've spoken with a customizer who will set it up to my specifications."

"But what about your job?" Julie asked before plucking a cookie from the tray.

"I spoke with my editor and ran my proposal past him. He thinks it's a great idea. I'll record converting the van and blog about the van life. Ripley said with my years of trucking, I can make a comparison between the two, which will make in more interesting."

"Well, this is news." Replied Audrey, dabbing her lips with a napkin.

Maggie smiled. "I also think I'll write a book. I don't know what it will be about yet. It's just an idea."

"What about your house and condo?" Aunt Julie asked.

"When I get back, I will clean out the condo and put it up for rent again. I'll hire the manager to check in and let me know if there are any issues, just like I did in the past. The house I will clean and lock up. After Liam died, I installed some security cameras. I can monitor them from where ever I am, and I know Mrs. Cameron watches everything. I'll leave her my number and she can call if she sees anything suspicious. But I won't be gone forever. I'll be travelling back and forth, and depending on how many stops I make, I'll be back every few weeks. Uncle Bobby, you know a trip in a semi only takes seven days from Halifax to Vancouver, weather permitting."

"That's true. If you're not driving a rig, you can stop in every time you go by Cobden. No excuses now. It sounds like you've put a lot of thought into this. I know you'll be fine. You always are." Uncle Bobby said, giving her a big hug.

"When are you planning on leaving?" Julie asked.

"I figured right after New Year's. I'll watch the weather forecast first, of course. No need to head out into a snow storm."

Audrey remained quiet. It wasn't until later, after Julie and Bobbie retired for the night, that she voiced her opinions.

"Be honest with me, Maggie. Are you planning on a new vendetta? Do I still have to worry about you?"

Maggie chuckled, "No Audrey. I'm going to do exactly what I said, write a series of articles and work on a book. Maybe I can title the book 'My life as a Serial Killer'." She joked.

"That's not funny." Audrey snapped.

"Audrey, I'll call and stop in. We can both keep working the Facebook page until we find out who those last two hair clips belong to. In the meantime, we can continue looking in other avenues. I can stop at libraries across the country and check old news articles. Maybe that will help."

Audrey frowned. "I know you better than most people. Can you promise me you won't do anything risky?"

"Audrey, you know I can't make that promise. If I find someone in need, you know I'll help them. I can't change who I am."

"What about Noelle's ashes?"

"I plan to scatter her ashes. I'll start at the Atlantic Ocean and end at the Pacific. She loved the ocean so much, it's what she would want."

"Agreed."

Audrey stayed a while longer and wondered if there was something else behind Maggie's sudden need to travel the highways again. Maggie sat sipping her drink, lost in thought. It was Maggie's dark side that terrified Audrey. Not because she thought Maggie would harm her or anyone she loved, but because she worried one day Maggie would come up against someone she couldn't beat. The thought of burying Maggie tore at her deep in her soul. She'd become family, almost a surrogate child, but didn't know what to do to prevent Maggie from avenging wrongs. So far, no one she'd killed was innocent, but that didn't justify her actions. A part of Audrey's fear was based on the thought that one day, Maggie could make a mistake and an innocent person would die. Something she knew Maggie would never come back from.

After a while, the silence between them thickened the air and Audrey excused herself. Maggie was so deep in thought, she barely noticed when Audrey left the room.

15

On January 3, with a few clear days of weather ahead, Maggie left Cobden and started home. Her plan was to head to her house first and check on things. Then go into the city to work on the next items on her list, which included picking up the Sprinter van, cleaning out the condo, and listing it for rent. But first she had a side stop to make on her way, something she didn't tell anyone else about. She was picking up the Christmas present she bought for herself.

Maggie followed the instructions on her GPS and pulled up in front of a weathered farmhouse. Outside were several dog runs lined up around the back of the house. When she turned off the engine, she heard barking from multiple dogs alerting the owner of her presence. Smiling she pulled on her gloves, stepped out of the car, and went to the front entrance. A sharp rap on the door with her knuckles and a portly woman swung it open before stepping out to greet her.

"Maggie Murphy?" She asked, and at Maggie's nod, continue. "I'm Cathy." Her hand was outstretched.

Maggie took the hand, liking Cathy's firm grip. "Hi Cathy! Yes, I'm Maggie."

"Come on up. I have the one you picked out all ready for you." She smiled.

Maggie entered the house to the sweet aroma of cedar chips and the musky scent of many animals. She could hear smaller yips along with the deeper sounds from the older dogs. She waited in the kitchen as Cathy went off to another room.

Upon returning, she held a wiggling brown ball in her arms. As soon as Maggie saw it, her heart melted. Cathy held out the pudgy brindle boxer boy, with his white blaze and motley pink and black nose.

"Watcha calling him?" She asked, as Maggie took the pup from her and pulled him close, nuzzling him.

"I'm not sure just yet. I thought I'd meet him first and see what fits."

Cathy smiled, "He's a little imp. I'm going to suggest crate training. This breed is on the anxious side. If you leave them alone, they'll get into a whole mess of trouble."

"I have a small crate in my car to get him home in. From there we'll see, but I'll keep it in mind. I don't expect to be away from him often."

Maggie signed the contract, handing Cathy the rest of the breeding fee, then Cathy handed Maggie a bag containing a blanket, a toy, and some dog food to get her started.

"I had him chipped and gave them your information, but when you name him, you'll have to update it. He's up to date on his shots, but you'll need to get him vet checked soon to set up a schedule for more. I've included his vaccine records in the bag. If you have questions, call."

"Thank you so much. Don't worry! He's in good hands."

Maggie made her way back to the car, gave the puppy a kiss on the head and slipped him in the travel crate on the front seat. He looked up at her and whined, tearing at her heart.

"It's okay boy. The crate is for your safety." Maggie cooed as she stroked his head.

Feeling him shaking, she stuffed the blanket and toy Cathy gave her in the crate beside him. His woeful eyes stared at her as she closed the door. It wouldn't be long before he outgrew it, but it would be fine for the next few weeks.

With a deep breath, Maggie started the car. Liam would have loved this pup. He often talked about the boxer his family had when he was a boy. The playfulness, energy and the fierce need to protect the family endeared the breed in his heart. Maggie never forgot this and when deciding on a dog, she knew it had to be a boxer. Her last nod to Liam's memory.

There was a thin dusting of snow on the ground when she arrived home. Her house looked forlorn without the glow from Christmas still burning, like those of several of her neighbours, but at least the sensor lights came on when she pulled in.

She turned off the ignitions and noticed something laying on the front porch. A ball form in the pit of her stomach. She stepped out of the car with wooden steps and approached the door. On the stoop was a bouquet of roses. This time, there were four black buds in the centre. *'Did I miss one?'* Maggie thought as she bent over and picked up the bouquet. She looked through the flowers and for the first time found a note. She pulled the card out of the envelope and read the typed words **'Welcome Home!'**

The flowers slipped from her hands, landing on the porch with a splat. Maggie spun around. *'Is someone watching me? Who knew I'd be home today?'* Her mind buzzed with unanswered questions. *'I wonder what happens when there are 12 black buds?'*

Her hand shook as she stooped and picked up the bouquet again. This time, walking straight to the compost bin and tossing them. She almost threw out the note, but held on to it. Someone was sending her a message, and she needed to figure out who, and this may be the clue. She slipped the card into her back pocket and headed back to her car to take her puppy out and unload her luggage.

Maggie lifted her still unnamed puppy from his carrier, attached the leash to his collar, carried him to the snow dusted grass and put him down. He wiggled about, playfully bouncing up and down, his white-tipped tail wagged from side to side, then he peed. It was lucky the breeder had started house training, but she'd bought a package of puppy pads for inside the house, just in case. She knew it would take a while before he caught on and became fully house broken. From everything she'd read, consistency was the key, and she knew it was a good thing she wasn't leaving on her coast-to-coast adventure right away. She still had to see the van, figure out what changes needed to be made, to make her comfortable on the road, plus plan everything with the customizer, clean out the condo, to get it ready to rent.

She lifted the puppy and looked into his dark brown eyes and tried out a few names on him. He cocked his head from side to side while listening. Nothing felt right. She put him back inside the crate and carried it into the house. He'd be safe from harm in there while she unloaded the rest of her things from the car.

16

When she finished unpacking and had put everything away, Maggie pulled out the salad she picked up at the Superstore for her supper, and added the dressing. She sat at the kitchen table eating while the puppy played on the floor at her feet. She'd barricaded the entrance to the kitchen to contain him and placed some pee pads on the tiles. This was the only room that was tiled other than the bathrooms and laundry room. The rest was carpeted. Until she finished training him, he couldn't have free range of the house.

She paused while eating and looked down at him, enjoying his antics, and small pearls of glee escaped her lips, startling him. For the first time since Liam died, the warmth of happiness enveloped her. Then the puppy pounced at a piece of lettuce she dropped on the floor, picked it up and spit it out. Maggie laughed again.

"I guess that won't be on your menu." She said, before bending over to pick up the lettuce and toss it out.

Maggie was cleaning up her dishes when the doorbell rang, sending the puppy into a fury of yips. She stepped over the barricade, and went to answer it. Glimpsing Colby through the sidelight, she smiled. She'd texted him she was home, and the speed at which he arrived afterwards showed her how much he missed her.

Maggie swung open the door with a wide smile on her face and said, "Well, hello stranger!"

"Hello yourself." He greeted, leaning over to kiss her cheek. "I hope it's okay, my just dropping in."

Colby heard the skittering of claws on the kitchen floor and turned, a quizzical look on his face, "What's that?"

"That's my new puppy. Come meet him."

Colby followed Maggie to the kitchen and looked over the barricade at the tiny puppy, jumping up to say hello.

"He's adorable. What's his name?"

Maggie frowned. "So far, I haven't chosen one. I only picked him up on my way home today. I've never had a dog before and thought he'd make a good companion for me. His name is important, as he'll have it for life. So, I'm searching for the right fit."

Maggie stepped over the barricade and scooped up the puppy, kissed his brow, and held him out for Colby to get a better look. Colby took the puppy from her and rubbed his ears.

"Evelyn will love him. If it's okay, I'd like to bring her over soon to meet him."

"Sure, but I'll have to think of a name before then. I don't want her to call him 'dog'." Maggie teased, taking the puppy back and putting him on the floor. "He's pretty smart, watch this." Maggie went to the counter and grabbed a couple of pieces of kibble.

She lifted her right index finger into the air and said, "Sit." The puppy sat, his tail wagging behind him. Maggie rewarded him with a treat. "I don't know how long training takes, but he seems pretty quick."

"It's like a light bulb went off," Colby commented.

"That's it!" Maggie exclaimed.

"What's it?" Colby asked, confused.

"Edison. I'll call him Edison." Maggie rubbed his ears. "How do you like that, boy?" To which Edison's tail wagged.

They left Edison in the kitchen, asleep on a soft mat, and went to the living room to talk.

"So, where's Evelyn tonight?"

"She's with my mom. I debated bringing her, but it's a school night and I didn't want to keep her out too late. Plus, we haven't seen each other since our dinner."

"Is your mom at your place, or is Evelyn at hers?"

Colby frowned, "At my mom's place. She's spending the night. Why?"

"I wondered if I should open a bottle of wine for us to share while we talk."

"Talk? Good talk or bad talk?" Colby asked. "And yes, wine would be nice."

"Good talk I think." Maggie replied as she picked out a bottle of chianti, opened it, and attached the aerator before pouring them each a glass.

"I wanted to tell you about my plans."

Colby listened as Maggie laid out her plan to travel coast to coast and write a blog. They hadn't come up with a title for it yet, but she explained her editor loved the idea. She told him about the Sprinter camper van she purchased and explained there were some modifications that needed to be done to set it up for her as she'd be living in it while she travelled. Her excitement was evident.

When she'd finished talking, Colby sighed. Maggie looked at his frown and wondered what was bothering him.

"That sounds very exciting, Maggie. When would you leave?"

"Oh, not until Spring. I have a lot to work out first. Plus, I'd like to see where this goes." She replied through hooded eyes.

"This?" He asked.

"This," she said, motioning between the two of them.

A broad smile swept across his face, and he grabbed her hand. "I'd like that too, but how would it work if you're on the road?"

Maggie took a sip of her wine, to pause while she gathered her thoughts. "Well, before I leave, we should spend time together. We already know we like each other. Evelyn adores me." She winked. "When I'm on the road, we can FaceTime. I don't plan to be on the road forever. I figured I would go out, maybe for a few weeks, and return for a few weeks. It will depend on how the blog goes. I'm also setting up a YouTube channel to video different things. But one thing I want to do is write a book. I have some ideas for a crime mystery."

"I like the sound of that."

They continued chatting, and when the first bottle was empty, Maggie offered to open a second one, but Colby declined, saying he had to drive. Maggie replied, "Or do you?" The meaning behind her words hit him, and he hesitated.

"You said you wanted to take things slow."

Maggie chuckled, "And you pointed out how brief life was. Of course, if it's too soon…"

A deep sound rumbled in his throat as he leaned forward and kissed her, his lips gentle at first, until the need deepened. He broke away and asked, "Are you sure?"

Her voice was husky when she whispered, "Yes."

17

Colby left early the next morning, giving Maggie a kiss and promising to call. Maggie languished in bed before phoning Audrey. The flowers she found on the porch continued to bother her. The latest bouquet had four black buds. She realized she missed one containing three, and wondered if it had arrived before they left for Ontario. If so, Audrey would know.

Audrey answered the phone on the second ring.

"Hey Maggie, how are you? Did you get yourself settled in?"

"Yes, I'm good, and I even had a visitor last night."

"Do I have to guess, or can I assume it was the handsome Detective Tate?"

"Yes." Maggie felt heat in her face as the colour rose to her cheeks. She wouldn't tell Audrey he just left. That was something Audrey didn't need to know.

"You sound happy, so I won't warn you to be careful."

Maggie rolled her eyes before proceeding. "When you were here, was a bouquet of roses delivered?"

Audrey hesitated. "Yes. Why?"

"Let me guess, nine red roses and three black buds?"

"Yes." Audrey whispered. "How did you know? I tossed the black buds because they creeped me out. The rest I put in water. I said nothing to you at the time because you had so much going on. Does it mean something?"

"I'm not sure. I got home yesterday to find a bouquet with four black buds and for the first time there was a note enclosed that said, 'Welcome Home'. Whoever sent them typed it. If it was handwritten, there may have been a clue. But I already received one with one bud and another with two. No cards."

"Maggie, this is serious. Someone is trying to scare you. When did it start?"

"Shortly after Liam died, but before I got involved with the Dark Enders, so it can't have anything to do with them or Carter."

"You need to be careful, Maggie."

"I will Audrey. If I learn anything, I'll let you know."

Wanting to change the subject, Maggie snapped a picture and sent it to Audrey. "Check your phone. He may not look like much now, but he's going to be a big boy based on the size of his paws."

"Awe he's adorable Maggie. What's his name?"

"Edison, he'll travel with me and alert me to trouble, plus keep me company."

"I'm sure he will. Knowing you have him with you will put my mind at ease. But do me a favour? Keep me in the loop. If you get any more flowers, I want to know, especially if there's another card enclosed."

"I will. Okay Audrey, I have to go take Edison out, then we're heading to the condo to clean and prepare it for renting. Chat soon."

Maggie pressed end and scooped up Edison to take him to the fenced backyard. On the way, she found a small pile of poop on one of the puppy pads and told him what a good boy he was.

Later that morning, Maggie arrived at the condo, and a sense of unease overcame her. It wasn't anything she could put her finger on. There was nothing out of place, but something felt off. She put Edison on the floor to explore and made herself a pot of coffee. She'd spend the next few days cleaning and sorting through things, plus it was easier to be in the city while she worked with the customizer. The van needed a few more luxuries than just a bed, tv, microwave and fridge like she had in her rig. If she designed it right, it could have a small shower/toilet combo, which meant no more bucket! The idea thrilled her.

The first article for the blog series would describe the prep work needed before hitting the road. Everything had to be documented, from the design process to the finished product, meaning she needed lots of pictures. She made a mental note to request the customizer take pictures for her as well, because she couldn't be there full time.

Maggie placed the groceries she brought on the counter before turning to see where Edison had gotten too, only to find him curled up on the throw rug in front of the patio doors, enjoying the sunbeam that stretched across the floor. She smiled and put the groceries away. Then she put a bowl of water and food on the floor in the kitchen for Edison and scattered some pads out for him to use.

After putting away the groceries, she headed to Noelle's room. Although she packed up Noelle's things after she died, the need to clean this room first was overwhelming. She opened the door and looked around before stepping inside. Maggie swiped her finger along the surface of the dresser, leaving a trail in the layer of dust. The boxes containing Noelle's belongings lay stacked on the floor of the cupboard. When she first packed them up, Maggie couldn't bring herself to donate them, which was why they were still there.

Staring at the two small boxes, a tightness formed in her chest. Somehow, she had to do right by Noelle, even in death. Maggie took a deep breath, pulled out the boxes, and stacked them by the front entranceway. Edison lifted his head and yawned as she went by, but then curled up and went back to sleep.

In Noelle's room, Maggie changed the sheets on the bed and put fresh towels in the bathroom before starting the laundry. By the time she finished, everything gleamed. Now it was time to tackle her room. She packed her clothes to bring down to the garage and put them in the trunk of her car. During one of her outings, she'd drop them back at the house.

The two bedrooms and bathrooms were clean, leaving the kitchen, living and dining rooms, but first she needed to take Edison out for a walk. She grabbed the leash and harness, slipped them on him, and headed out. As soon as his paws hit the grass, he peed and pooped. Maggie cleaned it up and tossed the bag in a garbage bin on the street. Then took him for a walk around the downtown core.

The crisp air helped to clear her mind. Moving Noelle's belongings had left her emotionally exhausted, and the fresh air made her feel better. She looked down at Edison and felt gratitude at having him in her life, or today she'd have wallowed in her emotions instead of getting outside, which did her a world of good. Maggie noticed Edison enjoyed the walk and the attention he received as he pranced around with pride. Watching him filled a tiny part of the hole left by losing Liam and her child. She smiled down and said. "How's my good boy?"

People stopped her to ask about Edison; how old he was, what breed, etc. Edison jumped with excitement every time someone bent over to pet him, his tail whipping back and forth. He marked a few more spots before they returned to the building, leaving Maggie feeling refreshed from the break, as she carried a tired Edison back.

18

Exhaustion washed over Maggie after she returned to the apartment. She looked down at Edison, who was snoring on the mat, and thought a nap was a good idea. So, instead of finishing the cleaning, she ordered in something for supper and curled up on the sofa. After eating, she picked up Edison and put him on her lap to watch a movie. She'd clean the rest of the apartment in the morning and take the boxes with Noelle's belongings to a drop box or shelter on her way to see the customizer. The box containing Noelle's ashes was still in the closet. She'd bring it to the house until she was ready to deal with that.

Not wanting to remain on her lap, Edison begged to get down. Soon, a skittering noise brought Maggie's attention to the kitchen. The puppy pads lay in disarray across the floor. Edison had his front paws on the ground and rump in the air, looking to play. He'd shredded two of the pads. Maggie laughed, but before going to bed, she taped new pads on the floor. He was going to play and it would keep them in place. She kissed his blaze and put Edison in the kitchen with his sleep mat. Any mess he made, she could dispose of it in the morning. As she walked away, he whined, and a small wave of guilt tickled her spine. One day he could sleep on a bed in her room, but for now, containing his accidents was more important, but she reassured him, "Don't worry boy, I'm in the next room."

In the morning, Maggie slipped off the bed and stepped into a puddle of puppy piddle. She cursed to herself and realized the barricade hadn't kept Edison in the kitchen. His accident wasn't something she could fault him for. She had to remember he was still a baby and learning to signal her when he needed to go out. Maggie mopped up the mess, got dressed, and went in search of him. She found him in the living room, playfully destroying one of her throw pillows. There was fluff scattered all over the room. It took everything in her not to laugh, as he looked so comical and proud of himself as he turned to her with a bit of fluff stuck to his lips.

She had to scold him. It wasn't something she wanted to do, but he had to learn it wasn't acceptable behaviour. Then she harnessed him to go out. It was time for a crate and made a note to get a soft-sided one where he could sleep. She wasn't a fan of the metal crates. In a soft sided crate, he wouldn't be able to get into trouble at night, but still be contained. She could keep him near her, and her home wouldn't get destroyed.

It was close to lunchtime when she finished cleaning the apartment, so Maggie grabbed a quick bite to eat, then took Edison and the box with Noelle's ashes down to her car. She'd already brought down the donation boxes containing Noelle's belongings.

While she was out, she needed to replace the destroyed pillow, maybe even buy a new set, stop at the pet store and head back to the house after stopping in to see the customizer.

At the pet store, Maggie looked at the various soft sided crates before deciding on one that folded up flat for storage but would still fit in the floor plan of her camper van at night. It had two zippered sides and a zippered top, but she planned to leave the top open like a playpen. Then, he could still use it as a safe space when he got older. Before checking out, she added some training treats and toys for him to 'destroy'.

When her errands were done, Maggie arrived back at her house late in the afternoon and called Colby. They'd chatted several times since she returned from Ontario, but their busy schedules made it difficult for them to see each other.

"Tate here."

"Hello Tate," she purred, "do you have any plans this evening?"

"Maggie?"

"Of course. Who else were you expecting?"

"I thought you were going to love me and leave me." He teased, "Yes, I'm free. What did you have in mind?"

"I think it's time Evelyn met Edison. I can make some homemade pizza, pull out the board games, maybe we could even take Edison for a walk."

"Evelyn would love that, and so would I. What time?"

"As soon as you're finished work and can get here. We'll build the pizza together, but I'll chop everything up beforehand. I think Evelyn will enjoy adding the toppings."

"Yes, she will. Okay, I'll send a text as we're leaving the house. Evelyn is going to be so excited. All she has done since I told her about Edison is ask when she can meet him."

"Sounds good. See you soon."

Maggie set up the crate as soon as the call ended. Edison could nap in there while she worked the dough. Maggie left the dough to rise while she chopped peppers, onions and other toppings and place them in covered bowls. One contained a mountain of freshly shredded mozzarella. According to the clock on the stove, she had enough time to get changed and take Edison out before Colby texted he was on his way.

Maggie fussed over what to wear and settled on a pair of jeans and a sweater, which she laid out to put on after her shower. Her hair didn't need washing, so she clipped it up out of the way and let the water wash away the stress from the last few days. After dressing, she pulled her hair into a low ponytail and finished with some light cosmetics.

The diamonds on her left hand caught the light, and for the first time since Liam placed them there, took them off. Her eyes welled, but before the tears could spill out, she brought them to her lips, kissed them, and whispered goodbye to Liam. Her future had changed, and it was time to look ahead.

19

The sound of Edison's barking dragged Maggie from her sleep. Curious about what set him off, she got up, threw on some clothes, splashed water on her face and looked in on him. He was sitting up in his crate, his tail wagging a mile a minute as he watched her approach.

"Who's a good boy? Do you want out?" She cooed, stroking him behind the ear and fastening him into the harness for their walk.

When she returned and fed him, she caught sight of the board games still piled on the table and smiled. Colby and Evelyn were just what the doctor ordered, even if the doctor had warned her to be careful. Evelyn fell in love with Edison immediately, and he loved her back. Colby admonished her, explaining he was now going to be bombarded by requests for a puppy, so Maggie had better be prepared to share hers. Maggie had laughed and assured him she'd bring Edison over as often as she could.

While Edison crunched away at his kibble, she put away the games and flicked through the pictures on her phone, first at the ones she took last night, then the ones over Christmas and then she came to a set she'd forgotten she took. The ones from Colby's house.

Maggie remembered taking them, but couldn't remember why. She airdropped them to her computer so she could have a better look. Maggie sat down at her desk and pulled up the photographs on her iMac. The pictures were from a murder scene and included the file with notes on the investigation. One picture was of the police's primary suspect, Wesley Zimmerman.

She frowned while flicking through the pictures, trying to remember why she took them. The only recourse was to read through the file, and it wasn't until she came across the handwritten notes on the suspect that she remembered. On the back of his mugshot someone had written in bold block print **'GUILTY'**. They'd even underlined the word several times for emphasis.

Maggie looked at the evidence in front of her and felt the familiar sensation curl in her stomach. Here was another guilty man the police couldn't arrest. Taking care of it herself would be easy. But what would Audrey say? Audrey, who'd supported her in everything she'd done so far. Would something like this be too much?

Tapping her finger on her desk, she searched google for any information or articles she could find about the crime and the suspect. Even checking out his social media accounts, learning where he lived, but nothing stood out. The woman they suspected him of killing was on his list of friends, but she needed proof before taking action. Then it hit her. She'd follow him. It was a way to learn more about him, who he was and if he was capable of the crime. Killing him had to be justified. Following him was the only way to be certain.

There were too many injustices in the world, and Maggie's body shook in her struggle to control the bloodlust that boiled beneath the surface. "Only the deserving." She reminded herself.

20

Before the first streaks of dawn filtered through the sky, Maggie packed up Edison and headed towards the street Wesley Zimmerman lived on. His apartment was in a shared house in the downtown core. Under the cover of darkness, she left Edison in the car and walked the perimeter of the house to investigate. There were two exits, one in the front and one in the back. She noticed only one car parked in the driveway and wondered if it belonged to Zimmerman. She peered over the gate to the fenced-in backyard and assumed he'd leave through the front.

Maggie sprinted back to the car and took Edison out for a short walk along the street, looking into the parked cars as she passed, trying to determine which one was his, or if he even had a car. Returning to her vehicle once Edison had finished and not wanting to draw attention to herself, she put Edison into his crate and leaned back in the driver's seat to wait. She watched the house for signs of life, pulled her ball cap low over her eyes and slouched down, hoping not to be noticed.

Vibrant rays of pink and orange streaked the sky before the first lights went on inside the house. Soon, both floors were alive with light and movement. Maggie rolled her shoulders and wondered how long it would take before someone emerged from the house?

There was no need to pull up his picture for recognition as he exited the front door. The light from the screen lit his face up as he stepped out of the building, hunched over his phone. He was so absorbed in what he was doing; he didn't notice the car start. Maggie waited until he got to the end of the street and turned right, then left the curb to follow him. The stop sign enabled her to pause and look up the street before turning. He was waiting at the bus stop. To the left, she saw the bus approaching and a sigh of relief escaped her lips. Staying parked at the stop sign too long would attract unnecessary attention.

Maggie checked the rear-view mirror, to ensure no one was behind her, then waited for the bus to pass before she slipped in to follow it. She kept to a slow pace, waiting to see who got off each time the bus stopped.

She watched as he transferred buses a few more times before ending up at the docks. Maggie smiled when she realized he was at work and would be there for the day. She checked the time and estimated when his shift would end, and left, knowing she'd return before he was done.

There were plenty of things on her to-do list, and waiting until he got off work wasn't one of them. She'd check on the progress of the van and stop by the condo for one last check before listing it. The property manager already had a set of keys and her instructions. He would contact her with successful candidates. Maggie planned to continue renting to students because the short-term lease was convenient in case the unit needed repairs or she listed it. So far, she'd been lucky with the students she'd rented to, but anything could happen, so chose to keep her options open.

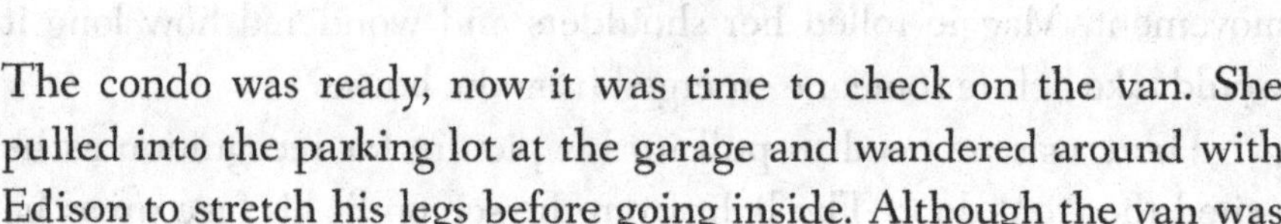

The condo was ready, now it was time to check on the van. She pulled into the parking lot at the garage and wandered around with Edison to stretch his legs before going inside. Although the van was in a bay being worked on, and she was eager to check the progress, Edison needed a break from being in the car for so long.

When Edison was back in his crate, she made her way to the bay where they were working in the interior. The original double bed took up the whole back of the van, leaving room for little else. She had the bed changed to a single that flipped up into a dinette. This made room for a small shower/toilet cabinet. She figured she'd use the showers at truck stops and get a hotel from time to time to stretch out her water supply, but wanted to shower in the van if facilities weren't available. Plus, the toilet would replace her old bucket system from her trucking days. She had them remove the passenger seat to house Edison's soft crate and make more room for her kitchen and work space, but had seatbelts installed in the dinette just in case she ever had a passenger.

The garage manager saw Maggie approach and greeted her.

"Hey Maggie, how are you? Did you come to check out how we're doing?"

"Hi Tim, I'm good, thank you. Yes, I was curious to see how things were coming along. Any idea of when it will be ready?"

"We will have everything hooked up and ready to go for the end of next week."

Maggie beamed, "Wonderful! Can I see how the shower cabinet looks?"

"I think you'll be pleased. Come see."

21

Prior to the end of Wesley's shift, Maggie found herself parked within view of the bus stop at the port. She wasn't sure what she was going to accomplish by following him, but everything she read in the police file indicated he was trouble. The darkness in her pulsed with excitement and possibilities. Unsure what she'd face, Maggie brought her gun with her. She stowed it under the seat and slipped the hunting knife into her pocket. Carrying them became a habit during her vendetta with the Dark Enders.

Her eyes never left the exit of the warehouse as she fed Edison a few pieces of kibble while she waited. She spotted him leave the building and walk past her car before getting on the waiting bus. Maggie breathed a sigh of relief that he didn't look her way. Edison growled a soft, low growl as Wesley went by. "That's right, boy, he's not nice." She said, feeding him another piece of kibble. After Wesley climbed onto the waiting bus and it departed, she slipped in behind it to follow him home.

Keeping her distance, even as he walked down his street, she parked where she could watch the house. Her stomach rumbled, and she knew it was well past supper. She considered heading home to eat, thinking he was in for the night, when she saw him step out on the porch and light a smoke. Maggie sank down low in her seat and watched as a cab pulled up. He tossed the cigarette into the garden and hopped into the back seat.

Maggie pulled out and followed until the cab stopped at a bar near the boardwalk. Wesley got out, paid the driver, and went inside. She glanced down at Edison on the seat beside her and considered her next move. Leaving him in the car while she went inside wasn't an option. The condo was only a couple of blocks away. Figuring she had time, she went back, parked her car and left Edison barricaded in the kitchen, then walked back. She'd observe him and see what kind of man he was.

Maggie pulled up a stool at the bar a few spots away from Wesley. Out of the corner of her eye, she noticed him take a swig from his beer. Her proximity to him would allow her to watch and eavesdrop on his conversations. She waited and observed as he hit on every woman who came by and bought drinks at the bar. He even attempted to pay for them, but was rejected every time he did.

'What was it that alarmed them?' Maggie wondered, *'he's average looking, clean, was it his approach?'* Maggie opened her cell phone and brought up his picture. *'It's his eyes. They were the dead black eyes of a shark.'* The women sensed the man he was.

As the night wore on, following each rejection, he became more aggressive in his approach. He grabbed the arm of the last woman, forcing the bartender to intervene. Maggie frowned and allowed her fingers to tighten on her glass. *'He's suspected of killing a woman he knew, but would he go after a stranger if he got angry enough?'* Maggie wondered. *'Maybe that woman wasn't his first victim?'*

She noticed he didn't ring up a tab, but paid for each drink as it arrived, so she followed suit. If he made a move, she needed to be prepared. Out of the corner of her eye, she saw him staring at her. She picked up her phone to feign disinterest. She wasn't sure if he looked her way because he suspected she was watching him or if it was because she was the only one in the bar he hadn't hit on yet. Whichever it was, she needed him to ignore her.

Hoping to prevent him from hitting on her, she pretended to take a call. "Hi honey, yes, I'm here. I'm waiting for you at the bar. See you soon." She knew he was listening and figured he'd get the idea.

It wasn't long before he hit on someone who'd already rejected him, and he snapped in response. Maggie saw the change in him. It was like someone flicked a switch. She recognized the ire that took over, having felt it every time she confronted a monster. Now she was certain his character was flawed. Somehow, he felt entitled to the women he approached. It didn't matter if they were interested in him or not. She'd seen this behaviour before, and her body tingled with excitement. Her hand slid into her pocket and touched the hilt of her knife. Wherever he went tonight, she would follow.

As fewer women approached to order drinks, he began using her trick of watching the room through the mirrored glass behind the bar. Maggie wondered what he was waiting for. Then a woman got up and left on her own. He slid off his seat and followed with Maggie close behind.

Keeping at a safe distance, Maggie saw the woman turn and enter an underground parking garage. Wesley's pace quickened, and so did hers. She was thankful for the soft-soled shoes she'd put on before leaving the house. The clunk of his boots echoed on the pavement. Maggie saw the woman turn and look over her shoulder, but the sight of a man being followed by a woman didn't seem to worry her.

Maggie watched the woman fumble with her car keys and tsked to herself. A woman alone needed to be prepared. It was just enough time for Wesley to close the distance between them. She stood back behind a pole, not wanting to alert him of her presence, while she waited. She had to be sure before she made a move.

He grabbed the woman's arm and spun her around. Her eyes flickered with recognition when she saw him, then narrowed.

"What do *you* want?" She sneered, oblivious to the potential danger.

He slapped the woman hard across the face. The sound echoed in the underground. Her hand cupped her cheek, eyes wide as she stepped back against her car.

"You!" He hissed.

The woman screamed. The shrill sound bounced off the concrete walls as Maggie sprang into action. She lifted her hood, hiding her hair, covered her face with her scarf, and pulled out her knife.

Maggie rushed up behind him, her knife clenched in her hand, as he shoved the woman to the ground. She swung her arm, and the blade found its mark, sinking into the soft flesh above his hip bone. He howled in pain and spun around. Anger flashed in his eyes rather than alarm.

"Leave!" she hissed to the woman, who, wide eyed, scrambled up and got into her car. Wesley tried to stop her, but she slipped past him. The engine sprang to life and the tires spun, squealing as they found traction and she drove away.

Wesley stared down at the hand he'd pressed to his abdomen, blood seeping between his fingers. His shock registered in his expression.

"Who the fuck are you?"

"I'm the piper and it's time to pay." Maggie replied.

He jabbed his fist at Maggie, but she stepped back out of the way, bouncing on her toes, ready to fight. He raised his fist and thrust another punch, which she sidestepped with ease. As much as she'd like to fight him, draining the pent-up energy that vibrated within, there wasn't time. A guttural sound escaped her lips as she rushed towards him, stabbing him several times in quick succession. He grabbed his midsection and slumped to his knees; eyes wide. She raised her hand and sliced the knife across his neck, finishing the job. Blood pulsed out, covering her hand and soaking the arm of her coat.

She locked eyes with his, smiling as his eyes glazed over and rolled back. Her chest heaved from the frenzy of her attack. The sound of fast approaching footsteps alerted her to imminent danger. She scanned the area for an escape and spied a door a few feet away. Her feet caught traction, and she ran towards it and freedom.

22

Sirens wailed as she raced from the building. She kept her hood up and her head low as she went. Holding the blood-soaked knife buried in her pocket, her hand gripping it tightly. Back on the street, she blended in with the crowd. There, she lowered her hood and scarf. Knowing the woman Wesley attacked would report it and describe her saviour as a person wearing a hooded coat with their face covered. Maggie doubted the woman noticed her stature, or that she was a woman, so she didn't feel the need to hide or bring undue attention to herself.

Maggie slowed her stride as she made her way back to the condo. She needed to get inside, wash the blood from her clothing and knife, and change. The blue/red flash of lights filled the sky as police cars descended on the area. She'd be home long before the police started investigating what happened.

Maggie used the sleeve of her left arm to open the door. Being careful not to leave a bloody trail. She didn't plan on confronting him. But she also didn't expect him to follow that woman and attack her.

As soon as she entered her apartment, Maggie stripped out of her clothes, stuffed them into the washing machine and started the load.

She stepped over the barrier to the kitchen, with Edison jumping around her feet in excitement as she headed to the sink to wash the knife. When she finished, she wiped it down with bleach, then pulled out a scrub brush and cleaned the blood from under her nails.

Maggie padded to the bathroom and looked in the mirror, and noticed a spot of blood on her cheek. She ran the water and washed her face before checking for more. Then she slipped into a pair of yoga pants and a sweatshirt, brushed her hair into a ponytail, and went back to the kitchen to look down at Edison's sweet face. He had a look of expectation and goofiness in his upturned mouth.

"Okay, my sweet boy. Give me a second and I'll take you out."

Maggie grabbed the harness and put it on Edison, picked up some sanitizing wipes, and left the unit. She'd retrace her steps and wipe down any surface she touched. The elevator buttons, the front door, whatever she could remember as she walked Edison towards the parking garage to ensure Wesley was dead.

There was no need to hurry, so she allowed Edison to take his time sniffing the ground. He had yet to learn to cock his leg. Instead, he squatted and marked his territory on every blade of grass they came to, including producing a small poop. She discarded this along with the used wipes in a trash can on the street.

By the time she was close to the parking garage, the EMTs were wheeling out Wesley's body. Maggie scooped up Edison, thankful he was still small enough she could do that, and watched. She wanted to verify Wesley's death, watching for the body bag.

She let out the breath she held as she watched his covered body loaded into the back. To her left, she saw the frightened woman he attacked giving her statement to an officer. Satisfied they couldn't connect her to the crime, Maggie put Edison back on the ground and turned to leave.

"Maggie? Maggie? Is that you?"

Her heart sank at the sound of his voice, but she plastered a smile on her face and spun around to greet Colby.

"Colby!" she replied, leaning in and kissing his cheek. "When I saw the commotion, I wondered if you'd be here."

Colby leaned over and rubbed Edison's ears. "What are you doing here?"

"I'm taking Edison for a walk."

"No, I mean downtown. What are you doing downtown?"

"Oh." Maggie paused, frowning. "Didn't I tell you I have a condo down here?"

Colby shook his head. Maggie noticed the dark circles under his eyes and realized he wasn't sleeping well. She wondered if his lack of sleep had anything to do with her, but held her tongue.

"I bought a condo downtown when I started university. My parents left me some money, and I saved a lot during my career as a truck driver. I wasn't the traditional student, and knew I didn't want to live in student housing, so I bought the condo. Now I rent it out to students for the school year. I was just there cleaning it. I didn't rent it this year because I considered selling it, but I've changed my mind."

"Oh," was all he said.

"Is everything okay Colby? You don't seem yourself."

"I'll explain everything as soon as I'm finished down here. Why don't you give me the address of your condo and I'll stop by so we can talk?"

Maggie chimed her address off and touched Colby's arm before leaning in to kiss his cheek again. This time, he turned and captured her lips and kissed her back. A smile played at the corner of her mouth as she turned and walked back to the condo. It took every ounce of restraint not to run. She needed to check that she'd covered her steps and left nothing out to arouse his suspicions.

23

Once out of Colby's eyesight, Maggie scooped up Edison and picked up her pace. There was a lot to take care of before he arrived.

Her impatience was evident as she repeatedly pushed the call button for the elevator. When the doors opened, she puffed out a breath of exasperation and sagged against the back wall of the cubical as the elevator rose.

The bell chimed, and the doors slid open when it reached her floor. She put Edison back down and hurried to her door, inserted the key, and opened it. The smell of bleach was the first thing she noticed. It wasn't too strong and she could explain it away by the fact she was cleaning, but she didn't want the smell in the apartment. She lit a scented candle and cracked a window, hoping to dissipate the aroma to something more pleasant.

The knife was still in the dish rack, so she picked it up and hid it on the shelf in her closet at the back. Her eyes scanned the apartment for drops of blood. Satisfied there weren't any, she checked the laundry to see if the blood came out of her clothes and threw everything into the dryer.

She put the barricade into the front hall closet and noticed that Edison had soiled the puppy pads she laid down before deciding to go after Wesley, so she tossed them out and put fresh pads down.

She glanced at the clock on the stove and figured she had time for a quick shower. Her hair was clean, so she tucked it up in a shower cap and stepped under the steaming water and scrubbed her skin. Washing away the aroma of sweat and fear that permeated her flesh.

Still wrapped in a towel, she pulled clean underwear out of her bag and slipped back into the yoga pants and sweatshirt she was wearing when she saw Colby. They were clean, and changing her clothes would arouse his suspicions. She desperately needed a drink and grabbed the bottle of red she'd left in the unit and opened it. If he'd finished work for the night, maybe he would share a glass with her. If not, after the night she'd had, she could use one. The last thing she did was to close the open window so the aroma from the candle would fill the room and flopped down on the sofa to wait.

The adrenaline that pulsed through her body had dissipated, and Maggie dozed off when the intercom sounded, sending Edison into a round of barks, alerting her to Colby's arrival. Startled, she jumped up and answered it. The tension that wracked her body eased when he responded to her question. "Who is it?"

It didn't take long before Colby knocked on the door. Maggie peered through the peephole, checking that he was alone before opening it. Colby seemed unsure as he stood on the other side with his arms dangling. She stepped towards him and he wrapped his arms around her, pulled her tight against his body, and gave her a deep kiss.

"Ever since I saw you outside tonight, I've wanted to do that." He said as he lifted his head and looked around. "This is a nice place. I can see why the university students want it."

"The location is prime, but it also has two bedrooms, both with an ensuite. That's why the students want it." She chuckled. "Come in and have a seat. Are you done for the night?"

"Technically, no, but my partner will cover for me. Why? What did you have in mind?"

"I just opened a nice red and thought we could share it. You look like you could use some downtime, and I'm assuming Evelyn is with your mom if you're working nights."

Colby smiled. "Yes, she is. It's been a rough week. Let me call the station and let them know I'm off the clock. Then I'll ask my mom to stay, if that's okay."

"That's perfect." Maggie grinned, knowing he wouldn't stay if she was a suspect.

Maggie poured them each a glass of wine and sat down on the sofa, waiting for Colby to finish with his calls. She smiled to herself, pleased that she put on a cute bra and panty set after her shower. Colby would think she dressed like that all the time, especially since she had the same yoga pants and sweatshirt on overtop.

She watched Colby slip his phone into his pocket after finishing his calls, then turn and make his way to her. He reached for the glass she offered, took a sip, and sagged back onto the sofa.

"Why don't you tell me what's on your mind?" Maggie suggested as she crossed her legs underneath her.

"Are you sure you want to know?" He asked, watching as she nodded, then sighed before continuing. "I don't even know where to begin."

"Why don't you start with tonight?"

"What are you talking about? The crime scene? That's easy. Guy tried to grab a woman after she left a local bar, then some vigilante saved her but killed the perp. But here's where it gets strange. He was the prime suspect in another murder investigation. We knew he was guilty but couldn't prove it. So, in a sense, his death is poetic justice."

"Do you know who the vigilante is?"

Colby shook his head. "No. The woman was too terrified to get a good look. Whoever it was saved her life. But we can't have some random vigilante killer out there, so we'll be looking for witnesses and at videos from surveillance cameras in the area."

Maggie swallowed a large gulp of wine and sputtered. Before coughing to clear her airway. Colby rubbed her back. *'Shit!'* She thought, *'I forgot about the street cameras.'* She prayed there wasn't any footage of her removing her scarf and hood that would identify her.

"I hope you find out whoever did this, but didn't that person save the woman? Could it be self-defence?"

"Not likely. The repeated stab wounds could have been part of a fight-or-flight situation, but the perpetrator sliced the attacker's throat. That was deliberate and demonstrated forethought."

"I see. Well, I'm sure you'll figure it out. What else is on your mind?"

"Us."

The word hung in the air between them. Its power caused Maggie's eyes to flick up to his. She licked her lips, but her mouth felt dry, so she took a sip of wine, then responded.

"Us? What do you mean?"

"I've been wondering how there could be an us, what with you leaving on your cross-country blog trip."

Maggie hesitated before responding. "Colby, if you want there to be an us, we will make it work. I'm coming back. Plus, we can video chat, have phone calls, check in by text. I explained all this to you. It's not like I'm moving away." She replied, cuddling into him.

"I'm falling for you, Maggie, hard. And so is Evelyn. That's why, if you're not all in, you need to let me know."

Maggie put her glass on the table, turned to him, put her hands on either side of his face, and kissed him. Then she stood up, took his hand and said, "Let me show you how all in I am." As she led him to the bedroom.

24

The next morning when the alarm on her phone sounded, Maggie rolled over and snuggled into Colby's warmth, who wrapped his arms around her and kissed her forehead. They set the alarm early so they could enjoy coffee together. Colby's mom would take Evelyn to school and although he had some things to do at the station that morning, he was off for the next few days. Maggie popped out of bed and started the coffee while Colby jumped in the shower.

"I have an idea. I have nothing pressing for the next couple of days, and you're off. Why don't you take Evelyn out of school and we plan some fun activities for her? I'll even cook for you both. What do you say?" Maggie asked, curling her legs up beside her on the sofa.

"More time with you and Evelyn, plus I'm going to get fed? Why not? Let me give you the code for my house. You can see what staples I have and what you can work with and then pick up what you need."

"The code to your house?" Maggie hesitated before taking a sip of coffee.

"You said you were all in." Colby teased.

She beamed back at him. "Yes, I did!"

"While you're doing that, I can go to the station, finish what I need to, pick up Evelyn and let the school know she'll be absent for a couple of days."

"Sounds good."

"Do you have anything in mind?"

"Why don't we wait and ask Evelyn? But I'll make a list of possibilities. One thing I think she'd like is the Discovery Centre. Of course, we both know at some point we'll be going to the park." Maggie chuckled.

"The Discovery Centre? That's a great idea. Evelyn will love that." Colby put his cup in the sink. "I'd better get going or I won't get back until suppertime."

"Okay. I have to take Edison out and clean up here. I'll stop by your place to see what I need, shop and go home to change. Should I pack a bag? Or is it too soon?"

"Pack a bag! We can turn the living room into a camp. I'll put an air mattress on the floor, we can watch movies and make popcorn. Evelyn will be in heaven." He said, kissing her cheek. "See you later, Maggie."

Maggie washed and put the dishes away, emptied the garbage, changed the sheets, and took the dirty ones home with her to wash. There wasn't time to run a load at the apartment and she didn't plan on returning. She made a quick stop outside with Edison and thought, *'Oh drat, I forgot to check with Colby if I could bring Edison with me. I can't leave him.'*

Maggie fired off a quick text.

Grinning, she sent the thumbs up emoji. Then stuffed the laundry into the trunk of her car, put Edison in the crate, and headed to Colby's house.

Maggie left Edison in the car as she went through Colby's cupboards and fridge before putting a list together of what she needed. She was about to leave when a thought struck her and headed to his office. Maggie took a picture of the disarray so she could put everything back as it was and looked through his files. She'd done the police a service by killing Wesley Zimmerman. Maybe there were others.

A few files had potential, so she photographed everything and put the office back the way she found it. Guilt prickled at the back of her neck as she searched through his files, but doing so could both help the police and curb her bloodlust.

Maggie would upload the pictures to her computer and delete them from her phone when she got home, in case Colby had any reason to look through it. She knew he wouldn't snoop, but if there was a reason to look at pictures, he might discover them.

Satisfied the office was as she found it, she went to the kitchen and wrote a note on the white board for them.

Colby and Evelyn, I'll see you soon! :) Maggie

With a smile on her face, she locked the door, went out to her car, took Edison out to relieve himself, and headed home.

The flash of moving blinds across the street alerted Maggie to the fact Mrs. Cameron was peeking out of her living room window. A mischievous grin swept her face as she stepped out of her car and waved. Laughter escaped her lips as the blinds snapped shut. Scooping Edison up and dragging the sheets from the back, she went inside.

Maggie didn't bother with the laundry, it could wait, instead she stuffed the sheets in the hamper and went to the kitchen. There she opened a grocery tote and filled it with items from her cupboards and went to her bedroom to pack a small bag. As an afterthought, she grabbed the sleeping bag from the basement, the one she bought for her camping trips with Liam, knowing it would be handy in their living room fort.

It took two trips to get everything in the car and a third to get Edison, but soon she was on her way to the grocery store to get what she needed before heading back to Colby's house to set up. Her body tingled with excitement at the prospect of a genuine family and everything it meant. She wondered if she could have it all.

25

She'd spent the last two days with Colby and Evelyn, which passed with a blur of activity. Maggie realized she hadn't felt this much happiness since before Liam died, and it scared her. Her heart ached with what might have been, and now wondered if their child had been a girl and if it was, would she be like Evelyn? Evelyn filled the ache in her heart, but Maggie didn't know if she could give up her blood lust and settle down with Colby and Evelyn. She did it once. Maybe she could do it again and they could become a family.

At home, she checked her messages and found the customizer had called to let her know the van was ready to pick up. Her heart soared. It was almost time to set out on her adventure. It was then that the realization hit her. She *wanted* to be a family with Colby and Evelyn, but she wasn't ready to give up her blood lust, not just yet. There were too many people who deserved to meet their end with the slice of her knife. Wesley Zimmerman proved that. This cross-county trip and blog might help her get the need out of her system, and gain some clarity, because she wanted to be a part of their lives.

She called the customizer back and arranged a time to pick up the van. Then she called for a cab and barricaded Edison in the kitchen. She considered asking Colby for a lift, but decided against it. She knew how he felt about her leaving and how he'd figure into her life, even though she'd reassured him multiple times she was coming back. When she started her journey, she'd have to make a point of keeping her word and maintaining regular contact.

Tim walked with her while she completed her inspection of the van, pointing out the attributes and she knew she'd made the right choices with the upgrades. The interior compartment was small but versatile, ensuring her comfort inside. Travelling the highways in a rig was in her blood, and her van was pure luxury by comparison. It had everything she'd need. A small kitchen, toilet/shower combination, bed, work station and storage. It even had an awning she could pull out for shelter when she parked. The bed flipped up and became a sofa during the day with a pop-up table to eat at, and there was even an entertainment system.

Because the construction process was part of her blog idea, she'd recorded everything, from purchasing it, the customizing, and now to the finished concept. She contacted Ripley before leaving the shop and told him she'd stop by. He needed to see this in person.

Maggie pulled up in front of the building, parked, and called Ripley to come down. If things went according to plan, this was going to be a profitable endeavour for both of them. She'd also set up a YouTube channel to post live videos. If it gained popularity, she could earn a residual income from it. Maggie would write a blog linked to the magazine, but she would also have a more personal one on the side.

She ran the idea by Ripley first, to avoid a conflict of interest, but he was fine with it as long as the magazine had first dibs. Maggie promised she would pass anything she wrote past him before posting. Fewer people were buying print magazines, and the future was in online subscriptions. Ripley was excited to have something to move the magazine forward and told her so.

She'd just finished setting up and opening the doors for Ripley when he exited the office building with several members of staff who clamoured behind him. Maggie smiled, knowing their curiosity got the better of them and they wanted to see it, too. She was proud to show off her new travel accommodations.

"It's great, Murphy!" Ripley said after looking inside. He always used her last name when he addressed her. "I hope you photographed the entire building process. A photo spread of it would be a great way to kick off the blog."

Maggie smiled, then laughed. "Of course I did! I have tons of pictures. I figured I'd go home, sort through them, and write the first piece for your approval before I leave."

Ripley nodded. "Are you worried about your safety out there? A woman alone on the road?"

Maggie frowned. "You remember I was a truck driver, right?" She watched as he nodded. "Then you know that I'm well prepared for life on the road. I've done it before; I know the routes and best places to park. But I won't have the same issues of stopping for the mandatory breaks like I did when trucking. This beauty will be much easier to manoeuvre. I should come up with a name for her. It will add some flavour to the blog."

"As long as you're sure. I don't want you getting hurt out there. But, don't just stick to your familiar routes, explore a bit. The readers are looking for excitement. Interesting things they can't see in every city. You're creative. Try looking at this with fresh eyes. Pretend you didn't have a career travelling coast to coast. What did you want to see/know when you started?"

"Okay, I get the idea Ripley. My first run will be the familiar.

Maybe I'll run into some of my old road friends and they can add some colourful commentary, but I'll also be doing some exploring. Stopping and seeing things I couldn't in my rig."

Maggie took a lot of teasing from her coworkers about the size of her toilet/shower cupboard. One commented, 'only someone who was as tiny as her would fit inside'. The consensus was the set up appeared comfortable. Of course, she proudly showed everyone pictures of Edison as well. It was hard not to when his crate took up the space for the passenger seat, creating a lot of questions. They wished her well before going back to work. Maggie closed up the van and headed home. Edison needed to be let out. She was sure there'd be a mess on the kitchen floor by now. Hopefully, he'd hit the puppy pads, so all she'd have to do was roll them up.

As she pulled into the driveway and her eyes scanned her front porch, her heart sank; another bouquet waited for her. She parked and stepped out of the van before making her way to the front door. Maggie scooped up the flowers and, out of habit, looked around to see if anyone was watching.

She peered down at the now familiar mixture of red and black buds with disgust. Inside, someone had hidden a small envelope. Her hands shook as she plucked it out and opened it. In neat type was the following message:

ENJOY YOUR HAPPINESS WHILE YOU CAN

Fear prickled along the base of her neck, causing her to stumble in her hurry to unlock the door. After several failed attempts at the key hole, it went in and turned. Her breath hitched, as she stepped in and locked the door behind her. Maggie peered through the sidelight at the surrounding neighbourhood, noting the cars on the road and recorded their make and colour. She was now certain someone was following her. Maggie knew the sensible thing to do was report it, but it would raise too many questions she couldn't answer, and if she reported it, Colby would find out.

With the flowers still in hand, she greeted Edison and took him and the flowers out to the backyard. While Edison took care of his needs, she dumped the flowers in the green bin, but kept the note to add to the previous one. One thing was certain: she needed to move up her departure date before Colby and Evelyn got dragged into whatever mess this was.

Maggie let Edison back inside, cleaned up the puppy pads, laid out fresh ones, and changed his water. She played with him to wear out some of his energy. When he settled on his mat, she listed what she'd need for her road trip, but with limited space, had to choose only the essentials. Maggie went through her wardrobe, looking for versatile items, then laid everything out on the dining room table and packed them in the van. Next, she dug through her cupboards for food and sundries for her trip. Satisfied she was ready, she sat down and wrote the first two blogs, so they'd be ready to publish. The last thing was to contact Colby and show him and Evelyn the van before she left.

26

Even though he had reservations, Colby wished her a safe trip. They said their goodbyes the night before she left, with the promise of regular phone calls and texts. Edison was now curled up asleep in the soft sided crate beside her. The crate took up a lot of valuable floor space, but she had brackets installed to secure it in the place where the passenger seat used to be. When she parked, she could fold it up flat and slide it out of her way if she needed to. She felt safer knowing the crate offered protection for him while she drove and would continue using it until he was van/house broken and maybe longer if he found comfort inside. She'd already discovered he wouldn't go to the bathroom where he slept, so using the crate also prevented accidents. His proximity to her meant she could hear him when he pawed at the mesh and whined if he needed a pee break. She had to be aware of his cues as she continued to train him.

The flowers nagged at the back of her mind. Who sent them and why? It was all she could think about. Before she visited with Colby, she'd even gone over to Mrs. Cameron's house to see if she saw who delivered them. Being the neighbourhood 'Gladys Kravitz', she enjoyed sharing the gossip of the neighbourhood but only saw a man in coveralls and a baseball hat get out of a white van to deliver them. Maggie was sure she'd gone over to the house to look at what he had left, because Mrs. Cameron kept patting her arm, asking if everything was okay. In the end, Maggie asked her to monitor the house and to contact her if she noticed anything suspicious, explaining that she was leaving on an assignment. Her noisy neighbour was happy to help.

Between them, she and Ripley spent a lot of time deliberating what the first road trip should comprise. In the end, they reached a compromise and decided that a true coast-to-coast trip was the best option, so she'd start her trip from Newfoundland. Ripley arranged for her to catch the ferry from North Sydney, Nova Scotia, to Port Aux Basques, Newfoundland, taking the night ferry so she could sleep on board and wake up refreshed. He booked a berth for her as passengers couldn't remain in their vehicles during the crossing. She might have to share the berth with another female passenger and had arranged for a pet friendly one so she could bring Edison out of the van.

Taking the night ferry meant she could shower on board and sleep through the crossing. It was a seven or eight-hour trip, depending on the weather, but it would also take a full day of driving to get to St. John's. She'd crossed many times before as a driver, but this would be different.

Maggie woke early on the day of her departure and loaded Edison into a well-stocked, fuelled van. Without Edison, she could have made the trip to Sydney without stopping, but he was still training, so she'd have to make several stops along the way. She wanted to arrive in plenty of time to line up for the ferry and get him out to stretch his legs before embarking.

When she was on board and settled in her berth, she sent texts to Colby, Audrey and aunt Julie, letting them know she was okay and off on the first leg of her journey. She opened the sandwiches she packed for her supper, ate, showered and then sat down to write in her blog about her first day on the road and the details about the ferry and her berth. She was fortunate and didn't have to share her space, so she and Edison enjoyed the peace and quiet.

One thing Maggie remembered from her trucking days was how cold the boat was and brought a thick blanket up to her berth, allowing Edison up on the bed to snuggle with her; his body adding extra warmth. As the boat rolled, Maggie drifted off to sleep and her dreams became filled with black roses and red ones dripping with blood.

After a fitful night, she awoke to the alert that they were approaching Port Aux Basques and found herself soaked in sweat. Maggie showered again and headed to the kennel area for Edison to relieve himself, before descending to her van and securing him in his crate as they prepared to disembark.

27

Maggie tapped the steering wheel while waiting for the vehicles to off load. The process of evacuating took forever. Once on dry ground, she began the day-long trip to St. John's, to the planned starting point of her coast-to-coast trip. There were many places she could pull off and take a break, which differed from her trucking days.

It was dark by the time she arrived at her destination, so she found a place to park for the night, took Edison out for a walk, and crawled into bed. She didn't even bother with supper. The lack of restful sleep on the boat and the trip across the province left her feeling exhausted.

In the morning, she awoke refreshed, with the possibilities of what lay ahead filtering through her mind. This was the first time her travels would take her coast to coast without an agenda or schedule. Yes, she had to write her blog, but she could be a tourist and stop and see all the things that interested her or she thought would interest her readers. Today she planned to check out all the local sights, write about them and clear her head. She had some soul searching to do.

Colby told her he loved her before she left, leaving her feeling confused. She loved him too, but the threats behind the flowers, her dark side and Evelyn complicated things. She loved Evelyn, but was afraid of being a part of her life and putting her at risk. Maggie had to decide how she could deal with the injustices of the world without taking action. More importantly, she needed to find out who was sending the flowers and what they meant.

Maggie opened her computer and wrote the blog about the ferry describing the various lounges. One that patrons had to pay to use, it had more comfortable seating, and accommodated those who didn't want a berth. The berths had two sets of bunk beds and a three-piece washroom, and supplied linens. These details people wouldn't know if they'd never crossed before, but describing them would help future travellers.

Maggie took her time to describe everything in detail. The on-board eating facilities, levels of parking and how the boat felt as it rolled with the ocean waves. Even the trek to St. John's deserved a mention as it wove through forest and flat lands, making her feel she was on top of the world. At one point, a bull moose crossed the road in front of her. He stopped, tossed his impressive antlers before disappearing into the forest with the echoes of cracking trees. When the blog felt complete, she sent it to Ripley for his approval.

With time on her hands, she clicked on the icon containing the folder she set up of the photos from Colby's house. As an RCMP officer, he had access to crimes across the country. She worried at a hang nail, feeling the shadow of her darkness hovering around the edges, and wondered if there were other criminals, she could take care of in her travels.

Smiling to herself, she began sorting through the pictures, organizing the case files by crime and then by location. It wasn't until she came to a file about murdered truck drivers that her heart sank.

Could he still be working on The Trans-Canada Killer case even though she set Carter up to take the fall? She scanned through Colby's notes and noticed that the killer used a knife, like she did, but he was messy. The victims fought back, which meant whoever confronted them did so face to face. There was no easy slice of the throat. Each kill was erratic, and the only thing tying them together was that the victims were truckers.

At the bottom of one page, Colby wrote, 'Trans-Canada Killer?', but then crossed it out. According to his notes, the biggest clue that it wasn't the same person was the lack of pink barrettes. She knew why the barrettes were at every scene, because she'd placed them there, but this killer wouldn't. Colby referred to all the victims in his notes by initials only, so she scrolled until she reached the victims' files, which were organized by death.

The files included crime scene photographs depicting multiple stab wounds to the chest and abdomen. She looked at the head shot of the first victim and realized she knew him, not well, but he was someone she'd talked to and greeted when they'd run into each other on the road. She flipped through a few more files and noticed a pattern. They were all people she knew from her trucking days!

It wasn't until she got to the last file that her eyes bulged and a chill trickled up her spine. Her body shook and tears filled her eyes, erupting and drizzling down her cheeks in crooked rivers. Her hands curled into fists around the edge of her work station.

"Oh God! No!" she screamed into the air. Then she pulled up the picture of Tom, one of her fellow drivers, and someone she considered a friend. "Tom, oh Tom, I'm so sorry. I didn't know."

"Who would want to kill you?" she wondered. "You were the sweetest man I knew. You wouldn't hurt anyone."

It wasn't until she enlarged the picture for a better look and noticed the black rose clutched in Tom's hand that her knees weakened and the connection between the roses she received and the killer became clear. Tom's death was her fault. Whoever was doing this was sending her a message and knew a lot about her past and present. He knew where she lived! Knew that she was dating an RCMP detective and would find the message he was sending her.

Her stomach clenched and the air inside the van closed in on her. She needed to get outside and breathe in the fresh air. Maggie put Edison in his harness and stepped outside. She had to think. Her strides were long and purposeful as her feet slapped the pavement of the downtown core, only pausing for Edison to relieve himself. Tears continued to flow, but the tension she felt eased with each movement. She needed to find out who was doing this and make him pay.

With a newfound resolve, she headed back to the van. Edison kept the pace, and she realized what a great edition he was to her life. He grounded her and might just be her salvation. As she approached the van, she noticed a small cone of paper stuck under her wiper. Her initial instinct was to investigate, but put Edison inside the van first.

The item was about 6 inches long and when she pulled it out, she noticed how light it was. She peeled back the paper to see what it was. Her mouth sagged and her eyebrows raised. Then she spun around, scanning the area for danger. Maggie knew whoever left it was long gone. Her body shook as she stared at the single black bud. Her hand tightened around it until blood blossomed on the paper where the thorns pierced her flesh.

She walked to the closest garbage can and as the rose slipped out of the paper, she noticed for the first time the words written on it. "COME FIND ME".

Crumpling the page, she tossed it in the trash and said to the wind, "I'm coming, asshole, don't you worry!"

28

aggie paced the pavement of the parking lot, wiping the blood from her hand on a tissue. Each step she took vibrated through her body as she worked out the anger that bubbled up within. She needed to find who this was. Was he following her, or did he have someone else do it? Her mind considered the possibilities. How could he know where she was? Then she realized he knew where she lived. Could he have put a tracking device on the van? If there was one, she needed to find it.

She turned on her phone, and it identified a tracking device. Her years of hauling exotic cars came in handy. Adam, her dispatcher, showed her how to do this to protect herself. Thieves often put trackers on trucks to highjack or steal the load. Knowing a device was there, now she had to find it. She threw open the hood and began checking the engine compartment. Then she checked the rest of the van, the wheel-wells, bumpers, even crawling beneath it to check the undercarriage. The problem was if he gained access to the van while it was in the shop, being customized, a device could be anywhere. She let out a sigh of relief when she found it up under the rear wheel-well, and debated destroying it, but thought better of it. If he was following her, then let him. It would make finding him easier, and if he didn't know she knew he was tracking her, she had the element of surprise.

Maggie went back inside, washed her hands and changed her clothes, then keyed in the code to the hidden lock box under the cabinets. Her handgun and spare ammo lay inside and, after checking that there were bullets in the barrel, she locked it back away. She didn't need it now, but it had to be ready.

Maggie sat down and rubbed Edison's head while she thought about the latest rose. Unless the killer brought it with him to The Rock, he'd have to purchase it somewhere local. Maggie pulled her phone out of her pocket and searched for florists in the area, figuring there'd only be a couple. The long list that popped up on her screen surprised her.

She'd thought she could just pop by and see if anyone had come in to buy black roses, but the sheer number of locations made that impossible. Instead, she called them all to find out which one recently sold a black rose, if any.

As she made her way down the list, she prayed he bought it locally and not on his way here from the ferry in another town. But she also hoped that whoever sold it would remember him. Halfway through the list, she found a store who sold not one, but two black roses to a gentleman first thing this morning. Maggie sucked in her breath. *'Two! That meant he planned to leave another one soon.'*

After verifying the store's hours, and that the person she was speaking with was the one who sold the man the flowers, she headed downtown to the shop. She'd park at a distance and walk the rest of the way. He couldn't know she was on to him.

The overhead bell tinkled, announcing her arrival as she entered the store to the heady aroma of an array of florals.

"Hello?" A voice called out from the back. "I'll be right with you."

"Hi. I'm the one who called about the black roses." Maggie replied.

The tallest woman Maggie had ever seen stepped out of a back room. Maggie had to crane her neck back to look up.

"Were you looking for black roses?"

"No, I'm looking for information about who bought the two you sold today."

"I'm sorry I can't give out that information."

Prepared for this response, Maggie allowed tears to pool in her eyes. Then she spoke again.

"You're my last hope. This man has been stalking me. I'm travelling coast to coast writing a blog for my magazine and I'm scared. Today, he left the most recent one under my wiper blade with a threatening note. He knows where I live, and where I'm travelling. I'm not safe anywhere." She sobbed as the tears broke free.

The woman's eyes darted around the shop before she placed a hand on Maggie's shoulders to comfort her.

"That's horrible." She paused as Maggie gave the woman her name. "Maggie, I don't have his name because he paid in cash, but I can do one better. I have surveillance footage."

"I thought you couldn't help me." Maggie sniffed, wiping away her tears.

"I shouldn't, but him stalking you is something different entirely. I can see how afraid you are. Let's look at the footage and see if you recognize him."

The woman locked the front door and put up a sign that said, 'Be back in 5 minutes.' Then she took Maggie by the arm and led her to the back of the shop, where a tiny office was located. A mountain of paperwork hid the surface of the desktop. A pile of papers served as a perch for the keyboard of the computer.

"Excuse the mess and please don't touch anything. It may not look like it, but I have a system and I can lay my hands on whatever I need in an instant."

Maggie just nodded. She'd never be able to work in such chaos. She thought about her tidy office at home and shrugged.

The woman, who said her name was Shirley, sat down and jiggled the mouse until the computer screen came to life. Maggie watched as she selected a file, typed in a password, and up popped multiple mini-views from the surveillance videos. Shirley scrolled until she found the one she was looking for and pulled it up. There were two views, one facing customers at the cash and another by the front door.

"We won't have to go through the whole day. He came in right after I opened, so I can fast forward to the first part of the day."

Maggie leaned in as Shirley slowed the video, skipping past other customers until she came to the time she wanted, then moved frame by frame until she found the best angle.

The man wore a ball cap which hid most of his face, but Maggie could see he was white, with no facial hair and what appeared to be short dark hair. He was of average build and was shorter than Shirley, with no visible tattoos. Maggie didn't recognize him.

"How tall are you, Shirley?" Maggie asked.

"6' 3", why?"

"I'm trying to guess how tall he is. I'd say 5' 10", would you agree?"

Shirley looked back at the photo and nodded. "Oh wait, I remember something!"

Maggie let her continue.

"It was his eyes. They were the same colour as a lion's, yellow and gold with thick black lashes that almost made it look like he was wearing eyeliner. It was a striking combination."

"Would you say he was attractive?"

"Nothing that stood out, but those eyes distracted me."

The printer sputtered and jumped to life as a page came out.

Shirley grabbed it and handed it to Maggie. It was the picture of the man.

"It's the best I can do. But if you come across someone with eyes like I described, it has to be him. There can't be too many men out there with eyes like his."

Maggie thanked Shirley and left the store with a small cactus for her van. She'd never bothered with house plants at home, but she figured a cactus would be hard to kill, even if she forgot to water it. But she couldn't leave empty-handed, not after all the help Shirley had given her.

Now that she had her answers and was downtown with nothing else to do, it was time to explore the area after checking on Edison. She needed to add some local interest to her blog and couldn't let the killer distract her.

29

When Maggie stumbled back to the van several hours later, she dragged herself inside and realized she was feeling a little tipsy after participating in a typical Screech-in ceremony at one of the local bars. She even had the certificate to prove it. She slipped the page into a file and tried to remember how many shots of Screech Rum she drank. Maggie thought it was an odd custom, repeating the local sayings and then kissing a cod, but it was worth it. The excitement that erupted in the bar when she did it proved her point and her readers would love learning about this custom.

Edison looked up at her with expectation, so she took him out for a quick pee. Then went to bed. She laid back on the bed as it spun, stuck her foot out of the covers and placed it on the ground, but it didn't help, so she opted to get up and drink some water to dilute the effects of the alcohol. She looked at Edison's sweet face as he lay in his crate watching her, his eyes almost saying, 'you did this to yourself.'

"Okay I get it," Maggie said to the dog, "I'll suffer in the morning if I don't take an Advil and drink lots of water."

Edison raised and cocked his head, then blinked at her before resting his chin on his paws. Maggie chuckled at the comical expression on his face and downed a bottle of Big 8 water and an Advil before settling back on the bed.

Maggie's head felt thick as she blinked open her eyes against the glare of the sun that blazed in the front window of the van. She'd forgotten to put the curtains up and Edison was whining to get out. Maggie splashed some water on her face, relieved herself before getting dressed and taking Edison out.

They went for a long walk to wear him out before packing up to begin the trip back to the ferry. They'd take their time, including a stop in the famed Gander for their kindness during 9/11.

She gathered her thoughts as she walked. Her mind kept slipping back to the man who was stalking her. She paused and looked around. *'Could he be watching me? Even now?'* She wondered. *'How could he have found me in the first place? Know where I live if I don't recognize him?'*

There was a part of Maggie that wondered if the killer knew what she'd done. Knew about the many perverts whose lives she ended. Maybe he witnessed her killing one of them. Knew who she associated with on the road and was going after them to get to her. The question remained: how had he found her?

She knew the roses were the clue. She thought about when she first received them and realized it was after Liam died. Then she remembered the article in the paper that posted pictures of both of them with their names after the shooting, and realization settled in. That's how he found her. He saw something she did and recognized her when her picture was in the paper.

In her grief, she'd forgotten about the article. She now realized how lucky she'd been that no one from the Dark Enders saw it and recognized her as the wife of their screwed-up hit. It was out there and she couldn't do anything about it now. She prayed no one from the gang ever saw it and connected the widow Maggie Murphy to the Maggie, who was Quinn's old lady. If they did, more than one evil entity would hunt her.

Maggie kept her eyes on her surroundings as she packed up the van to prepare for the next leg of her journey. When she got back to Nova Scotia, she'd go home for a few days. She debated surprising Colby, but ended up calling him to give him a heads up. Not everyone liked surprises. She told him when she planned to be back and he suggested a date night on her first night home, but warned her they'd also need a family night because Evelyn had been bugging him, wondering when Maggie and Edison would be back.

Maggie loved knowing Evelyn had warmed to her. The news gave her a newfound resolve to find out who this killer was and end his terror. She wondered if Colby had changed the code to his house. If not, she could go there and make a meal for the three of them. It would give her the opportunity to search his files and find out if there was anything new. Maybe she could mention to Colby that she learned someone was killing truck drivers again and see if he'd talk to her about it.

She estimated the side stops she planned to take would put her back on the ferry in three days. She called Ripley. He'd book her berth on the night ferry and make all the arrangements. She wrote the most recent instalment of the blog this morning after walking Edison and forwarded it to him. When they spoke, he teased her about having fish lips, which she took in stride, but also complimented her on the human-interest aspect of the story.

It was only about a 3 1/2-hour drive to Gander from St. John's, but she planned to make a couple of side trips. The first to Conception Bay and then a stop in Dildo, if for no other reason than the names were interesting. She'd take her time at each stop and planned to arrive in Gander by suppertime. There she'd find a restaurant and grab a meal after she had Edison settled instead of pulling something out of her freezer.

30

Three days later, Maggie stood on the deck of the ferry staring out into the moonlight that kissed the surface of the Atlantic Ocean. In her hand, she held a fist full of Noelle's ashes. Noelle came to Nova Scotia to see the Atlantic Ocean. It only seemed fitting that a part of her remained within the depth of the waters. She held up her fist as the breeze lifted the ashes from her hand with a swirl. Watching the ashes scatter, Maggie said the first of many farewells to Noelle. "Goodbye, my friend. You didn't deserve what happened to you." She brushed away the ashes that clung to her skin over the edge of the rail and, with a heavy heart, headed below deck to her berth and Edison.

When the ferry docked in Sydney, Maggie and Edison made their way, with the crowds of people through the stairwell down to the car hold. She got Edison secured in his crate and something on the windshield caught her eye. She walked around to the front of the van to investigate. Once again, under the wiper, was a single black rose. This time the note said, *'Josh says hello.'*

A ball formed in the pit of her stomach as she spun around and looked at the faces of the various people entering their vehicles. There were so many she couldn't differentiate one from the next. She crumpled the note in her hand and dropped the rose to the ground, grinding it beneath her toe. She wouldn't engage with him. Not here. Not now.

Her mind whipped to Josh. What did he mean by, 'Josh says hello?' Her heart raced and beads of sweat dotted her brow. When she got home, she'd call Josh to check on him. Then she'd call all of her trucking friends and warn them. This was personal.

Maggie struggled to keep her emotions under control as she drove home from the ferry. She cursed herself for not keeping in touch with her road family since Liam's death. If she had, maybe none of this would be happening. When she stopped trucking, it was to distance herself from the person she was and start a new life. The only one she maintained regular contact with was Ryan, because he saved her life and had a special spot in her heart.

Ryan! If the killer wanted to hurt her, killing Ryan would do it. He was her closest road friend. Her stomach clenched and her eyes welled. She had to warn him first. It couldn't wait until she got home. If the killer was going after truckers who were important to her, Ryan was a walking billboard. She called out Ryan's name to her Bluetooth and waited as the phone rang.

"Hey Maggie! It's been a while. How're you doing?"

"Ryan!" Maggie sighed. "It's a relief to hear your voice. I'm good. Picked up a dog. His name is Edison. He's a purebred boxer, and I'm hitting the road again."

"A dog? Well, that's something. The kids have always wanted a dog. Maybe it's time. Wait! Did you just say you're hitting the road again? As in trucking?"

Maggie's laughter filled the line as relief wash over her. It felt good to hear his voice and know he was ok. "No, not trucking, but I may run into you on the highway. I'm doing the van life thing. Picked up a Sprinter van and converted it for my comfort. I'm writing a blog about my travels and experiences on the road. Maybe you'll read it. They've published the first few instalments already. When I stop, I'll send you the link."

"You amaze me, Maggie. Is there anything you can't do?"

Maggie's breath caught as she remembered the one thing she'd never be able to do, bring a child into the world. The thought haunted her and a small gasp escaped her lips.

"Ah shit! I'm sorry Maggie. Me and my big mouth." Ryan mumbled.

"It's okay Ryan, I'm coming to terms with it. It's not something I can change, but that doesn't mean I can't have children in my life. Did I tell you I'm dating a widower with a young daughter?"

"That's wonderful! They're lucky to have you in their lives. You're a special woman, Maggie."

"Well, thank you. Anyway, the reason for my call is this guy I'm seeing is RCMP, and he told me there's someone killing truck drivers again. He's already killed someone, I know. I just wanted to warn you."

"Killing truckers? I thought they found the Trans-Canada Killer."

"They did. This is someone new. Just be careful, Ryan. I don't want to see anything happen to you."

"Sheesh, if there wasn't already enough to worry about with all the untrained drivers on Highway 11 and 17, now I have to worry about an unknown killer!"

"Let's hope they catch him soon. If I hear anything more, I'll call. Say hello to Krissy and the kids."

"Will do. And Maggie..."

"Yes?"

"Make sure you let me know where you're at. Maybe we can sit down somewhere for a coffee."

"Read my blog and you'll get a general idea of where I am. If we are in the same area, call me and I'll meet you. I'm driving a slate grey Sprinter Van."

Maggie pushed the disconnect button as her own words echoed in her head. The blog! Whoever this killer was, he could keep track of her by following her blog. He didn't need the tracker he placed in the wheel well. Her next call was to the man she bought her gun from. She needed more bullets before going on the road again. The future was uncertain, and she wanted to be prepared.

Maggie thought about her safety while she drove and pulled off at a plaza to pick up a dash cam. Thinking it would help provide a better visual of the killer's appearance when he dropped off another rose. While searching the electronics, she also picked up a nanny cam for the inside of the van. Figuring if anyone broke in, she'd know.

Before unpacking, Maggie hooked up the dash and nanny cams. Edison watched her from his crate with interest. When she'd set everything up, she grabbed her laundry, and Edison, and went inside.

With the dog settled and the laundry started, Maggie worked her way through her list of highway friends. Relief spread through her like a warm blanket with every answered call. She saved calling Josh until the end. Deep down, she knew he wouldn't answer his phone.

She listened as it rang and rang, then the voicemail kicked in. The deep roll of fear crept through her core. His mailbox was full. Her guts clenched as she disconnected the call. None of the others mentioned Josh, but maybe if anything happened to him, it wasn't common knowledge yet.

She debated calling Adam, her old dispatcher, but thought better of it. How could she explain the inside information and why she was calling? Her best bet was to wait until tomorrow. Colby had already agreed that she could let herself in again and set up for a family night. If she was lucky, she'd find the file, and any updated information still on his desk.

31

Maggie lay on her bed and stretched, catching the aroma of Colby's cologne that clung to the sheets. Her body was still raw from their night of passion after their dinner date. She slipped out of the bed, and headed straight for the shower. Colby left an hour ago to get home before Evelyn woke up and take her to school. A smile played at the corner of her mouth, relishing in the feelings Colby had awakened.

With nothing else on her agenda, she had plenty of time to plan the family events for later today. Colby didn't tell Evelyn that Maggie was back and planned to pick her up from school and surprise Evelyn with Maggie already there. Maggie thought she'd prepare a teddy bear picnic for Evelyn's after-school snack. She slipped into the room that was to be the nursery and pulled out the plush teddy bear Liam brought home after she first confirmed her pregnancy.

Maggie held it to her nose and sniffed at the new toy scent. Confirming it didn't smell like Liam, she put it on the bed to pack and bring with her to Colby's house. There was a picnic basket in the basement that belonged to Liam's mom, including a gingham blanket and dishes. Everything else they'd need, she'd picked up on her way over. There was plenty of time to look through his office, pull out Evelyn's teddy bears and get set up.

Edison's time in the van helped him learn to hold off going to the bathroom, and now he was housebroken. He learned to ask to go out by placing his paw up on her lap, so there was no need to worry about him at Colby's house. She no longer needed to pack puppy pads wherever she went. Maggie looked down at him as he followed her around the house and couldn't believe how big he was already.

She grabbed a few more things and packed an overnight bag, figuring if Colby didn't want her to stay, she'd sleep in the van, especially after a couple of glasses of the wine she'd packed.

On her way to Colby's, she stopped at Pete's Frootique in Halifax for the specialty items she wanted to add to the picnic and for the dinner she planned. She even picked up a beautiful potted violet for Evelyn. The window in her bedroom would provide the perfect lighting. She'd just have to remind Colby to water it from time to time.

She arrived with plenty of time to set up. But before she got started, she put Edison in the fenced-in backyard and made a mental note to look for any presents he might leave behind when she brought him in. Then she unloaded the van, put the groceries away, and placed the picnic basket in the living room.

Deciding it would be best to set up and prepare everything first, she went into Evelyn's room and picked out a few teddy bears, including the graduation bear she made for Evelyn after she graduated from kindergarten, and brought them out to the living room.

After moving the coffee table to one side to make room for the picnic, she laid the gingham blanket down on the floor and set up the teddy bears as 'guests'. She placed the bottle of wine on the end table and bought grape juice for Evelyn. She even had adult styled sippy cups for them all. The ones for her and Colby looked like wine glasses inside a plastic tumbler.

Maggie went to the kitchen and got busy preparing for the picnic. A bowl with Teddy Grahams was the final touch to go with the theme, but snacks also included celery cheese boats, apple slices, carrots and dip. Everything needed to stay in the kitchen for now or Edison would help himself and ruin the surprise. Then she started on supper. Diced up the vegetables, potatoes and seasoned the chicken. She searched until she found a large rectangular baking dish to put everything in. When Colby returned, she'd turn the oven on, for the roasted potatoes, veggies and chicken, a one dish supper. Maggie checked the time and realized she had a couple of hours left to search Colby's office. She checked on Edison, who was racing after a squirrel in the yard, put a bowl of water outside for him, and headed down the hall.

Her step faltered when she entered the room and noticed how tidy it was. The last time she was here, there were files all over the desk. Now none was visible. He'd put everything away. She wondered if Colby suspected she'd gone through his files and that was why it was tidy. If that was the case, then he was on to her, but if so, why allow her to have access to his house? Maggie was quick to dismiss the idea and went to work.

She sat down at his desk and began opening the drawers, expecting to find some of his files inside, but other than typical office supplies, she didn't find a single file. Her eyes flicked to the corner of the room where the filing cabinet loomed. Even before she checked the drawers, she knew she'd find them locked. Cursing under her breath, she considered her options.

She could jimmy the lock, but then he'd know she'd snooped. He couldn't know this side of her. Even if he suspected, she couldn't expose herself. She looked back at the desk and considered the drawers. It made sense to lock the files away, especially with a young, inquisitive child around. If that was the reason, then the key would be close at hand.

Maggie rummaged around in the desk until she found a small wooden puzzle box. She shook it and could hear something rattling inside. She carefully examined it before locating the small trigger that opened it. A drawer slid out and inside; she found the key.

Checking the time on her phone, she realized she needed to hurry, or Colby would catch her. She unlocked the cabinet and began rummaging through the files until she found the right ones. A large rubber band held them together. It appeared thicker than the last time, so she pulled out her phone and began snapping photos of every page, picture, and note within the file, not caring if she duplicated anything . She wrapped the elastic back around it, slipped the file back in the correct spot, locked the cabinet, and returned the key to the puzzle box. With the box back in the drawer, Maggie took a deep, calming breath, rolled her shoulders, and released the tension that built up.

Needing to keep the pictures out of sight, she created a hidden file and moved them into it. Edison was barking, so she went out the back door to let him in and clean up after him. Once inside, he raced to her picnic set up and sniffed the teddy bears, pulling one aside to cuddle, before curling up in the centre of the blanket. Maggie chuckled, but scolded him to get on his own mat. They didn't want dog hair on the picnic blanket.

There was just enough time to set out the snack foods, pull out the Teddy Bear Picnic book to read to Evelyn, and find the song on her phone. She opened the wine and poured a glass for her and Colby and a grape juice for Evelyn and sat on the blanket to wait. Edison was within reach, so she petted him. He inched forward and place his head on her lap.

The beep from the code being entered alerted Edison, who jumped up and began barking. Excitedly, Evelyn raced in to be greeted by a lick from Edison, which she brushed off before wrapping her arms around his neck and squealing, "Maggie!"

32

Colby beamed as he followed Evelyn into the room, his eyes scanned how Maggie had set things up, from the teddy bears, the picnic on the blanket, to the odd-looking wine glasses and said, "What's all this?"

"We're having a Teddy Bear picnic!" Maggie exclaimed as she started the song on her phone.

Evelyn ran to Maggie, grabbed her hand, and pulled her up to dance to the music. The sparkle in Evelyn's eyes lit up the room and Colby's face split in a grin, mouthing, 'you're great with her.' Pink rose to Maggie's cheek at the compliment.

"What's in the glasses?" He asked, nodding to the three sippy cups.

"Grape juice. Adult grape juice in ours and regular grape juice in Evelyn's."

"I have actual wine glasses, you know."

Maggie grinned, "Of course I know, but with a picnic on the floor, a glass could get knocked over. 'Grape juice' is horrible to get out of carpeting."

"Good thinking."

The next morning, Evelyn sat on Maggie's lap while she brushed her hair into two tidy pigtails. Maggie's heart warmed as Evelyn ran to show her father her hairdo. As Colby helped Evelyn get into the car, Maggie prepared to leave. She already told Colby she was heading back on the road later today, but promised to arrange regular video chats for the three of them and private ones just for them. He smiled and kissed her on his way out the door and told her to stay safe.

Maggie waved goodbye, her eyes sparkling, with Edison at her heels. While she packed the van, her eyes followed Colby's car as he turned right towards Evelyn's school. Before starting her trip, she wanted to get home and look at the pictures on her iMac, thankful her devices synced and the pictures would be there waiting for her. She made a quick stop to restock her food and top up her gas tank before she pulled into her driveway.

Maggie fiddled with the collar of her coat as she took Edison out and locked the vehicle, turned and looked up and down the street and noted the cars parked nearby before entering the house. Her nerves were raw from the constant checking of her surroundings, but knew *he* could be out there, watching. She hurried to the house, locked the door, and sagged against it, letting out the breath she held. Maggie took a deep, cleansing breath and slowly released it as she kicked off her shoes. One thing about owning a dog, you knew if anyone approached.

She padded to her office with Edison at her heels and turned on her computer while her spunky pup jumped up and curled into a ball on the armchair in the corner. Maggie clicked the photos icon and then the hidden file, to retrieve the pictures she took at Colby's house. She felt a twinge of guilt at sneaking around his office copying files, but he didn't know the connection between herself and the killer. The killer was killing her friends and taunting her with it. This was personal, and she suspected she was the only one who could stop him.

It was easy to scan the pages, ignoring the ones she already looked at and paused at the new ones. There were two more victims, one a driver she didn't recognize, and the other caused her stomach to clench and bile to rise in the back of her throat. It was Josh. Her hands curled into fists, and she smacked them down on her desk, causing Edison to jump. Tears pooled in her eyes and a sob escaped her lips, "Josh, I'm so sorry."

Her body awash with a mixture of emotions, struggling to gain control, she wiped the tears from her eyes and read the recent hand-written notes. The killer was scattering rose petals with his victims. His methodology had progressed and his kills were cleaner. A single slash across the throat. The police felt the weapon he used was a switchblade.

"His leaving a calling card may make him easier to find," Maggie said to Edison, who cocked his head as he listened to her. "He'd have to buy the roses somewhere, and my guess is it'll be near where they found each victim."

Maggie closed the file, added a password to protect its contents in case anyone accessed to her house, and logged out of the computer. Her phone pinged with a text from the contact she bought the gun from. He had the bullets for her and could meet her in an hour. She responded she'd be there and went to gather the rest of her gear to be ready to leave immediately afterwards.

Prior to leaving, she locked the windows and doors and reset the cameras, allowing her to view them while on the road. She ran her thumb along the blade of her hunting knife, to check the sharpness. At the last minute, she grabbed the sharpening stone, planning on keeping the blade razor sharp. She may not have the gun handy when she ran into *him*, but she could always carry the knife.

With Edison secured in the van, she sent Colby a quick text telling him she was leaving, then drove straight to meet with her contact. He was discrete, and the transaction was quick, no questions asked. Once alone, she opened the safe, inserted the ammo, double-checked the gun, closed the safe, and concealed its presence by sliding the panel into place. These little tidbits wouldn't be in her blog.

Before leaving the parking lot, Maggie turned on her Sirius Radio, picked a station and cranked the volume as 'Life is a Highway' by Tom Cochrane filled the air. She slid her sunglasses in place and belted out the song along with Tom as she merged onto the 102 heading west. She'd make Enfield her first stop, as she wanted to check out the trucks, see if she knew anyone there and begin searching for the killer before he killed any more of her friends.

Of course, the other reason for the stop was to write about it, let travellers know the facilities and compare it with the eyes of a typical tourist instead of a truck driver. She'd ask questions to see if they treated her differently now that she wasn't a trucker and if the rates for showers etc. were different.

One thing she liked about the Big Stop, as the truck stop in Enfield was called, was that they didn't allow overnight parking for RVs. She knew it was an inconvenience for regular travellers, but meant the 54 truck spots were always available for the drivers. Truckers didn't have the luxury of booking into a campground and most plazas allowed RVs, but not trucks. Drivers needed the spaces to do their job.

She'd also grab a coffee at Tim Horton's, fuelling herself up on her way out of the province. In the notes file on her phone was a list of the stops and touristy things she planned to see along the way. Colby told her he read her blog to follow her travels, and she'd keep that in mind when picking places to stop at night. If she only chose trucks stops, it would raise his suspicions and make him worry about her, so she'd be sure to find other places to park. Enjoying the side stops on her list would only get her as far as Amherst tonight, but there was a lot to see.

33

It was well after dark when she turned into the parking lot near the Canadian Tire in Amherst. Maggie rolled her head from side-to-side, to ease the aching muscles in her shoulders, then took Edison out. She'd gathered some interesting information to write about in her blog, including a stop in Springhill where Anne Murray grew up and at the Masstown Market along the way.

Edison pulled on the lead in his hurry to get off the pavement and find some grass to relieve himself. The amount of pent-up energy he displayed made her decide to take Edison for a long walk and ignore the exhaustion that wracked her body.

Edison had calmed down by the time she returned to the van, so she threw her supper in the microwave and sat down to write the latest instalment. It could wait until morning, but she wanted to get her ideas out while they were fresh. After forwarding the blog to Ripley, she sent Colby a text, telling him where she was and included a heart emoji.

Next, she sent a quick text to her aunt, then pondered the killer's identity and his connection to her. There was only one person she could talk to about this, and that was Audrey. Maggie checked the time before calling her.

"Hi Maggie! It's good to hear from you. I see from your blog you've started your cross-country road trip. I loved the pictures from the inside of the van. It looks wonderful."

"The van's comfortable and Edison is keeping me on my toes. I've only made it as far as Amherst, but this isn't a race. It's about living in a van and seeing the country."

"I assume you've stayed out of trouble."

Maggie hesitated wanting to talk to Audrey about the killer, but knowing how much Audrey would worry, concerned her.

"Maggie? I know you. What's going on?"

Maggie sighed. "Do you remember the roses? The ones with black buds mixed in with the red ones?"

"Yes, of course I do. Why?"

"The sender started sending single black roses with notes. Audrey, he left them on the windshield of my van!"

"What! Maggie, this is serious! Tell me everything."

Maggie sighed and told Audrey about her trip to The Rock. Starting with the notes, the file she found at Colby's, her suspicions that whoever left the roses was the killer and that he was killing her friends. Audrey remained quiet, giving Maggie the opportunity to speak, and get everything off her chest, for which Maggie was thankful.

"Audrey, there's one more thing. He wants me to find him."

"Maggie! Tell me you're not considering looking for this maniac? You promised not to go looking for trouble."

"Audrey, I said I wouldn't go looking for trouble. I didn't say I'd ignore trouble if it came looking for me."

"Okay Maggie, but you know that's just semantics." Audrey sighed. "Tell me what you know about him. I'm assuming you haven't told Colby about this."

"No, of course not."

"I thought as much. I'll make a few calls to some of my contacts on the force and see if I can get them to feed me any information. That way, if something new pops up, I can keep you in the loop. But Maggie, that works both ways. If you learn something, let me know."

"Deal."

"Oh, and Maggie, remember I know you, so I want you to check in with me daily. Don't hide things from me and if you need me, I'll be on the first flight out."

"Audrey, you need to be careful too. So far, he's killed two of my good trucking friends, but he knows where I live, so he may know where you live. Aunt Julie has full security around the house and shop, but you don't. I'd feel better if you put up motion detectors and cameras in the front and back of your house and out by the road. That way, you'll know if anyone approaches."

Audrey let out a breath. "Okay."

They continued chatting and Audrey updated her on the status of the remaining barrettes, informing Maggie that the Facebook page had helped move things along. But there was still one lost soul whose family didn't have closure. Before she hung up, Maggie told Audrey she thought it was time to mention the last barrette on their page, describing it to see if it led anywhere. It was risky, but they were running out of options. Audrey said she'd consider it, and they should discuss again at a later date.

34

The next morning the sun glistened in the sky, creating prisms of colours through the windshield as Maggie prepared to leave for the next leg of her journey. Instead of making herself a coffee, she went up the street to the Tim Hortons, grabbed herself one and included a snack pack of Timbits in her order. As promised, she sent two texts, one to Colby and the other to Audrey, before leaving.

Highway 104 turned onto Highway 2 after a few kilometres, marking her entrance into New Brunswick. One stop on today's agenda was the Magnetic Hill, a place she'd often passed on the road. Many of the places she planned to visit this trip were the ones she saw from the highway, but didn't have the time or availability to stop.

Instead of taking Highway 2 straight across New Brunswick, she'd detour down to Saint John. She'd delivered there in the past, but never walked around to see the sights. Then she'd continue on to Highway 1 and end at St. Andrews, where she'd find a place to park, and allow time in the morning to explore the area. The extra stops would add a couple of days to her trip across New Brunswick, but it was about the journey, not the destination.

By the time she found a place to park, one where they wouldn't tow her, and had taken Edison out, she fell into bed as exhaustion settled into her bones. Throughout the night, she awoke several times from a fitful sleep filled with dreams of her fallen friends. Finding herself wide awake, she laid staring at the ceiling as the sun rose, and as it did, something on her windshield caught her attention. There was a crushing sensation in her chest as she stared at the single black rose.

Maggie threw back the covers, her body vibrating, and hopped out of the van, stumbling on the gravel in her bare feet. With her feet planted in a firm stance, she looked around but saw no one. She grabbed the rose and unfurled the attached note 'I see you,' was all it said.

Maggie cursed to the wind as it rose and dragged tendrils of her hair across her face. He'd been so close and she missed him. She clenched onto the fender of the van, trying to gain control of her emotions, and wondered how Edison had missed alerting her to his arrival. But then she remembered how strong the wind was last night and the multitude of outside noises. The van shook and even she had a difficult time getting to sleep. It would have been hard to differentiate the sounds from wind knocking the van with those of someone leaving a rose under her wiper.

Then she thought about the dash cam. It recorded incidents on the road, and should have recorded someone approaching her van. She pulled up the footage and began reviewing it frame by frame. She saw the black clad arm that lifted the wiper and place the rose underneath and her heart sank. He knew she was recording. Her jaw slackened and her eyes widened as the figure moved to the front of her van, hood up, and a bandana full of skulls covering his face while he stood there and waved, mocking her.

She clenched her teeth as her hand crashed onto the work surface, causing Edison to jump. '*He was so close, and I missed him.*'

But now she wondered if he was a trucker or not. Of course, he could be bob-tailing, making it easier for him to find a parking spot in the remote place she parked. But there wasn't truck parking here. He must have followed her. In the future, she'd have to be more diligent. She wouldn't say anything to Audrey about this when she sent out her morning texts. There was no need to worry her.

Maggie put the note with the others he'd left. It was a game of cat and mouse, and this time, she was the mouse. That concept didn't sit well with her. She was more feral and embodied the hunting feline. It was then that Maggie decided she'd stop at every truck stop she came to and put-up posters. Truckers needed to know a killer was out there. Using the picture the florist gave her and describing his eyes, she set to work designing something to post. He might tear them down as fast as she put them up, but someone would see them and she hoped it would save a life.

He killed for the pleasure of it, and that infuriated Maggie. At least her victims had been the dregs of society and deserved their fate. But Tom and Josh? You could fly to the moon and back and not find two more honest men. She'd known them both for years. If there was something off about either of them, or with her sixth sense for the criminal, she'd have known.

It took her about 15 minutes to design the poster and print out a half dozen copies to get started. She tucked them away, knowing there wasn't a truck stop in St. Andrews, but she still needed to walk around and see what was available for her blog. Killer or no killer, she had a job to do.

After harnessing Edison, Maggie paused at the box containing Noelle's ashes and dumped some into a baggie. St. Andrews was a beautiful place on Passamaquoddy Bay. Noelle would have loved it. Maggie took Edison with her and walked to the water's edge and stared out at the midnight depths of the water. The baggie weighed on her. It was time for another farewell. Maggie glanced around to ensure she wasn't being watched and opened the baggie. As the ashes scattered and lay floating on the surface, Maggie said, "You didn't get to see much in life. You deserve the beauty of the world in death." She stayed there, watching as the particles of what was once Noelle melted into the water and ebbed with the tide.

35

By the time Maggie arrived at the Grey Rock in Edmundston, she struggled to keep her eyes open. She'd stretched her day out to do the touristy things and still stop at all the truck stops on the way, even talking to a few of the drivers she ran into. The drivers she spoke with had heard there was someone targeting truckers, but didn't seem concerned and that worried her. The original posters she made were now posted at each truck stop, and she'd printed more.

Maggie glanced over at Edison and rubbed his head, he turned out to be a great traveller, but still needed his walks, so Maggie put him in his harness, walked him, got him settled before heading inside to use the washroom and put up a poster. She stifled a yawn when she tacked the poster to the board, and turned to find a driver behind her.

"A killer who's after truck driver's, eh? That's new. The media always makes us out to be the bad guys."

Startled, Maggie looked hard at the man. As soon as she saw his red beard, she relaxed, and the tension that erupted eased out of her body.

"You're preaching to the choir." She responded, "I drove a truck for several years, even owned my rig."

The man paused, looked her up and down and replied, "A bitty thing like you?"

Maggie laughed, "Didn't we just establish you didn't like stereotypes?"

"Shit, sorry. That came out wrong. Name's Tucker." He said, extending his meaty hand.

Maggie took his outreached hand and shook it. "I'm Maggie."

"So, Maggie, what's your interest in this killer? If you don't drive trucks anymore, I'd think you'd be safe."

"I'm travelling coast to coast in a sprinter van writing a blog, so although I'm not in a truck, I could be a target. But the biggest reason is he's already killed two of my friends. I figure the more people who know he's out there, the faster he can be caught."

"You might have something there." He said, stroking his beard. "Well, have a good night. I have to hit the head before bed."

"Stay safe."

"You too."

The sky was still dark when the sound of sirens dragged Maggie from a deep sleep. Edison lifted his head and howled at the sound. She checked the time and saw that it was 3 am. The sirens were getting closer. Maggie pulled on her clothes and peered out the curtains as a barrage of police, fire and ambulance descended around the back of the truck stop.

Maggie rubbed Edison's head, told him she'd be right back, slipped her hunting knife in its sheath, and went out to see what happened. She cut through the building and up the back stairs, instead of going around, to find the emergency team surrounding a truck in the far back. Officers were busy setting up a barricade to keep the onlookers away from the crime scene.

She slipped into the crowd and worked her way to the front just as they pulled a body from the truck. Maggie listened to the gossip and discovered that someone saw the driver's door was ajar and when they went to check on him, they found him dead inside, with his throat slashed.

The hairs on the back of Maggie's neck prickled as she looked around at the sizeable crowd and searched the faces for the killer. She knew he was here somewhere. Her eyes flicked back to the body and bile rose in the back of her throat. The police were zipping up the body bag and she glimpsed a flash of red beard. Her stomach clenched. She knew him. It was Tucker, the man she'd spoken with earlier that night. An anguished sound escaped her lips as she saw the bloody gash across his throat. She looked at the ground surrounding his truck and saw the killer's trademark. Dozens of dried rose petals lay scattered on the ground, lifting and swirling with the movements of the EMTs.

Tucker was killed in the safety of his own truck. Her hand found her knife, undoing the safety snap that held it in place. Her eyes darted from side-to-side as she stepped back away from the mass of people. Quiet strides led her to the street instead of the building; afraid he'd be waiting for her in the shadows of the drive-thru at the bottom of the stairs.

She made her way back to the van, sticking to the well-lit areas. The sound of Edison's anxious barking from inside sent a chill through her body. Her step faltered when she saw the rose on the windshield. The killer was taunting her, daring her to come find him, and she vowed to do just that.

Maggie pulled her knife out and squatted down to ensure he wasn't under her van or any of the nearby vehicles. Then took the rose and tossed it away. There wasn't a note this time, but his threat was terrifying. She unlocked the doors, climbed in and calmed Edison, then after one last glance around the area, she locked them.

Maggie tossed and turned as sleep evaded her for the rest of the night. In the end, she sat in the darkened van with her knife in her hand and waited for the sun to rise, her eyes scanning the parking lot for movement.

As the first flashes of orange and pink streaked the sky, Maggie slipped Edison's harness on and walked the perimeter of the parking lot, taking pictures of the trucks that were still there. She needed a guide to work from and figured if one of these trucks belonged to the killer, she had better familiarize herself with them and maybe a pattern would arise.

A truck that always showed up at various locations, or one that was there when there was a victim or a rose was found, could be his. Then a thought struck her. *'The rose he left last night! I wonder if I can find it. It's time to send a message back.'*

She deposited Edison in the van and searched the ground for the rose, praying no one picked it up. When she saw it, she grasped it and felt giddy with glee. She was going to turn the tides in her favour.

Maggie pulled out her notebook and tore off a page and wrote, THE HUNTER BECOMES THE HUNTED, then wrapped it around the stem of the rose and fastened it in place. She doubted he'd approach her van in the daylight, but she'd put in under the wiper just in case. If it was still there when she was ready to leave, she'd put the rose in the fridge and put it on her windshield tonight and every night until he took it.

Maggie debated mentioning Tucker's murder in her blog or not, but felt it was important. She sat down and wrote about it and mentioned meeting him only a few hours before he died. She described the scene, but out of respect for Colby and the case, she didn't mention the rose petals she saw fluttering in the breeze. This was something the average person wouldn't notice, and she didn't want to reveal this detail. She knew the police were keeping it under wraps.

Maggie hesitated before submitting the article to Ripley and gave both Colby and Audrey a heads up before they read her blog and worried. She called Colby first because he didn't know her truths and the dark secrets that haunted her, which meant the conversation would be more about her safety.

"Hey sweetheart, I thought you might call today."

"Oh? And what made you think that?"

"Because I know you miss me." Colby retorted.

Maggie almost replied, *'With every bullet so far,'* as she used to jest with Liam, but Colby wasn't Liam and their relationship wasn't there yet, not for jokes like that.

"Yes, I miss you." Maggie hesitated.

"Is everything okay Maggie?"

"I'm fine. I just wanted to warn you before my next blog comes out."

"Why? Are you declaring that you love me to the world?" He teased.

"I'm serious, Colby."

"So am I. Wait, did something happen?"

"A trucker died. No, not died. Murdered. Near where I parked last night. I even spoke to him in the driver's lounge earlier in the evening. If the sound of the sirens didn't wake me up, I wouldn't have a clue there was a killer nearby."

"But you're okay, right?"

"Yes, I just wanted my blog to be real, so I wrote about it. There was something weird, though."

"What was that?"

"Well, Tucker, that's the driver's name, died inside his truck, so either he knew the person, trusted the person, or the killer surprised him. But the weird part was there were all these rose petals on the ground by the stairs of his cab."

Maggie heard the hiss of breath Colby took. She knew she was correct in telling him. Maybe if he worried about her, he would feed her some information about the killer.

"Did you mention the petals in your blog?" he snapped.

"No, of course not. I wasn't sure if they're connected, but if they were, I didn't think the police would want that getting out. If this person has killed before, it could be a calling card. But it could also be a jealous lover, so I didn't think it pertained to my blog."

"That's probably a good thing. No need to get people upset, especially now that your blog is getting a lot of traction."

"Look at you, Mr. Detective, using the lingo." Maggie teased, hoping to lighten the mood. "I'm still in Edmundston, and my next stop will be Rivière-du-Loop. I know it's not far, but because I don't have an agenda, I can end my day anywhere." And for the first time, she ended with, "I love you, send Evelyn my love."

36

Colby stared wide eyed at the phone in his hand. Did he hear her right? Did Maggie just tell him she loved him? He couldn't believe it. A ripple of joy spread through his core. He'd said it to her before she left, but she only replied with 'Me too.' Colby couldn't keep the smile from his lips as he keyed in the information she gave him. In his happiness, he didn't notice his partner approach.

"Ok Tate, you look like the cat who swallowed the canary, what gives?" His partner, Mark Carlson, asked as he plopped onto his desk chair and spun around to face him.

"She loves me." Colby replied, his grin stretched wide across his face.

Carlson smacked Colby's desk. "That's great. We are talking about the sexy redhead, right?"

"Yes, we're talking about Maggie and no, it's not necessarily great."

"Don't tell me you're having reservations? Not after all the time you spent persuading her to take a chance on you."

"No, nothing like that, but now I have to worry about her, about

143

her safety. Not that I wouldn't have anyway, but now it's deeper. I told you she's travelling coast to coast in a Sprinter Van, right?"

"Yup."

"Well, she just called me. She parked in Edmundston at the Grey Rock last night and a trucker got killed."

"Well, if it was a trucker, you don't have to worry."

"You don't get it. Maggie was a trucker. Not only that, she spoke to the victim earlier in the evening before he died. Now she's written about it in her blog. But get this, she mentioned there were rose petals on the ground by the victim's cab."

"Sshhiiittt." Carlson muttered. "That's our guy."

"Ya, shit." Colby ran his hand through his hair. "I think we need to take a fresh look at the file. If this is the same guy, that means he's in the area. We'll also need to talk to the local detectives and have them send over the case files for this latest crime scene."

"Okay, I'll make the call." Carlson turned back to his desk and dialled the Edmundston police department, while Colby searched the database for everything they had on the killer and his victimology.

"They're sending everything they have from last night over. You're right. It's got to be the same guy. Same MO, knife across the neck and the rose petals scattered around on the ground. If we didn't know who the Trans-Canada Killer was, I'd say this was him. As it is, it may be a copycat. Someone who didn't know about the barrettes. Or maybe we got the wrong guy and the barrettes aren't the signature anymore because now the victims are random? What are your thoughts?"

Colby rubbed the whiskers of his goatee before responding. "I considered Carter wasn't the Trans-Canada killer, many times. Finding him dead in his burnt-out cab, with all the evidence scattered in the ditch nearby, seemed too perfect. Almost as if someone wrapped everything with a tight little bow and left it for us to find. But then the killings stopped. I even watched reports from the US to see if maybe our killer was stateside, but there was nothing. This killer only just started. I think the chances of it being a copycat are greater. Maybe he knew The Trans-Canada Killer left something at the scene, but not what, so he chose rose petals."

"Have you considered that with the rose petals, the killer might be a woman? Before you say anything, hear me out. Rose petals, is a feminine touch, not a lot of dudes carry rose petals. But then there's the trust thing. This guy that was killed last night was in his own truck. He'd have to trust the person to let him get close. So maybe it's a lot lizard?"

Colby thought back to the file about Maggie and her father. That was a man, and he somehow gained access to the truck, killed her father and raped and left Maggie for dead. He knew there were many scenarios where someone could gain access without trust.

"My gut is saying it's a man. I think he gets access by using the element of surprise. Someone who's hiding nearby and caught the driver off guard before he closed his door. Or maybe the driver stood on the step of the cab and took a piss. It happens more than you'd think."

"Maybe you're right, but I don't think we should rule out the possibility of a woman," Carlson said, turning back to open a new email.

"I'm not ruling anything out yet."

"Edmundston PD, just sent the file over. I think we need to see the captain."

Both detectives gathered what they had on the killer. Carlson stopped at the printer to pick up the information the Edmundston police sent over, and they went to the captain's office to present the latest victim and their theories.

37

After disconnecting with Colby, Maggie called Audrey. Now that she'd retired from seeing clients, Audrey had plenty of time on her hands and Maggie was counting on her being available. Audrey answered before the second ring.

"Hi Maggie. If you're calling so soon, it can only mean one of two things: you've found the last family, or there's trouble. My money's on trouble."

"Thanks a lot Audrey. I don't go searching for it."

"Really? You're forgetting who you're talking to. What happened?"

Maggie rolled her eyes and let out a deep breath. "There was a trucker killed near where I parked last night."

"A trucker? Can I ask if there was a barrette found by the body?"

"It wasn't me, Audrey!" Maggie replied in exasperation. "It was the killer who's been taunting me."

"Was it someone you knew?"

"Sorta, I met him last night inside the truck stop. I was putting up posters to warn drivers there was a killer out there and he stopped to

146

talk to me. Later on, the sound of sirens woke me up, and I went to check it out."

"Of course you did," Audrey replied, her voice dripping with sarcasm. "I thought this van thing was supposed to keep you out of trouble."

Maggie plopped down on the bed in a huff. She was getting angry. Audrey was being testy, and she didn't know what was bothering her, so she changed the subject and asked.

"Okay Audrey, I only called to tell you what happened because it's in my blog and I didn't want you to worry. But obviously, I shouldn't have bothered. Why don't you tell me what's wrong?"

The soft sound of sobs that drifted across the line shocked Maggie. She waited and allowed Audrey to release the sorrow in her heart before saying anything else.

"I'm sorry Maggie." Audrey whispered.

"Tell me what's wrong Audrey."

Between sniffs, Audrey told Maggie what today was. "It's the anniversary of Sara's murder. I know it's been years, but it still hits me hard."

Maggie sighed, "Audrey, I'm sorry I'd forgotten. But that's no excuse. I've had so much drama in my life, I forget that I'm not the only one who has suffered."

They continued talking for a few more minutes until Audrey felt she had control of her emotions. Maggie suggested she go out and log into their Facebook account to see if there was anything new as a distraction, and she heard Audrey shuffling around as she got ready.

"You're right Maggie, that's just what I need to do. It will be a pleasant distraction and also a way to honour Sara." Audrey paused, "Oh, and Maggie, stay safe. I'm sorry I was so short with you before."

Maggie stopped and looked in the driver's lounge before she started down the road. She wanted to check that the poster she put up was still there. As she approached, she could see that someone had written on the bottom of the page. The writing was so tiny she had to get right up to it to see what it said.

'You're a resourceful woman Maggie. This just became more interesting. See you in Hell.'

Her guts clenched as she read the words and realized how much he was enjoying this, but she vowed to find him. This game wasn't new to her; it's one she'd played many times herself. She tore down the poster. No need for the police to connect it with a woman named Maggie, and put up a new one.

One of the fundamental differences between herself and this killer was she stumbled upon her victims. They deserved their fate and presented themselves to her. Going after the Dark Enders was different. That was personal. But the truckers she killed made the world a safer place. This killer didn't care. He killed for the sheer pleasure of killing, and to taunt and hurt her.

When she returned to the van, the rose was gone, and with it, her note. There was a sense of satisfaction knowing he got her message as well. They were both now hunters and killers.

38

Maggie sat in the van and considered her next move. Just before starting the engine, she sent a quick text to Audrey.

Audrey, I'm sorry I was so thoughtless earlier. If you need anything, just let me know.

Thanks, don't worry, I'm ok. I took your advice. Right now, I'm at the library looking at our FB page. I'm going to add some details about Sara, see if it helps find the last family.

That's a good idea. It also might be therapeutic.

I thought so too. Stay safe Maggie.

You too Audrey

Maggie turned the key, put the van in drive, and turned up the radio as she maneuvered onto the highway. It was later in the day then she'd normally leave, but her plan didn't include Tucker being murdered, either. It was a good thing she was only going as far as Rivière-du-Loup.

She was belting out the lyrics to a Luke Bryant song when her phone rang. She clicked the button on the dash to answer it and a voice bellowed at her before she could even say hello.

"Holy Fuck Maggie!"

"Ripley?"

"Don't Ripley me. If you're going to include murders in your blog, it might be nice for a heads up or some kind of warning before I read it."

"Um, hello to you, too."

"I'm serious Maggie, not that I don't love the piece, but I wasn't expecting to worry about you while you're out there. Who knew the road had so many dangers?"

Maggie laughed, "You have no idea Ripley. You knew I was a truck driver. I did that while The Trans-Canada Killer was travelling the highway."

"I remember that case. Didn't the killer end up dying in an accident and saving the world the expense of a trial?" Ripley asked.

"It was something like that, yes. I was at the same truck stop during the last murder. That was just before I left trucking and went back to school."

"You've led an interesting life, Maggie. Just do me a favour. In the future, if you're going to include murder in the blog, give me a heads up?"

She could hear his fingers on the keyboard and figured he was looking up what happened at the truck stop. If she was lucky, maybe he would stumble on something that would help her find out who this killer was.

"Sure, I will, and Ripley?"

"Yes?"

"If you hear anything about other truckers getting killed, can you let me know? It might be nice to have a heads up if I park where someone recently died."

"Of course, Maggie. Drive safe and keep those blogs coming. You're garnering quite the following."

Maggie leaned forward and disconnected the call. In her mind, she reviewed everything she knew about the killer. She'd reached out to everyone she could think of to warn them. Now that she knew the killer was watching her, she'd be careful who she spoke with. She didn't want a repeat of what happened to Tucker.

It would only take her an hour and a half to get to her destination, which was why she planned to stop there. She hoped that by ending her day early, the killer would continue on. She wanted to run into him at some point, and planned to confront and kill him, but she needed more information first. Taking some time off in Rivière-du-Loup would give her the opportunity to figure out what was next and start writing her book, now that she decided what it was going to be about.

She smiled at the working title she came up with 'My life as a Serial Killer.' In her case, it wouldn't be a full work of fiction, but no one else would know that. She would write about how it felt the first time she killed a man. Give away details that no one else would know, but her life experience would make it realistic. She wasn't sure if she was going to use a pseudonym or not, but she felt the excitement fill her at the possibilities that awaited.

39

Staying in Quebec wasn't her first choice. She didn't speak the language and found the barrier difficult. But because she was self-sufficient, Maggie stretched out her time there to work on her book. She didn't stay at a truck stop, choosing a shopping centre instead, and hoped the killer would continue on down the highway, putting distance between them. He didn't scare her, but his unpredictability of appearing and killing anyone she spoke to bothered her. She couldn't continue putting others at risk. This man was a different type of killer; killing for the effect it had on her.

During her time off, she made good progress in her book, jotting down notes to weave in as she went along, writing it as a work of fiction, but pulling from her own experiences in her hunt for Carter to add to the believability.

When she started, she thought back to the first time she killed a man and the sensations that ran through her. She hadn't planned on killing him. It was a crime of passion and opportunity. She overheard him boasting to someone that he preferred his females on the younger side. After what happened to her as a child, she couldn't help but feel the rage as it bubbled up within, and then she embraced it. Relishing in the sense of accomplishment rather than the guilt at taking a life, it wasn't what she was born to do.It was her experiences that turned her into this person.

The pages flew from her fingertips as she tapped the keyboard. She chose not to write in chronological order, but to write the thoughts as they came to her, awash in the sensations she felt, as she remembered each victim and how the world was a better place now that they were gone.

Reliving each kill brought back her rage, something she could harness in her search for the rose killer. Not the rage of vengeance that led her to kill Butch and Quinn, that was something deeper and more personal. This was the basic instinct bubbling deep inside, that forced her to right the wrongs created by an unjust world. A smile crept across her face as her hand furled and unfurled, clenching the knife she imagined there.

There was no sign of the killer since leaving Edmundston. But one thing she knew, he hadn't killed again. She had Ripley and Audrey watching the news for dead truckers and she was certain if they didn't hear of anything and Colby did, he'd be the first to warn her.

Maggie finished her writing for the day and put away her laptop. She looked out the window at the grey drizzle that pebbled its surface and pulled out her raincoat. It was time to take Edison for a walk. He wagged his tail in excitement when she pulled out his harness and stepped into it without issue. As soon as his paws hit the wet pavement, he turned and looked back over his shoulder as if to say, '*really mom? You're making me get wet?*' Then he did a full body shake before continuing, while bubbles of laughter escaped her lips at his antics.

She tightened the hood around her face and hoped he would be quick to find his spot, but there were too many places to smell, even with the rain-soaked pavement. After a few laps around the block, he found a place, and now she carried the bagged bundle back with her while she looked for a trash can to deposit it in. There was no way she'd bring that back to the garbage inside.

With the trash disposed of, they were both happy to be back in the dry warmth of the van. She wiped down Edison's paws and rubbed his coat dry, thankful he had such short fur. She put some fresh water down for him and topped up his kibble before starting on her supper.

While she cooked, she sent a text to her aunt Julie and Audrey telling them she was going to stop in Cobden for a few days before continuing on her travels. Audrey responded first and asked her to park in her laneway and spend a few days so they could discuss the hair clips. Maggie agreed, but knew she'd have to divide her time between her aunt and Audrey, especially when she found out her uncle was on his way home as well.

<h1 style="text-align:center">40</h1>

The sun crept into the sky early the next morning. Gentle golden rays flicked across her face, waking Maggie from a deep sleep. She rolled over onto her back and stretched, taking her time until she heard Edison whine indicating that he needed to go out. After slipping out of bed, she went to the washroom and pulled her hair into a ponytail before donning a pair of yoga pants and a tee-shirt. She only had a few hours to drive today to get to Cobden, but she wanted to give Edison a nice long walk beforehand.

They set out into the fresh crisp air to the smell of fresh baked bread from the nearby bakery. She could see the playfulness in his eyes when she looked down at his upturned face and said, "Let's go for a run." He bounced into the air, caught the leash in his mouth, growled at her and tugged. She engaged him in a game of tug-of-war for a couple of minutes before ordering him to 'drop it' and felt surprised when he did.

Feeling limber, they started out at a good pace, her feet slapping the pavement with Edison beside her. It had been a while since her last run, but she needed to get back into shape for the battle she knew was coming. In his excitement, Edison tried taking off, but his butt tried to

155

surpass his front end in comical pursuit. Maggie couldn't help but laugh at the sight and knew he was going to be a great exercise partner.

After half an hour, Maggie slowed her pace to a light jog. She didn't want to suffer from cramps while she drove, and as they got closer to the parking lot, she slowed down again to a brisk walk. She had to consider Edison as well. He wasn't used to the running and may cramp up. The walking would allow for a slow stretch, which she incorporated into full stretches on the steps to the van. As she leaned into the stretches, Edison jumped up at her, thinking it was playtime. She took a hold of his front paws and did a quick 'dosey doe' with him until he leaned over to be released.

Maggie took a few minutes to rub him down, then fed him his breakfast, made her bed and cleaned up the van before she poured coffee into her travel mug and started the ignition. She still had to get past Montreal, and couldn't go around on highway 30 unless she wanted to backtrack. She smiled as she merged onto the highway, knowing she was going to introduce Edison to her family for the first time. She hoped they'd love him as much as she did.

Although she promised to park at Audrey's for a few days, Maggie knew she had to see her aunt first or suffer her wrath, plus she felt a couple of hours working in the shop would do her some good. She pulled into the parking lot and parked off to one side so she wouldn't be in the way of the big rigs, and put Edison into his harness.

After relieving himself, he pulled her towards the shop, eager to see what was causing all the noise. He stuck his nose in the open bay and jumped back as soon as one of the power tools started. Maggie laughed at him and said, "Come on now, boy, don't be a nervous Nelly."

When the power tool paused, Edison ventured in with caution, first his nose, then his body, and then his butt and wagging tail. As soon as the mechanics saw him, they stopped what they were doing and came to meet him. He jumped up and licked at their faces, enjoying all the attention.

It didn't take long for Julie to notice the lull in work and come investigate.

"All right, boys, stop your lallygagging. We've got work to finish." As she turned the corner first noting the boxer that was greeting her mechanics with excitement and then her niece on the end of the leash, she added, "Well, when the prodigal daughter returns and brings a friend, I guess we can all take a break."

Julie waltzed over to Maggie and pulled her into a big hug. "So, who do we have here?"

"This is Edison! He's the best decision I've made since Liam's death. I even started running again because he has so much energy, it might be the only way to wear him out."

Julie crouched down to greet him and he put his paws on both of her shoulders and leaned in for a hug as she rubbed his body with vigour.

"Look at that," Maggie said, "he likes you!"

"You sound surprised? I love dogs."

"No, I'm not surprised. I've just never seen him do that to anyone but me."

Julie cast Maggie a sideways glance. "I know you too well. I can bet you haven't been around anyone since you got him."

"That's not true. I've brought him with me to Colby's house. He loves Evelyn."

"Colby, eh? That's the detective you told me about. I guess you decided he was worth a second look." Julie teased, then turned to her mechanics, who were still standing around and snapped, "Now get back to work. Maggie's off the market and you've already said hello to her dog."

The mechanics turned, but took their time going back to their workstations, muttering amongst themselves, good-naturedly, about how disruptive visitors were

Maggie watched them go and turned to Julie. "I'll put Edison back in the van, but I'm hoping you have some things for me to work on. I need some good old-fashioned physical labour to make me feel useful."

"Why don't you let Edison hang out in the office with me? Then you can go change the oil on that Kenworth in bay 4."

Maggie handed the leash to her aunt, donned her coveralls, clipped her hair up, and got to work.

When quitting time rolled around, Maggie felt exhausted after a full day's work. She went over to the wash station and cleaned up with the rest of the mechanics. Out of the closest window, Maggie saw Julie taking Edison for a walk around the compound, so she asked the mechanics if they wanted to see inside her van. When they nodded, Maggie beamed, and led them over, chatting about their day. They stood back while she opened up the doors for them to see and took turns looking inside and asking questions.

41

After showing the boys the attributes of her van, Maggie sent Audrey a quick text telling her she'd be by sometime later tomorrow. Hearing the rumble of an approaching rig, she turned and watched Uncle Bobby pull in for his 36-hour re-set. The mechanics were still hanging around her van, and he joined them, both to see what was going on and greet his niece. She planned to spend the night and part of the next day with her aunt and uncle because once she left Cobden; she didn't know when she'd return.

With his arm around Maggie's shoulder, Bobby took the leash from Julie as they made their way up to the house. Edison's excitement at all the goings on prevailed, and he tugged on the leash, hoping to run, but Bobby held firm. Maggie could tell Edison was tired, but didn't know when to give up. She suspected he'd crash as soon as they were inside.

"I don't know what we'll do for supper," Julie said, "but I can guarantee there's beer in the fridge."

Bobby looked at his wife. "How long have we been married?"

She swatted at him. "You know I get by on frozen dinners when you're on the road. I planned to do some grocery shopping, but time got away from me."

"Well, then it's a good thing I stopped on my way home. We're having chicken parm tonight. Maggie can give me a hand with it while you set up her room."

"Oh, don't go to any trouble. I can sleep in the van."

Bobby scowled at her. "Sleep in the van? I rarely get my whole family under one roof. You're sleeping in the house."

Maggie knew better than to argue with him. They got to work on supper with Edison laying on the floor between them, hoping for food to drop. In the meantime, Julie went upstairs to shower and set up Maggie's old room. While supper cooked, Bobby and Maggie took turns showering.

Preferring to don comfy clothes after their showers, they sat down to a delicious supper, enjoying the opportunity to catch up and appreciating each other's company. Edison lay curled up on the floor by Maggie's feet with his paw touching her foot for comfort.

After a night of conversation and storytelling, they all headed to bed. Maggie noticed that neither her aunt nor uncle asked her about the dead trucker from her blog, but stacked it up to their typical avoidance of matters they didn't want to face. What they didn't know, they didn't worry about. Edison followed her upstairs and sniffed around her bedroom. She noticed he seemed out of sorts, but put a blanket on the floor and hoped he'd make himself comfortable. Maggie didn't feel like going out to the van and getting him his sleeping crate.

She closed the door to her room so Edison wouldn't wander around the house at night, slipped between the covers and turned out the light. It didn't take long for Edison to hop up on the bed, come up and sniff her face before curling up in a ball beside her. She reached down, patted him and said, "Don't get too comfortable. We won't make a habit of this." Then Maggie rolled over and tugged at the covers pinned to the bed by Edison's weight and went to sleep.

In the morning, when the first light filtered through the curtains, Maggie opened her eyes. She tried to stretch but found Edison had made himself very comfortable on the other side of the bed by extending his full length, leaving her on the edge. She scolded him for being a bed hog. He responded by looking over his shoulder and yawning.

Maggie slipped out of bed and into her street clothes before heading to the washroom. She came back to the room, and found Edison standing by the door, waiting for her. "Come on boy." She said and motioned for him to follow her downstairs to where she'd hung up his harness, slipped it on him and took him outside.

When she came back in, Maggie smelled the aroma of bacon in the air fryer.

"Something smells good." She called out as she hung up the harness.

"I know you're heading over to spend some time with Audrey today. I just wanted to be sure you had a substantial breakfast first."

"Where's aunt Julie?"

"Oh, you know your aunt. She's already at the shop working. She hates goodbyes, but I know you'll pop in and see her before you leave. Do me a favour?"

"Sure what?"

"Give her a great big kiss on the cheek when you do."

Maggie chuckled, "I'll be happy to."

"Good, now go set the table. Breakfast will be ready in a few minutes."

Maggie gave Edison some fresh water and kibble, then set the table as Bobby asked. She helped bring the food out as Bobby favoured eating family style, never wanting to assume how much someone was going to eat. They took their time, and even lingering over a second cup of coffee before cleaning up. Maggie wanted to do the clean-up considering Bobby cooked, but he wouldn't hear of it, so they compromised and washed up together.

It wasn't long before Maggie decided it was time to head over to Audrey's house, so she said her goodbyes to her uncle, knowing he needed some alone time with Julie, and headed down to the shop to plant a big kiss on her aunt's face. Her aunt bristled when she did, but turned, gave her a big hug, and said, "Please be careful out there."

"I will." Maggie promised.

42

Maggie pulled into the laneway at Audrey's and parked close to the house. She'd sleep in the van because of Audrey's two Siamese cats, Blue and Ash, knowing there was no way Edison and the cats could be under the same roof. Edison, she was sure, would learn to adapt to the cats, but the Ash and Blue were a different story. They were older and set in their ways, and it would devastate Maggie and Audrey if anything happened.

Edison needed a walk first to stretch his legs and get settled before she knocked on the door. Feeling a tinge of guilt at leaving him, she made a mental note to go out to the van at regular intervals so he wouldn't be lonely. At least this was his home away from home, so he'd feel comfortable. Before leaving, she set Sirius to radio classics, so he'd hear the voices and wouldn't feel so alone.

With Edison settled, Maggie made her way up to the house. She lifted her hand, poised to knock, when Audrey opened the door and threw her arms around Maggie, pulling her into a big hug, walking backwards to close the door behind them.

"You're here! I'm sorry I was so moody the last time we spoke. You'd think after all these years it would get easier."

"Oh Audrey, you don't have to apologize to me. I know better than most what you're feeling."

"I saw you walking your dog. He's a handsome one, isn't he?"

"Yes, and he knows it. He's also so full of energy that he's like a firecracker that went off in a tin can, banging on the walls with nowhere to go."

Audrey laughed. "Will he be okay out in the van?" She asked, sending a worried glance towards it.

"He'll be fine. Don't worry. It's not like a regular vehicle. I have the temperature set and I don't have to leave it running to maintain it because of the APU. After we have a visit, I'll take you outside to show you."

Maggie made herself comfortable on the sofa and one cat, she didn't know which, jumped up on her lap and purred, rubbing itself against her. She rubbed its head and scratched under its chin and was about to pick it up and put it on the floor when Audrey came back in with a tray of tea and biscuits.

"Blue, get off her. Shoo him away."

"I'd better. I don't want Edison to think I'm cheating on him."

Audrey smiled and poured the tea. "Speaking of men..."

"No. We weren't speaking of men."

"Well, we are now. How's that handsome detective of yours?"

"It never fails to amaze me how quickly you can change the topic to one that you want to discuss."

"You still didn't answer me." Audrey replied.

Maggie sighed. "Colby is fine. We text every morning and every night, plus we've had a few video chats, both alone and with Evelyn."

"Video chats? What's the point?"

"Seeing each other face to face, so to speak. It makes the calls more personal."

"So, are you falling for him?" Audrey smiled over the brim of her teacup.

Maggie made a face, then said, "Yes, I've fallen for him."

"Thank God!"

Maggie swung her head up and stared into Audrey's eyes. "Wait, what? Aren't you the one who told me to be careful?"

"Because of your past, yes. But you're falling for him is self-serving."

"Um, how's that?"

"I can't imagine you continuing to kill while you're in a relationship with a detective. The more involved you become with him, the less likely you are to kill again. Then I can finally stop worrying about you."

Maggie let out a breath and chose her next words with care. "Audrey, you know there's a killer after me."

"Yes, I know."

"How do you think I can avoid confronting him? He's taunting me, and I know he's following me. You know I'm going to figure out who he is and kill him, right?"

Audrey placed the tea cup on the coffee table and leaned back. "Yes, I know that, and if you're going to get on with your life, you need to do it soon. I just want you to promise me when this is over, you'll be done with killing and enjoy the family you can make with Colby and Evelyn."

Maggie crossed her fingers beside her leg and replied, "I promise."

When they finished their tea, Maggie excuse herself and took Edison out for a short walk and refilled his water bowl. Her phone went off, and she pulled it out of her back pocket to check the message. It wasn't a text, but a messenger message from the Facebook account they'd set up about the barrettes. So far, it had helped them locate two of the last three families. Now there was only one barrette left. Based on its condition, they figured it was the oldest one from the collection.

She read the message and then reread it. *'Oh my God!'* she thought, closed the door to the van with Edison inside and ran back to the house.

43

Maggie burst through the front door, calling out for Audrey. "Audrey! Audrey! Did you see this?" She asked, holding up her phone.

"See what, Maggie?" Audrey questioned as she entered the room, drying her hands off on a tea towel.

Maggie handed Audrey her phone. Audrey stared at the message and then looked back up at Maggie, her mouth agape. "It can't be."

"I think it is. Go get your laptop. We need to sign in and see what's going on and if this person is real."

Audrey rushed to the other room, grabbed her laptop, and set it up on the coffee table in front of them. When it fired up, Maggie navigated it until their page was up on the screen. Before checking the message again, Maggie searched the various posts to see if, Debra, the woman who contacted them, had made comments on any of the other posts. They found several likes, but no posts or comments.

Maggie went back to see when the first like was and noticed that Debra joined three weeks ago. She couldn't remember accepting her join request, but either she or Audrey must have for her to be a member.

167

"I think she's for real. It looks like she's been following what's going on before reaching out. I'm going to respond to her."

Maggie typed a response to Debra, asking if she was a survivor or if she'd lost a family member. They waited, hands interlocked, watching the dots on the screen, indicating Debra was writing a response.

> Hi. One of my friends heard about your site for survivors. I reached out privately before posting my story. I don't want to get the rest of my family's hopes up that someone out there can tell us about Wanda.

> Who is Wanda?

> Wanda was my sister. She died when I was an infant. I'm the youngest of 7 children and Wanda was my oldest sister. I have two brothers who are older, the rest of us are girls.

> What do you know about what happened to Wanda? If we think it fits the profile of the rest of us, we'll help.

> Wanda disappeared when she was 9. My parents talked very little about it, but my siblings did. She was missing for over two months before the police found her body. The police said the evidence indicated that she died on the day she disappeared.

> How long ago was this?

> 55 years ago, this month. I never knew her, but her existence and then the lack of it, haunted my family. It changed our whole dynamic. When my parents died, my siblings and I began looking for answers. They never caught the man and when I was told about your site, I hoped we could put an end to the mystery once and for all.

> I'm sorry your parents aren't alive to get
> closure. What makes you think this is the
> right site and we can help?

> The hair clips. Whoever took Wanda kept
> her hair clip. At least that's what we
> assumed, because the police never found
> it. It was unique because my mom made it.
> It was a robin's egg blue with braided
> ribbon and a bow with streamers.

Maggie and Audrey gasped in unison. Audrey fumbled her way upright and went to her desk to retrieve the pouch containing the last barrette. When she came back to the living room and put it on the table, all they could do was stare. The barrette was identical to the one Debra described. The ribbon on it had faded and was grimy from Franks touching it over the years, but it had to be the same.

> Do you have a picture of the ribbon? Maybe
> we could post it for you and field all the
> questions. It would allow you to see if
> anyone knows anything about Wanda, and
> if whoever has been returning the clips sees
> it and has Wanda's, maybe they will
> return it.

> I don't have a picture of the exact barrette,
> but I do have pictures of duplicates. My
> mom made them for each of us girls,
> although never again in robin's egg blue. I
> have a picture of me wearing a violet one.
> Give me a few minutes and I'll upload it.

"I can't believe we've found the last family. It's heartbreaking that her parents won't have the closure they deserved, but at least the rest of the family will. Something like this shadow's over a family forever." Audrey said, walking to the liquor cabinet and pulling out a bottle of gin.

"I can't believe Carter began killing over 55 years ago and never got caught. He must have been in his early 20s when he started."

"I'm sure it started before that. Wanda's barrette may have been the first trophy he took and kept. My experience says there'd be a lot of 'tells' into the type of person he would become. Either no one cared or no one bothered to connect the dots." Audrey poured them each a shot.

"What's this for?"

"When Debra sends us the picture, we need to toast to a job well done. We have been searching for so long to bring closure to the families, and it looks like we finally have. We deserve it."

Maggie nodded in agreement as Debra's message came in. They looked at the picture and compared it to the barrette in front of them and knew they were the same. A sense of relief washed over them. It was over.

> If you'd like Debra, I can post the picture. I'll blur out your face and include a brief history of Wanda and what happened without giving her name. Hopefully, the person who has been returning the clips will see it.

> That sounds good. Can I give you my address? That way, if the person contacts you, you can give it to them and maybe my family can let Wanda rest.

> Of course, we've done that before. I hope this helps bring your family the closure you deserve.

Maggie turned to Audrey and raised her glass. "Well, there's no doubt about it. We can finally bring the last barrette home to the right family. Cheers."

44

They continued chatting and celebrating. One drink turned into two, and soon Maggie excused herself to check on Edison. She felt bad for leaving him alone for so long, but she didn't expect things to go the way they had. She also knew she couldn't bring him up to the house, not with the cats there, but she hated knowing he was spending so much time alone. That's not why she got him.

As she approached the van, she could see it shaking and realized Edison must be playing. She smiled and thought, *'oh good, he's entertaining himself.'* She slid open the side door and her eyes widened as Edison, startled, turned to face her, a tuft of fluff clinging to his lips.

"Edison!" she scolded in a firm voice. "What did you do?"

He licked at his lips and tried to dislodge the piece of fluff. Maggie reached out and removed it and turned to see what he'd gotten into. She looked to the left and discovered she'd forgotten to put away her pillow and stuffing from it littered the inside of the van.

Maggie tried hard to hide her smile at his comical look and her own forgetfulness. She put him in his harness and attached his lead to the hooking mechanism just outside the door, which she installed for this purpose, and began cleaning up the mess. When she'd bagged the 'offending' pillow remnants, she pulled out the vacuum and cleaned up the floor and crevices. Edison kept trying to get back inside while she picked up the fluff, but pulled to the end of his lead at the sound of the vacuum, only coming back to the door when she turned it off and put it away.

Maggie packed Edison back into the van and headed to town to replace the pillow. She didn't want to end up with a stiff neck the next morning. She fired off a quick text to Audrey, explaining what she was doing, and promised to bring back something for supper.

When Maggie returned to Audrey's, she'd restocked her food cupboards to prepare for her departure. For tonight's dinner, she picked up the ingredients for Chicken Alfredo, with Caesar salad and garlic bread. She pulled into the laneway and took Edison for a long walk after sending Audrey a text, letting her know she was back and coming up to make supper after walking Edison.

A half hour later, she returned to the van, pulled the bed down and covered it with a dog friendly sheet, put the pillow in storage, turned on the radio and grabbed the dinner fixings. She hid some treats for Edison to find as a way of entertaining himself and left the van after telling him to behave. All she could do was hope.

Back at the house, Maggie got to work in the kitchen. She grilled the chicken and put a pot on to boil for the pasta. Audrey set the table and fussed in the kitchen beside Maggie.

"I'm not used to others cooking in my kitchen." Audrey grumbled as she stood to one side, watching Maggie stir the sauce. A little annoyed that Maggie wouldn't let her help.

"Then enjoy it. But you could open the wine I picked up and pour us each a glass."

Audrey went to the fridge and pulled out the bottle of white. Holding it up, she said, "I thought you drank red?"

"I'm a non-discriminating wino," Maggie joked. "I like both red and white. But white is the better choice with the chicken."

"I agree, I like both too. I like that, 'non discriminating wino!' Who'd have thought you made jokes?" Audrey teased, handing Maggie her glass.

"Supper won't take long. I thought maybe afterwards we could look at the post we made earlier. If it's getting noticed, we could prepare the parcel for shipping. Then I could take it with me and drop it in the mailbox somewhere along my route."

"That's a great idea. I hate having to wait for your uncle to get back to ensure the postmarks are random. But I understand why we've had to do it. This being the last one, it would be nice to do it sooner than later."

Maggie nodded as she turned to mix the sauce into the pasta, then she added the chicken and some fresh chopped basil before putting it on a platter.

"Maggie!" Audrey exclaimed. "That's a lot of food."

Maggie looked down at the platter and shrugged. "We both may end up with leftovers. At least it reheats well. The salad won't be nice tomorrow, though. Can you grab that, please?"

Together, they placed the food on the table, dished out the amount they wanted, and chatted while they ate. Maggie felt a cat as it weaved between her legs and reached down to give it a rub.

Taking the last bite of her dinner, Audrey leaned back and patted her stomach. "That was delicious, Maggie."

Maggie put her fork on her plate and thanked her. Audrey stood up and gathered the dishes while Maggie put the leftovers on the counter to be divided up. There was enough pasta leftover for each of them to have another meal. So, it went into two containers. Then they split the last of the wine between them and went to the living room, where the laptop was still on the coffee table. Audrey signed into the computer and they checked on the post they'd made earlier.

It only took a couple of minutes to bring up the post and, according to the notifications, there were over 40 new posts and comments. They began reading them, noticing others had posted pictures of their returned barrettes, calling whoever sent them a hero.

Maggie chortled, "Hero? Far from a hero."

"But Maggie, to those families, we are heroes. We brought them closure and told them the monster who caused them so much pain was dead. You were a child victim. How do you think your father would have felt if he survived, knowing the monster that attacked you was dead?"

"I guess because I killed him, I've always thought of myself as a different monster." Maggie replied with a shrug of her shoulders.

"Maggie, you've only killed the deserving. You're not a monster. When you were a little girl, you came to me, broken and scared. I've watched you become strong and independent. I think what you've done has made the world a better place, no matter why you did it."

Audrey wrapped her arms around Maggie and embraced her. "You're a survivor. Never forget it."

They packaged up the barrette to mail to Debra after reading all comments. The act was bitter sweet. Knowing they'd found the families of all the barrettes that belonged to the victims, filled them with a sense of accomplishment, but deep down, they both knew there were more victims out there. Little girls who weren't wearing barrettes when Carter found them.

45

Sunshine streaked through the front window of the van and placed a warm kiss on Maggie's face. She yawned and stretched her body under the covers of her bed before rolling over to look at Edison's dark chocolate eyes glistening with the reflected light. He was already sitting up in his crate waiting for her, his head peeked over the edge. She chuckled and greeted him as she swung her feet off the bed.

Maggie stood and arched her back in a full stretch, and noticed something out of the corner of her eye on the front window. Her jaw slackened and her stomach rolled when she realized it was a black rose. She clenched her fist and cursed before throwing some clothes on and stepping outside to investigate. Edison whined as she opened the side door and left him in his crate. She snatched the rose out from under the wiper blade, oblivious to the thorns that dug into the flesh of her palm, and unraveled the attached note.

She read the words, 'I'm always watching' and her head swivelled around to the forest behind her as she scanned for movement. The sound of a twig snapping turned her attention towards Audrey's house. The sight before her caused her stomach to clench. Bile rose in her throat. Her hand flew to her mouth as she dropped the rose and trampled it in her haste to get to the front door.

"Nooo!" She screamed at the sight of the bloody, furry mess on the front porch. She couldn't let Audrey find this. *'This will devastate her. Oh, my God! How did he get a hold of one of her cats?'* Maggie wondered. *'She never allows them out.'*

Maggie had to remove it before Audrey saw it. She grimaced as she bent to pick up the carcass, praying it wasn't Blue or Ash, but some other unfortunate animal with the same colouring. She could smell the metallic scent of the blood, but when her hand went under the remains, she discovered there was no weight to it. An animal would have weighed something, even dead. She lifted it up to discover it was a stuffed animal made to look like one of Audrey's cats. But she knew from the smell that the blood was real. She was all too familiar with the scent of blood.

Maggie carried the twisted mess to Audrey's trash bin and wondered where the blood came from and what or who he killed to get it. She'd have to tell Audrey about this. Her body sagging as she let out a sigh of relief that it wasn't one of her cats.

Her hands were streak with blood, as she went back to the van to wash them and take Edison out. She heard him whining and wondered if he sensed the change in her emotions. In her haste to check out the rose, she'd left the door ajar, so she used her hip to open it in order to avoid getting blood on the handle.

"It's okay boy, just let me wash my hands and I'll take you out."

She heard him growl, and the hairs on the back of her neck prickled. Her eyes narrowed as Maggie spun around and scanned the tree line. She couldn't see anything out of the ordinary, but her heart pounded in her chest, anyway. Something had set Edison off. Satisfied no one was there, she stepped inside and used some baby wipes to clean off the blood. She'd do a better job after she took Edison out. Walking him would help flush out anyone who was hiding nearby. If he got on a scent, she'd follow. Just to be on the safe side, she grabbed her gun and stuck it in her jacket pocket before they left.

As soon as they were out of the van, Edison dragged her to Audrey's front door, his nose barely an inch from the ground. He sniffed where the stuffed animal had been and whimpered. Then he pulled and tugged her with his nose to the ground, only stopping when he relieved himself. Maggie struggled to keep up with him as he yanked her along with his nose on a scent.

She stumbled behind him, her arm jerking every time he lurched forward, as he made his way down the laneway towards the main road. At the apex of the laneway and the road, Maggie saw some tire tracks and realized a vehicle had parked there recently. Then she noticed a cigarette butt on the gravelled shoulder and thought, *'Another clue! He's a smoker.'* She bent down to check the brand and made a mental note to keep an eye out for the familiar white and blue packaging when she saw someone smoking.

After gaining control of Edison, she guided him back to the van for his breakfast. She sat down at the table and wished she hadn't thrown her last package of cigarettes away after finishing her business with the Dark Enders. This incident pulled her nerves, stretching them to the breaking point and coffee would just cause the thread to snap. She closed her eyes and took a few deep breaths. She needed to figure out a way to tell Audrey what happened without scaring her. One thing was certain: she needed to set up those security cameras and motion detectors around Audrey's property today.

Maggie stood at her sink, scrubbing the remaining traces of blood from under her fingernails and was rubbing her temples when she heard Audrey call out for her.

"Maggie, are you up?"

She took a deep breath, pasted a smile on her face, and opened the side door.

"Good morning, Audrey. I've been up for a while. Edison and I already took a walk, and he's enjoyed his breakfast."

Audrey bent over to rub his head. "Good morning, boy. I've got a pot of coffee on. It looks like another nice day. Bring Edison up to the house, and we can have our coffee outside on the deck."

"I'll be right up. Just give me a few minutes."

Audrey nodded and went back to the house.

"Well, Edison, here goes nothing. My fear is that Audrey will blame me for bringing the killer to her house."

46

Maggie hooked Edison back into his harness and brought him around to the backyard. There she found Audrey had made a tie up for him. She fastened him to it, allowing him to move around within range of his lead. To make him comfortable, she laid a mat down on the ground for him to lie on. Edison sniffed it and curled up on it in the sunshine as she sat herself down on a chair. Soon, Audrey came out with a tray laden with coffee, croissants warm from the oven, and a platter of fruit salad.

Maggie gasped. "You amaze me! When did you have time to get up and make croissants this morning?"

Audrey laughed, "If I'm being honest, I got them from Costco and all I had to do was bake them. They're in the freezer section, and they're almost as good as fresh made."

Maggie bit into one smothered with butter. "Mmm. I'll have to keep a lookout for these. They're fantastic."

Maggie took her time as she nibbled on the croissant. Thoughts whirled around in her head as she struggled to find the words to tell Audrey what happened and that the killer had been on her property.

"You were up early this morning." Audrey said, dragging Maggie back from her thoughts, "I heard you clattering around by the garbage as I was getting up."

Maggie sighed. There was no putting it off any longer. She hesitated before beginning, searching for the right words.

"I was looking around your property this morning and I didn't see a security system. We talked about this before. You're out here in the woods, far away from the main road. Aren't you worried about your safety?"

"I bought the cameras right after I promised you I would. I just haven't set them up yet. So far, I haven't seen a need."

"Unfortunately, I think there is a need. He was here."

Audrey turned towards Maggie, her face pale. "He?"

"The killer."

Maggie watched as Audrey's eyes widened and the rest of the colour drained from her face. Her voice was barely a whisper when she replied, "How do you know?"

Maggie took a deep breath and described what she encountered first thing this morning, starting with the rose on the windshield and finishing with the bloody mess of the fake cat that was on Audrey's porch.

"No, he wouldn't" Audrey sobbed.

"He kills without conscience. I'm sure a cat means nothing to him. You should know, the blood was real. I could tell by the metallic sent, which is unforgettable." Maggie paused. "We need to set up your cameras. It's the only way I can be sure you're safe. I'm sorry I brought this monster to your home. I also think we should set up some motion detectors as well. That way, they'll go off anytime someone approaches."

"Motion detectors? Won't those go off every time an animal comes by? I live in the forest. There are animals all over the area." Audrey complained, swinging her arm around at her sanctuary.

"I think having your motion detector set off by animals is a lot better than not knowing if somebody's here who means you harm.

How would you defend yourself? What could you do? Until I can find out who this is and stop him, I need to know you're safe."

Audrey took a deep breath and looked around her peaceful existence on the edge of the water with the forest surrounding. "Will I ever feel safe here again?"

"I'm sorry Audrey. This is all my fault."

"No. This is the killer's fault. Okay, I'll do what you asked, but that means I'll have to go into town and get some motion detectors. If you'll make a list of what I need, I can do that. In the meantime, can you set up the cameras? I don't have a clue on how to do that."

Tension filled the air as they sat back and drank their coffee in silence, both lost in their own thoughts. Maggie watched the way Audrey swung her foot over her crossed leg, and could sense her agitation. She reached over and put her hand on Audrey's knee. Audrey looked up, startled.

"It will be okay, I'll get him." Maggie reassured.

After they finished their coffee, Audrey went inside and pulled out the cameras from the back of a storage cupboard and handed them to Maggie. Maggie checked to make sure she had everything she needed, then she gave Audrey instructions on what to buy. Maggie suggested they should put motion detectors up along the laneway as well and estimated how many Audrey would need. That way, they'd illuminate her yard if somebody or something came close, alerting Audrey of their presence.

Maggie finished installing the last of the security cameras and checked to make sure that they worked when Audrey returned with the motion detectors. Audrey got advice from the man at the store and chose the solar models so they wouldn't need an electrician in to hard wire them or have to change batteries. This would allow them to hide the devices in the various trees that lined the laneway.

With Audrey's help, Maggie set up all the motion detectors in the front and the back of the house, as well as along the laneway. Only when she felt satisfied and they'd run out of detectors did she stop.

"Every time an animal gets near, my house is gonna be lit up like a Christmas tree." Audrey complained.

"Better to be lit up, than surprised by an unwanted intruder." Maggie retorted.

Audrey raised her hands in defeat. "Okay I get it. Listen, I bought some steaks for supper while I was out. Do you think Edison will be okay in the van tonight?"

"I'm sure he'll be fine. He's been outside with me all day while I set up your security. I should take him for a quick run, grab a shower, and make a salad before joining you. We also need to check what's happening with the post we made."

"Okay, but shower up at the house. No need to waste your resources while you're here."

Maggie nodded, and set off with Edison for a quick run along the tree lined country road, enjoying the warmth of the late afternoon sun. When she realized Edison was getting tired, she turned and walked back knowing he would sleep well and not get into trouble while she had dinner with Audrey, but to be on the safe side, this time she'd put her pillows and comforter in the storage cabinet out of reach.

When they finished eating, Audrey pulled out her laptop to check the posts. During supper, Maggie informed Audrey she'd leave in the morning and planned to take the parcel with her. Audrey agreed.

Bobby was already back on the road and they didn't know when he'd return. They were both eager for Debra and her family to have closure.

Audrey turned on the computer and pulled up the site before turning the laptop towards Maggie, who took over scanning the page.

"I can't believe how many people have posted pictures of their returned hair clips. Debra's picture started something. I think it's safe for us to mail out the barrette. Look at all these comments of support and sharing of information." Maggie said, turning the laptop around so Audrey could see.

Audrey read a few of the comments and smiled at Maggie. "It feels good to give people the answers they need, doesn't it?"

They continued to read through the comments, planning to delete any they found that were negative in context. That's not what the page was for and even though they were very careful about who had access, sometimes the wrong person slipped by. Before long, Maggie stifled a yawn and said good night. She needed to take Edison out before bed, and planned to get going early the next morning.

"You're not going to say goodbye?"

"I'm doing it right now. I promise I'll keep texting you daily so you know I'm okay. And I'll stop by again on my way back. Hopefully, I'll have caught up with my stalker by then and all of this will be over."

Audrey wrapped her arms around Maggie and pulled her into an embrace, telling her to stay safe. Then Audrey watched as Maggie made her way to her van, lights from the motion detectors illuminating her way. Maggie turned, smiled and gave Audrey a thumbs up when the first one went off. Audrey couldn't help but smile back at her.

47

The following morning, Maggie took Edison out for a long run as the first streaks of pink were filtering into the sky. Knowing she needed to put in a lot of miles today, it was important that he got his exercise. She didn't say goodbye to Audrey; they said their goodbyes last night. So, she packed the van and started out along Highway 17 on the route to Sault Ste. Marie. She figured it would take between 7 1/2 to 9 hours to get there, but that depended on traffic and the number of stops she needed to make. Taking Edison for a run this morning served a dual purpose. One, she hoped it would wear him out and he wouldn't need as many stops, and two, it gave them both some much needed exercise.

The hurry to get to Sault Ste. Marie today was to put as many miles between herself and her family as possible. The monster that hunted her was a threat to Audrey, and that meant he was also a threat to aunt Julie and uncle Bobby. Later today, she'd call Colby and see if there was any new information about the killer. She had to know what was going on and hoped that Colby would divulge some of the information he knew.

She looked up at her GPS, and her planned route that avoided the 401 and a stop in Toronto. Ripley would be furious that she took a different route, but she could always hit Toronto on the way back. She knew her blog would benefit from a stop there, but putting some distance between herself and those she loved was more important. The snarl of traffic leading into the GTA would slow her down, and it wasn't the most direct route from Cobden to Sault Ste. Marie, anyway.

Last night she included the information about the fake cat incident in her blog. She described what happened and how it felt to find what she thought was a mutilated animal. She didn't elaborate where it happened, but she had to assume the killer was reading the blog, so he'd know she got the message. As for her readers, they'd think that somebody out there thought it was a funny prank, and it would also gather more readers to her blog. People flocked to the macabre, and she hoped it would help her flush out the killer.

As Maggie pulled out onto Highway 17, she slid her sunglasses in place against the glare of the sun, and turned on her favourite Sirius station. She could tell Edison didn't like the first song, as he howled to the music. She chuckled to herself and turned the station, finding something a little gentler on his ears. He soon settled down.

Highway 17 wasn't as busy as the 401, but because it was only two lanes, it had more risks. The two-lane highway twisted and turned, creating blind spots, but also beautiful vistas. Running along that stretch of road was easier for a person with four wheels than a tractor trailer, but she knew she'd have to be diligent every step of the way. Too many drivers became impatient and tried to pass whether or not it was clear, so she had to stay alert. The sunshine and dry road were a blessing as she made her way to her destination.

Maggie pulled off in Sudbury to capture pictures of the Big Nickel. She needed something touristy to add to today's blog. A complete day of driving wasn't enough, and she wanted something upbeat after last night's post. She pulled up the post before leaving and noticed there were a lot of comments about the 'prank' of a dead cat. Ripley called and said he had to shut down the comment section on that post, and he asked her to include something of public interest in her next one, so the Nickel it was. She had to remind herself that although she'd been all across the country many times and had seen much of what it offered, the blog was for those who hadn't. It was for people who didn't have her experience and for those thinking of joining the van lifestyle, but also for general travellers.

After getting some beautiful pictures, Maggie uploaded them right away and wrote the blog. She figured she might as well do it while parked. It would save her time when she got to Sault Ste. Marie, knowing she'd be tired after a long day of driving. If there were any new and exciting developments, she could write about them in the next blog.

It was close to supper when she pulled in to the Husky parking lot in Sault Ste. Marie. Neither Colby nor Audrey would be happy she'd picked another truck stop, but the Husky was familiar to her. She could've parked anywhere in her sprinter van, but chose the truck stop for its comfort and familiarity. To her, truck stops were like a warm blanket that surrounded her like a friendly hug, even though she knew truck stops were also the killer's hunting ground. Where better to catch him than where he felt most comfortable?

Not wanting to take the parking spot of a truck, she picked one off to the side and out of the way. When she put the vehicle in park, she turned to Edison and told him they'd arrived. He responded by sitting up and yawning.

She slipped into the back and put Edison in his harness. It was time to take him out for a long walk to wear off his pent-up energy from travelling. They didn't need a run tonight. They did that this morning. She just needed to give him the exercise he required. She yawned and realized how tired she felt. So instead of making supper for herself, she decided she'd go into the restaurant, but before she left Edison alone, she'd be sure to put the pillows away so he wouldn't destroy them. No need for more fluff scattered across the van and an added shopping trip to replace them.

When they returned to the van, Edison's nose hit the ground, and he started sniffing, pulling on the lead as he went. It took all of Maggie's strength to control him. She wasn't sure what he detected as he led the way back to the van, but something put him on alert. Her senses were acute as she approached it, and Edison growled. Before she could investigate, she heard a voice call out.

"Maggie? Is that you?"

Maggie spun around towards the sound of the voice and a smile broke across your face, as she recognized Tammy, one of her trucking friends. She hadn't seen her since that last night in Chilliwack, which was also her last trip in her truck. She knew her road family had kept everybody informed on what was going on in her life, but this is the first time they'd come face-to-face. In Maggie's excitement, for a moment, she forgot about the killer.

"Tammy! I can't believe it's you!" Maggie replied, as Edison sat at her feet.

Tammy closed the distance between the two of them in a few quick steps and embraced Maggie.

"Are you trucking again?" Tammy asked.

"No, I'm living the van life." Maggie replied, motioning towards her van.

Tammy raised her eyebrows and shrugged her shoulders. "I thought you were a reporter now. What's with the van life?"

"After Liam died, I needed a change of pace, and this was it. I presented the idea to my editor and now I'm writing a blog about life on the road, but from a different perspective than when I was a trucker, I even make comparisons between the two in my blog. I'm surprised you didn't know. Haven't you run into any of the guys lately?"

"Run into who? Didn't you know most of the drivers we knew are already dead? There's somebody out there killing truckers again. He's picked off most of our friends."

Maggie swallowed hard as she looked around. Running into Tammy was wonderful, but she knew the killer could be nearby. Just talking with her put her at risk.

"I saw one of the crime scenes. It wasn't a friend, but it was a driver I'd met. It was in Edmundston as I started my trip. I even wrote about it in my blog. I heard about Josh and Tom. My heart broke with the news."

"Then you don't know about the latest victim." Tammy paused. "They found JD's body yesterday. I heard they think it's the same killer. The CB has been buzzing about it all day. It's all the drivers are talking about. Something about rose petals at every killing. You know how word spreads."

Maggie sagged back against her van, her knees felt weak and her hand flew to her mouth. Tears welled in her eyes. "No, not JD."

"You should probably go home and get off the road even though you're not in a truck. Or stop picking truck stops, they've become too dangerous. I'm only out here because I have to make a living. Otherwise, I'd fly to where I wanted to go. If I could, I'd go home, park and never get back out on the road, but Kevin is still out there and I'm worried about him. We talk every day, not just once, but multiple times, just to keep in touch with each other. I've almost considered teaming with him so we could be close all the time. But you and I both know we'd make no money doing that."

"I'm so sorry Tammy. I didn't know how bad things had gotten. Have you eaten? I'm putting Edison here back in the van and I was going to head inside for dinner."

"I was just heading inside when I saw you. It would be nice to have the company. Having a dog with you is a good idea. If my company allowed pets, I'd have one too."

Maggie unlocked the door and put Edison back inside, set out his dinner and refilled his water dish, forgetting about the scent that had him so anxious before she ran into Tammy. Then she checked the cameras and locked the van and headed inside. It was time to catch up with everything happening on the road and gather some information that would help her find the killer. The apprehension she felt about spending time with Tammy under the circumstances weighed on her, but there was nothing she could do about it now.

48

Sitting across the table from Tammy, Maggie noticed for the first time the state she was in. Her ragged nails were bitten to the quick. Her leg bounced with nervous energy and her eyes darted around the room after every sentence. Maggie had never seen her like this. Tammy's personality was more easygoing. She reached out and put her hand on top of Tammy's and gave it a squeeze. Tammy's eyes flicked from her hands up and Maggie noticed the dark circles that shadowed beneath them.

"Tammy, you're a wreck. You can't continue driving like this. Take some time off, get out of the truck. If you don't, you won't survive."

"Maggie, I can't calm down. Think about it. This killer seems to be focused on car haulers. Both Kevin and I haul cars. It's what we do. And we can't afford to stop. I mean, we can take a vacation, but what will that solve? That killer is out there and I'm guessing would still be there when we came back. The cops aren't saying anything. Let's face it, who cares about truckers?"

"I care."

"Maggie, that's because you're one of us, or at least you were. You get it better than most."

"Tammy, my friend is a detective with the RCMP. Because this killer is killing Canada wide, he'll know all about it, and he can find out some information. I think you and Kevin should take a vacation. Give yourself some distance from all of this. Maybe they will catch him by the time you get back."

Tammy chewed on the rough edge of a cuticle. "I'll talk to Kevin, see what he says. But when you talk to your friend, can you promise to call me?"

"Of course, I will."

Their food arrived, shifting the conversation, and Maggie continued to watch Tammy. Her behaviour worried her. She was tough as nails, but too many of their friends had fallen victim to this killer and she knew it was her fault. Tammy remained silent while they ate, relying on Maggie to fill the void with endless chatter.

When they finished eating, Maggie turned to Tammy and asked, "Do you have anything to protect yourself with?"

"What do you mean? You know we can't carry weapons."

"Wasp and hornet spray works just like mace in a pinch, also hairspray. They even have pocket ones you can carry everywhere with you. And I'm sure you have a sharp knife in your truck. Why not make a habit of having it on you?"

"Maggie, he's killing men. It's not me I'm worried about, it's Kevin. I can't lose him."

"Tammy, you don't know the killer only kills men. There aren't many women car haulers out there. But from what I've heard, he isn't just killing car haulers. Just do me a favour and protect yourself."

"Okay." Tammy mumbled. "Hey! Can you meet me for breakfast before you leave?"

"Sure. I'll walk with you back to your rig."

"Then who'll walk you back?"

Maggie chuckled and patted the hunting knife on her hip. "My friend will help me get back to safety."

The next morning Maggie noticed Tammy was calmer, a little more like her old self. It didn't take long for Maggie to find out why.

"I just got off the phone with Kevin." She smiled. "He's agreed to meet me back in the yard so we can take some time off together."

"That's wonderful news, Tammy. I'm so happy for you."

"Thanks for suggesting it. It's been too long since we've had a vacation of any kind. I think we're going to book something away. All we do when we're off now is work around the house. It will be nice just to relax and enjoy our time together."

"That's a good idea. Plan something exotic. If this situation has shown us anything, it's that life is short. I'm starving after my morning run. I think I'll get the pancakes. What about you?"

"Oh, that sounds good. I'll get the same." Tammy said, closing her menu and placing her order. "Now all I have to do is go to Vancouver and back before coming off the road. I have some deliveries along the way, but my pickups for my return trip are in Vancouver and then straight back to the yard. It would be nice to see you again if you can meet up with me somewhere on the road before I head back."

"I'll try to keep up with you. I'm writing a travel blog so I'll spend part of my days doing touristy things. But based on your picks and drops on your way west, I could meet up with you again in Headingley."

"If you get delayed, I'll find an excuse to hang around." Tammy grinned before taking a mouthful of her pancakes the server had placed on the table.

They parted ways after breakfast. Tammy had deliveries to make and Maggie had to get back to Edison. Maggie watched and waved as

Tammy wheeled her rig out of the lot and felt the tension ease out of her body. Tammy gave her a quick toot of her horn as she left, and Maggie sighed. She knew staying away from Tammy would be difficult if she planned to wait for her. She just had to be diligent about who was around them to keep her from harm. Maggie went back to the van and took Edison out before she got behind the wheel and called Colby.

49

Colby and Carlson spread the files out as they perused the case load that they'd nicknamed the Trans-Canada Copycat or TCC for short. This new killer was almost up to the same body count as the original, but he didn't have a specific victimology other than truck drivers. Up to date, all the victims had been men. The original TC Killer picked pedophiles, making him a vigilante killer. This one killed randomly, which made him more dangerous.

Colby pulled up the latest victim's information. Someone called John David Morgan, or JD to his friends. He noted the killing was personal and violent. The killer slashed JD's throat from ear to ear, the same MO as the original killer, but the weapon was different. He didn't leave barrettes at the scene, instead he left rose petals. By comparison, the new killer was sloppy. The telltale sign that it was the same person was the rose petals scattered near the bodies, and always red. If there was only one victim, Colby would assume it was the work of a jilted lover. What bothered him was the victims. Other than what they did for a living, there was no connection. Several victims hauled cars, but there was a flat deck operator, straight cargo and a refrigerated truck too.

He reviewed the information about the latest victim and the company he worked for. Something about it was familiar, so he pulled up the information he had from the other cases and found a similarity. Three of the victims worked for the same company. He wondered why the name of the company irked him. Then he realized he'd spoken with some of the victims during the interviews he conducted for the TC Killer case in Chilliwack. He remembered they were on some sort of car tour.

Colby went back to his notes and pulled out everything he had from the original case. He flipped through the pages until he came to his interviews with the victims. He paused when he came to Maggie's name in his notes and his jaw dropped. She'd worked for the same company. *'Could her life be in danger?'* He wondered.

"Carlson, come look at this."

Carlson stood up and moved closer, looking over Colby's shoulder to get a better angle.

"What have you got there?" He asked.

"Something nagged at me, and then I realized some of the victims worked for the same trucking company. The company name sounded familiar, so I pulled up my notes from the original TC Killer case. I discovered that I'd interviewed several of the victims during my investigation in Chilliwack."

Carlson grabbed Colby's notes and flipped through them. He paused when he came to Maggie's name.

"Maggie Hopkins? Isn't that the redhead you're seeing?"

"Yes." Colby choked on the word.

"She worked for the same company? I guess it's a good thing she's not trucking anymore."

"She's back on the road, remember? Writing that Van Life blog. The last I heard, she was leaving her family in Cobden and continuing west. I'm not sure if I should warn her? I mean, so far, all the victims have been men, but what does that mean?"

"Shit." Carlson exclaimed. "I think you have to warn her. Does she know what's going on?"

"She was in Edmundston when that driver," Colby paused, checking his notes, "Tucker Babcock was killed. Maggie saw the crime scene, even wrote about it in her blog. If you remember, we talked about it. What concerns me is if he's killing people who work for the same company as part of his victimology, could he know who she is?"

"You've got to tell her. Maybe you can persuade her to stay away from the truck stops."

Colby laughed with a tinge of bitterness. "You've never dated a redhead, have you? Maggie has a mind of her own. If I told her to stay away from one place in particular, she would show up just because. At one time I thought after her husband died, she had a death wish, but I don't think that's it. I now think it's the reporter in her, always looking for the next big story."

"Well, if she's that bullheaded, it's a good thing she's easy on the eyes."

"That and other things." Colby smiled as Carlson leaned back and laughed.

"Go call her, find out where she is, let her know what's going on. Then get your ass back in here. We have work to do."

Maggie picked up on the first ring.

"Hey Colby, I was just thinking about you."

"I hope you're always thinking about me." He teased. "Where are you?"

"I'm just leaving Sault Ste. Marie. I ran into a friend last night, so we had breakfast before she left for Vancouver. Is something wrong?" She asked.

"Not wrong, but I want to talk to you about something. Do you remember the guy killed in Edmundston?"

"Of course, I do. Why?"

"Well, there's been another body, and I think there's a connection between the victims you need to be aware of."

Maggie swallowed; last night she'd cried a lot over JD's death. His carefree manner and love of life. She couldn't tell Colby she knew there was another victim, but hoped that was why he was calling. If it was, it meant he was concerned and would keep her informed.

"A connection? Something on or off the record?" She asked.

He chuckled, "Always the reporter. This is off the record. There's been another victim. Someone I think you knew."

Maggie'a fingers tightened on the steering wheel as she braced herself to receive the official news of JD's death.

"A John David Morgan."

"JD? No, not JD!" She allowed a sob to escape her lips, realizing how fresh the pain still was.

"You knew him."

"Knew him? He saved my life in Chilliwack. You remember the time we met? Just before that, a man with a knife chased me in the parking lot. I didn't see him coming and JD got me to safety. I can't believe he's gone."

"Maggie, I'm sorry. I know how hard it is to lose a friend."

"You said a connection. What is the connection to Edmundston?"

"Oh, the only connection to Edmundston is that he was another trucker. The actual connection is there are several victims that worked for the same company. The same one you worked for."

"Oh my god!"

"I'm worried about you, Maggie. You need to be careful out there. I know you don't work as a trucker anymore, but if the killer is after people who worked for the same company you did, you may be on his list. Do me a favour and stay away from the truck stops."

"Colby, you know I can't do that. At least I have Edison. He'll let me know if anyone comes around. Plus, I put in a dash cam and security cameras inside the van for safety. I can promise I'll be careful."

Colby sighed and ran his hand through his hair. "I guess that's all I can ask for."

50

When Maggie ended her call with Colby, she thought about her options. He wanted her to stay away from truck stops, which she understood in principle: but she wanted to catch the killer. If she didn't, she wouldn't have a future with him and Evelyn. This trip was to clear her head and figure out what she wanted, and now she knew. She could give up the bloodlust to be a family with them, but in order to do that, she couldn't have someone after her, or it put everyone she loved at risk.

In her mind, she reviewed what she knew about the killer. He was average build with gold and yellow eyes, that were rimmed with thick black lashes. The killer smoked Belmont cigarettes and was about 5' 10". He also frequented flower shops, both for the roses he left her and the petals he left at the crime scenes. He either is or was a trucker, which made him familiar with truck stops. She knew if she ran into him, it would be his eyes that gave him away because of their distinctive characteristics.

Maggie cursed to herself for not asking Colby if they had any leads on the killer; a description or something. She was sure he'd tell her because he'd want her to be wary of anyone who matched that description. But the more she thought about it, the more she realized the police had little to go on. If they did, Colby would have told her something already.

Maggie noticed a convenience store up ahead and pulled off. She wanted to start a file of her own. There was so much on her mind she needed to sort out. After parking, she took Edison for a short walk to clear her head. The sun beat down on her. Its warmth radiated through her body and glistened off Edison's coat. Feeling refreshed, she pulled out her laptop and reviewed what she knew about the killer, even added some more notes to the file. Maggie scanned the picture from the surveillance camera and labeled the file 'Rose'. Then she checked her gun and the working mechanisms before locking it back in the safe. She pulled out her hunting knife, put it in its sheath, and attached it to her belt. She was going hunting. It was time to bring this man down before he killed any more of her friends.

When she felt ready, she closed her laptop and got back into the driver's seat. "Ready to go, boy?" she asked Edison, who cocked his head in response. Then she eased back onto the highway and continued west, with the radio blasting out some of her favourite songs. This time Edison wasn't in his crate; although she left the side open for him. Instead, he had curled up on the floor beside the seat to be closer to her.

He wouldn't sit up and look out the window, but she hoped to change that. It was why she installed the seat belts in the dinette area in the first place. She'd hoped he'd be interested in sitting there. Then she could buckle his harness to the seat belt. She knew he'd enjoy the trip more if he could see out the window. She'd even picked up a seat belt attachment to keep him safe. It was something she wanted to work on with him. Later, when stopped, she'd get him up on the seat and let him look around. She knew he got up on the driver's seat when she left the van, because she'd found him sitting there with pride, but he seemed to have an issue with the other seats.

Without an agenda, Maggie wasn't sure how far she'd get today. She knew Tammy was heading west and hoped to catch up with her again, as they agreed. But they had different schedules. Tammy had loads to deliver, and Maggie had a blog to write. This morning's blog talked about running into an old friend during her travels. She was careful not to mention gender or Tammy's name because she assumed the killer monitored her blog. Then it hit her. Maybe she could force him out by using her blog.

She thought of the power of her words and how she could leave hidden messages to him that only he would understand. Taunt him to come and get her. She figured he was in a vehicle, not a transport truck, because he didn't have a schedule, but she could be wrong. Maybe he owned his own rig and was bob tailing, taking his time to let her know he was near.

There wasn't any evidence to suggest that he was at the Husky in Sault Ste. Marie, but that didn't mean he wasn't nearby. She knew he was following her. Maybe passing her and stopping, waiting for her to pass him all along the highway. It would make sense and explain how he always seemed to be where she was. Tracker or no tracker, it was time to force his hand.

Maggie glanced at her GPS and decided she'd only go as far as Thunder Bay. She would spend the following day in the area doing touristy things and not drive as far. She had a job to do, not just a killer to catch. One thing she wanted was to get pictures of the Terry Fox Memorial and Lookout. Another thing was to find a mail box and send Debra the package containing the hair clip.

She'd pass the memorial on her way into Thunder Bay, and would have to back track to visit it, but it deserved a full entry in her blog. Tonight, instead of a truck stop, she'd park at a Walmart. They often allowed campers to park there, and if she found other RVs, she'd pull in close to them. A Walmart would serve two purposes. She could stock up her van in the store, be near people, and hope to keep the killer away.

If she spent a few hours in the morning looking around, taking pictures and notes, she could get on her way and be in Dryden tomorrow night. She wanted to get to Headingley the following day to meet with Tammy. Tammy said she'd wait for her, and Maggie didn't want her parked for any length of time.

When she pulled into the Walmart parking lot, she found two campers already set up. Parking close by, she pulled out a frozen meal and put it in the microwave to cook while she took Edison out to stretch his legs.

Maggie noticed an older couple sitting in folding chairs outside the camper closest to her. They waved when she and Edison stepped out, and Maggie had to fight to control him as he yanked on the leash, wanting to say hello. After a short walk, and finding a garbage bin to dispose of the baggie, Maggie returned to the parking lot. As she approached the van, the couple called out, "Is he friendly?"

Maggie nodded. "A little too friendly. He jumps up when he meets new people."

"Is it okay to say hello? I had boxers growing up. I'd have one now, but my hips aren't good and I couldn't walk one."

"Sure, but it would be better if you stayed seated. I don't want him to knock you over in his exuberance."

Edison's rear end vibrated with excitement when he realized she was taking him over to meet the people. As soon as he got close, he jumped up. Maggie scolded him, corrected his behaviour and told him to sit, which he did for about two-seconds, before jumping up again. The gentleman laughed.

"Yup, that about sums it up: too much excitement and deaf ears to what they don't want to hear."

Maggie laughed. "You definitely are a boxer lover. This is Edison. He's still a pup, but from what I've heard, boxers think they're puppies for life."

"You can say that again. Hey boy." The man said, rubbing Edison's ears. "He's a good-looking dog. I'm Jim, and this is my wife, Clara."

Maggie reached out and shook both of their hands. "I'm Maggie."

Jim motioned to her van. "Do you have that set up like a camper? Or are you roughing it?"

"Jim!" Clara scolded.

"What?"

"It's all right Clara, everyone's curious. If you want, come over and look. I'm driving across Canada, writing a blog about what I see and do and what the van life is all about."

"See Clara. She doesn't mind." Jim said as he struggled to get out of his chair, "I'd like to have a look-see. I've seen a few in my travels, but never inside one."

Maggie led the way and opened the side door of the van so they could have a peek. She'd left the bed folded away, and the table set up, but Maggie explained she had learned her lesson about leaving the bed down. It was too inviting for Edison when she had to leave him inside. He like pulling the fluff out of stuffed toys, pillows, etc.

"He'll never grow out of that," Jim teased as he stuck his head inside. "Something smells good. Whatcha cooking?"

"I was just warming up some leftovers from the freezer. Tomorrow I'll put something in the crock-pot to cook while I'm travelling around. I'm going out to the memorial in the morning."

"We saw that coming in. Clara had me stop to take a ton of pictures."

"I'll be doing the same. I plan to write about it in my blog."

"Come on, Jim, we've taken up enough of her time. Her supper's getting cold."

"All right, woman, hold your horses. Nice meeting you Maggie. Maybe we'll catch up again on the road." Maggie said good night and waited until they were back at their camper before stepping inside and closing the door.

51

The next morning when Maggie awoke, she peeked out the window and noticed Jim and Clara were gone. She checked the time and saw that it was only 7:30. They must have been up and out very early. She hoped when she retired, she never felt rushed to get moving like that.

"Well, Edison, what do you think? Should we go for a run before breakfast?"

Edison cocked his head and wagged his tail, smacking it against the door through the mesh of his crate, as she put on her running gear. A cool wind assaulted her as she stepped out and turned left towards the sidewalk. She set a comfortable pace as they continued on, her feet slapping against the concrete, Edison almost prancing to her beat.

She returned dripping in sweat. Grabbed a towel, wiped her face, fed Edison, flicked the switch on her coffee maker and showered in the tiny but useful shower/toilet cabinet. Afterwards, she checked the water/sewage tanks and made a note to find a dump station and a place to refill her water supply in the next day or so.

With her travel mug filled with a steaming hot cup of coffee, she headed to the monument to take pictures and gather the information she needed for today's blog. She took her time and enjoyed the tribute to the man of great spirit and determination the monument commemorated.

While in the parking lot, she pulled up Google Maps and found there were several more noted parks and attractions in the area, so she added them to her to-do list. Not all the areas were dog friendly, so she chose not to explore those, not wanting to leave Edison in the van too long. Maggie stopped by most of them, gathering information and pictures. She had more information than one blog entry would cover, but she could stretch it over two days.

It was getting late and if she was going to meet up with Tammy in Headingley tomorrow night, she needed to get moving. She uploaded her pictures to her laptop under the file TF, for Terry Fox, to make things easier when she stopped for the night and wrote her blog. After securing everything, she left.

Maggie realized she'd only get as far as Dryden before running out of steam. At least the crock-pot was cooking and when she stopped, she'd have a nice hot supper waiting for her.

She took the time to pull up her GPS and checked what was in the area, wanting to find a safe parking place away from the truck stop. When she saw that there was a Best Western, her decision to book a room was impulsive. Maggie checked it was pet friendly, as she wouldn't leave Edison alone in the van.

She called the hotel and reserved a room, informing them she was bringing Edison. Staying in a hotel room would give them some more space to stretch out for the night, and after talking to the front desk they told her there were a couple of dumping stations nearby, and one that had a bulk water option to fill up her tanks.

The traffic on the highway was light, with no mishaps until just outside of Ignace, where the traffic ground to a halt. Maggie flicked on the CB to see if she could determine what was holding things up. This stretch of the highway was only one lane heading east and one west. The slightest problem could snarl traffic for hours.

She listened to the chatter until she learned a truck made a wrong turn and was correcting its error, but in doing so, had blocked traffic in both lanes. She breathed a sigh of relief. At least it wasn't an accident. That could have taken hours to rectify. For now, all she could do was wait. Maggie thought about all the times she'd been stuck in traffic with Big Red. The frustrating thing was watching the time click by on her clock, knowing her hours of service were running out. There was one time she cut it so close that there were 53 seconds left in her day by the time she parked. There was no need to worry about that here, so, with her four ways flashing, she put the van in park and waited for the traffic to move, offering a couple of treats to Edison while she waited.

It didn't take long before the traffic flowed again, and she continued along Highway 17 until she reached Dryden. She knew she wouldn't have any trouble finding the Best Western. She picked it because it was right off the highway and easy to find. Spotting the sign, she pulled up front, parked the van, and checked in.

The first thing she did was take Edison out to stretch his legs, then went to the room to settle in. He hopped up on the bed and made himself comfortable right in the middle, looking at her with expectation, his mouth open in a comical smile.

Maggie scowled at him. "Don't get too comfortable there, boy. Mamma needs some room too. Ok, wait here. I'll be right back."

She went back to the van, packed a small bag, divided her supper into two containers, and put one in the fridge. She'd take the other one to her room to eat. Maggie added some water to the crock-pot and left it to soak. It was still too hot to clean and she could deal with it in the morning. Then she added Edison's bowls to her bag and locked up the van.

When she got back to the room, she found Edison still in the same spot, head tilted to one side, waiting for her. She tossed him a treat, filled his bowls, set her supper up on the desk, flicked on the television, and dug in to the hot meal.

<h1 style="text-align:center">52</h1>

I n the morning, Maggie looked out the window of the hotel room to find the sky was overcast. A quick check of the weather app on her phone showed sunshine in the forecast. Maggie hoped so, as the sky looked like it was threatening rain.

Before checking out, Maggie enjoyed the complimentary breakfast and the luxury of a hot shower with elbow room. There was no need to hurry today; it would only take her about six hours to get to Headingley. Since it was Saturday, and she knew Colby would be home watching cartoons with Evelyn, she decided to FaceTime them. It had been a while since she saw their faces.

Colby answered on the second ring, smiling as he greeted her.

"Hey gorgeous."

"Hey yourself."

"Wait, where are you?"

Maggie spun her phone round the room. "Edison and I took a hotel room last night. We're in Dryden."

"Lemme see," Evelyn asked, squeezing in beside her father. "Hi Maggie! Is Edison there too?"

"Yes, here he is." Maggie replied, turning the phone so Evelyn could see Edison.

"Hi Edison!" Evelyn called out. Edison turned and cocked his head towards the phone. "When are you coming back?"

"Oh sweetie, not for a while. I'm working. It will be a few more weeks at least." Maggie frowned when she saw Evelyn pout. "How about I plan a video chat the next time I'm somewhere interesting? Then you can see where I am and what I'm doing."

Evelyn nodded and went off to continue watching cartoons.

"I guess the novelty has worn off." Colby said.

"Novelty?"

"You know, chatting on video. She was more excited the first time you called."

"I know it's not the same as being there. But my blog is doing well, and there is the potential for residual income from it. I have a following now which thrills my editor."

"But you won't do this forever, will you?"

"Aww, it sounds like you miss me." Maggie teased.

"Yes, I miss you." Colby grumbled, leaning back and looking towards where Evelyn was watching tv, then lowered his voice, "I'm also worried about you. This killer has killed several people you know and worked with. I know that's the only link other than the victims being truck drivers, but you were already at a crime scene. That's a little too close for comfort."

"Then my staying in a hotel last night should put your mind at ease. I'm not taking chances. I'm parking in well-lit areas and I spent the night before in a Walmart parking lot with some campers."

Colby smiled at her. "Thank you. That helps. Where are you off to today?"

"Headingley, Manitoba. There's a friend I promised to meet up with. I only have about 6 hours of driving ahead of me, so I'll take my time. I have to hit the dump station and replenish my water supply first. The front desk gave me the name of a couple of options where I can take care of that."

Colby made a face. "That sounds like fun."

"I take it you're not much of a camper."

"Oh, I've camped. I just like room service better."

"I'll have to keep that in mind for when I get back."

They chatted for a few more minutes before signing off. Colby had to make Evelyn's breakfast and Maggie wanted to hit the dump station.

53

aggie was in good spirits when she got back on the highway. She'd had a pleasant video chat with Colby and Evelyn. The black/grey waste was gone, and she had fresh water on board. To top it off, the killer hadn't left a rose in a while. Maybe he was under a load and couldn't keep her pace? This helped put her mind at ease about meeting with Tammy in Headingley.

It frustrated her knowing he killed people she knew or was in contact with, and it's why she hesitated when Tammy asked to meet up again. Tammy couldn't know the truth, but meeting up with her could put her in danger. She'd focused her whole life on her need for revenge. Chasing down the monster who attacked her, the pedophiles who lurked in the dark corners of the world, and the gang that took everything from her. It was a daily struggle to keep the heinous urges that threatened to blow up her world at bay. Only Audrey knew how to help her. Her counselling helped find outlets for her darkness.

Maggie sighed. Audrey bound herself by patient/doctor confidentiality, but they were more than that. Maggie thought back to the weak, broken child who Audrey had first met. Healing physically was one thing, but the emotional scars ran deeper than her aunt and uncle knew. She didn't speak when they brought her home from the hospital. They'd hoped getting her back to a routine would help, but she became angry and withdrawn. Lashing out violently when anyone touched her. After punching a boy who bumped into her at school, they sent her to counselling as a last resort.

She and Audrey spent the first meeting in silence. Eight-year-old Maggie huddled on the chair in Audrey's office with her arms crossed and her head down. Unable to make eye contact and refusing to speak, the only sign of her anger was the swinging of her legs in defiance. Audrey greeted her, asked some questions, trying to create a connection, and when Maggie didn't respond, Audrey made herself comfortable on the floor and played with a toy semi. Soon Maggie slipped from the chair, took the semi and gripped it firmly, whispering 'daddy'. That was the first of many sessions they had over the years. Building a tentative bond of trust until Maggie responded to therapy. Now, they were friends.

She reprimanded herself for the brief texts sent to Audrey since leaving her house and decided it was time for a phone call. She needed to put her mind at ease that the killer hadn't returned and harassed Audrey again.

"Hi Maggie! I was just thinking about you."

"You know what they say, 'great minds'," Maggie chuckled.

Audrey laughed. "Okay, we'll go with that. So how has your trip been so far? Uneventful I hope."

"I was more concerned about you. Any unannounced visitors? Odd gifts?"

"It's been quiet here since you left. The motion detectors go off every time a raccoon comes around, but I feel safe, and I check the cameras every time to see what's set them off. That's how I know it's raccoons. But you still haven't answered me."

"Everything's fine. I stayed at one truck stop and ran into a friend. Unfortunately, she told me the killer got another friend of ours, which I confirmed with Colby. He's keeping me in the loop now because he's worried about me."

"He'd be more worried if he knew the truth."

"But he doesn't, and it's going to stay that way," Maggie snapped. She could hear Audrey sigh and Maggie rolled her eyes. "Audrey, you of all people know I can look after myself."

"Yes, but I also know it wasn't long ago you almost got yourself killed."

Maggie let the silence creep across the line. She didn't call Audrey to argue, so she chose her next words with care. "Audrey, I'm the only one who can stop this man. You and I both know it. I have my gun; I always carry my knife and I have fight training. The only thing I can promise is I won't do anything rash or stupid. But I have to stop him. You know I do. I don't know how far he'll go or who he'll kill to hurt me. It could be you, Julie, Uncle Bobbie, Colby or even Evelyn. I can't be responsible for that."

"Maggie, I know. I can't help but worry, but I won't add to your stress. From now on I'll try to be an ear, without giving you my two cents."

Maggie laughed out loud. "If you say so. I'm heading into Headingley tonight to meet up with Tammy again. I tried to dissuade her, but she's stubborn."

"Sounds like someone I know."

"Ha ha ha. Anyway, I'll text you when I stop for the night. Do me a favour?"

"Sure, what?"

"Stop by and check in with my aunt. She hasn't answered the phone the last couple of times I've called. She's texted me back, but I just want to be sure she's okay."

"I'll head over as soon as we hang up."

"Thanks Audrey."

It wasn't long before Maggie saw the sign for Manitoba ahead. The next few days of driving would be across the prairies. The flat land meant she didn't have to worry about traffic on hills and turns, but when the winds picked up, they could blow an empty trailer on its side, which included a high sided van like hers, but storm weren't in the forecast.

Her Sprinter van was high, but she wasn't worried. She'd driven through here for years during many weather systems. Today it was drizzling, but she could see sunshine ahead and the weather should be nice when she got to Headingley.

With only a few hours of driving ahead of her, she was glad she took the hotel room last night and could take her time on the road. She should arrive in plenty of time to take Edison out for a long walk, or maybe even a run, and then meet up with Tammy for supper. She'd put her leftovers from last night's dinner in the freezer to pull out at another time. The road was lonely and it would be nice to have some company again. Although she'd entertained herself well today with calls to Colby and Audrey, it wasn't the same as human contact.

54

Audrey stepped out of her car and walked up the laneway to Julie's shop. The first thing she noticed was the new fencing and security cameras and wondered what had happened. She peered through the windows into the bays to see if Julie was in there before heading to the office, where she found Julie sitting behind the desk, her unruly hair pulled back into a low ponytail and a smudge of grease on her nose. Julie looked up as soon as Audrey entered.

"Hey Audrey, what brings you by?" Julie asked, standing and reaching out to shake Audrey's hand.

"Oh, I just wanted to see how you were doing."

"Did my niece send you? She keeps calling, I've texted, but things have been crazy here this week."

Audrey chuckled. "Yes, Maggie asked me to look in. Something about the hard time you give her for not keeping in touch and now you're not answering your phone. Is everything ok?"

"Not really."

"What happened?"

"Someone got past the security cameras and messed with a few of the rigs parked here for servicing. We picked up on it right away, but we had to scramble to check all the trucks to be sure they weren't tampered with and now I had to beef up security, so I've installed a new system. There's a guard living in that trailer to monitor things at night, and the new motion detectors sound an alarm when they're set off. I'm sure you can imagine how that works with all the wildlife around here."

"When did this happen?" Audrey asked.

"A few days back. I think when Maggie was still visiting you."

Audrey pulled her shoulders back and wondered if it happened the same night the killer left the gruesome mess on her porch. He was sending Maggie a message. A part of her wanted to tell Julie it was a threat to Maggie, and now that she'd moved on, so had the threat, but in doing so, she'd break her promise to Maggie. It would also alert Julie to the danger Maggie was in and worry her more. So, she remained silent, but told Julie about the fake cat and Maggie setting up a security system at her place. Julie's eyes widened as she listened to Audrey's story.

"Thank God, I didn't see it. Maggie found it when she was out with Edison, but she knows how important my cats are to me and she thought the prank was a little vicious."

"It's a sick world, when people think leaving mutilated stuffed animals to resemble live cats is funny. My guess is it was a group of teenagers with nothing better to do. I bet if we checked, we'd find we weren't the only two people to have mischief done to their property."

"You're probably right, Julie. At least we are both protected from future teenage angst. My cameras have recorded many a vagrant raccoon making its way up my laneway."

Julie leaned back and roared with laughter. "I think between us we have the market covered in raccoon security."

"Well, if you've got everything back in order, take a few minutes to call Maggie. You can't complain about her lack of phone calls if you're not returning hers."

"You're right. I'll call her later today after I head up to the house. Well, I gotta check on the boys. Do you want me to walk you out?"

"No, I'm fine. Chat soon."

Audrey could feel Julie's eyes following her as she made her way back to her car. Julie was quick, and Audrey hoped she hadn't raised suspicions by mentioning the stuffed cat. She should have kept her mouth shut. It wasn't a far jump between the two incidents and the connection being Maggie.

55

Maggie pulled into the parking lot at the Flying J in Headingley as the first rays of pink from the setting sun streaked the sky. She took a quick drive through the truck parking lot to see if Tammy had arrived. Not finding her truck there, she continued on until she found a suitable place to park out of the way of both truck traffic and the regular vehicles frequenting the Flying J. With a Denny's on site there was a lot of transient traffic to the restaurant and the car parking was for them.

This travel stop had multiple showers, laundry facilities, and a well-equipped driver's lounge, which the drivers made use of. To avoid using the facilities here, she did her laundry when she was at the hotel. Maggie pulled up her blog and wrote a small piece for it, describing the amenities at the Flying J. The last words, *I'm trying to be a considerate traveller. As a past trucker, I know how valuable the parking spaces are. Also, if I used the laundry here, it would limit the washers for a driver on his downtime. If you travel and stop at truck stops, try to be cognizant of this.'*

After her walk, she'd finish it. She hoped not to offend any of her readers, but knew how frustrating it was when a camper stopped at a truck stop and used the laundry facilities instead of a laundry mat or one at the campground they visited. Truckers couldn't park just anywhere to take care of their needs on the road. They had to stick to truck friendly locations, and campers had more options.

Maggie popped inside to use the public bathroom. Having to find a dump station at regular intervals meant she limited the number of times she used the toilet in the van, preferring it for late nights and early morning usage if she couldn't wait for the public washroom. When she returned to the van, she'd take Edison out for a nice, long walk.

Exiting the building, Maggie noticed a large cloud mass on the horizon and figured a storm was coming, forecast or not. The wind picked up as she made her way back to the van where she found Edison sitting in the driver's seat, watching for her return. She laughed at the comical expression on his face when he saw her. She walked around the front of the vehicle, watching him through the windshield, and opened the side door.

"Where do you think you're driving off to?" She asked as she grabbed his harness. As soon as he saw it, he jumped off the seat and stuck his head through the harness opening. Maggie bent over, fastened him in and grabbed a poop bag, then Edison jumped out with his nose to the ground, tail wagging in search of a spot.

Maggie walked with Edison for about 45 minutes before heading back. She made her way through the truck lot, keeping close to the edge to see if Tammy had arrived. When she didn't see Tammy's truck, Maggie wondered if she'd gotten held up. She'd check her messages once she got Edison settled. If Tammy got delayed, she could spend another day here waiting for her.

Once his harness was offEdison went right to his water bowl and lapped up a large amount of water, splashing it on the mat on the floor. Maggie sat down and pulled out her phone to find a message waiting from Tammy. She was on route and would be there in less than an hour. Maggie responded, 'see you soon,' and pulled out her laptop. Now she had time to write the next segment of her blog.

"Well, boy, what should it be tonight? Should I talk about staying in the hotel instead of the van? Dumping waste? Face Timing with Colby?" She looked down at the puzzled expression on his face and responded, "Maybe all the above."

She set to work writing up the account of her travels since her last blog, including the mundane activities that are typical when travelling. Her blog had to be authentic, or her followers would notice. When she finished and uploaded it, she received a text from Ripley.

Hey. No stops? Sightseeing events?

No, it was just what I sent. I've hit the prairies, nothing much to see. But I'm meeting a friend for dinner, so maybe she can add some road stories. Don't worry, people know not every day is exciting.

Right. Just take your time. The more you see, the more exciting it can be.

She sighed when she signed off. Maggie could tell Ripley had different expectations of what her blog would entail than she did. There had been some explosive posts, the murder in Edmundston and the mutilated stuffed cat, for example, but that wasn't real life. The typical stuff on the road was boring mundane activities, such as looking for a dump station, refilling the water supply, groceries, and long periods behind the wheel. Maybe when she killed this killer, she should write about it. That would get Ripley excited. Unfortunately, it would also get her 25 to life.

Maggie positioned herself in the driver's seat to watch for Tammy and she found her mind drifting to thoughts of Colby when she spotted Tammy wheeling her rig into the lot. Maggie's face lit up with a smile. She continued watching as Tammy backed up into her space and parked her rig. She'd give her a few minutes to get settled and then head over.

56

Maggie swung the driver's door open when she noticed Tammy climb out of her rig and start across the parking lot. Based on her posture and stride, she was a woman on a mission, so Maggie closed her door and leaned back in her seat to wait until Tammy came back out of the building.

Twenty minutes later, a rap on her side window startled Maggie. She was so engrossed in her phone she didn't see Tammy approach. She looked up and saw Tammy with her tongue out, eyes crossed, holding her hands like antlers. Maggie pushed the button to roll down the window.

"Careful or your face will get stuck like that."

"It might be an improvement. Come on, I'm hungry. Will Edison be, ok?"

"He's had a long walk. Although he'll want you to say hello before we go inside. Let me give you a treat to give him. He'll be your friend for life."

Edison whined when they locked the door and headed towards the Denny's, but he'd be okay. Maggie felt a little guilty leaving him, but he had everything he needed except her. She even left the radio playing.

Inside the restaurant, they picked a booth to give themselves more room to spread out. Being a Saturday, they knew it would get busy, but so far, the restaurant was quiet. The server took their order, and they sat back to chat while they waited.

"So, tell me, how were roads?" Maggie asked.

"Roads were clear. But the jerk at the dealership was another matter."

"Oh?"

"Ya, he gets a little handsy. Acts like he thinks I'm some frail female in need of a big, powerful man."

Maggie snorted, "Maybe you should tell him about your big strong Kevin? I'm sure that would knock him down a peg or two."

Tammy laughed. "My thing is you'd think will all those Barbies they have working in the front counter there'd be enough women for him to harass."

"I'm betting he's been handsy with them before too and can't do it again or risk a lawsuit."

Tammy took a sip of her pop. "Do you remember JD telling us about the girl that worked at one of the Porsche Dealerships?"

"Oh, my god, yes. He said 'her cookie was out'." They finished in unison, laughing at the inside joke.

"I'm going to miss JD. I haven't been great about keeping in touch with the guys, but he was one of a kind." Maggie sighed.

"Do you remember when he saved you from the guy with the knife in Chilliwack?"

"I thought about that after we saw each other the other day. By the way, I spoke to my cop friend. He thinks it's a serial killer. Someone focused on the car industry. Although the killer has picked different victims as well, but all truckers. My thought is he's doing it to throw the cops off. I'm a little scared. It seems I know a lot of the victims."

Tammy reached across the table and covered Maggie's hand with hers. "You would know a lot of them, Maggie. You spent years as a car hauler. Now you understand why I've been so worried. Right now, Kevin is in the states, so I think he's okay, since according to my sources, all the victims have been in Canada."

"What about you?"

"I'm a woman. He kills men. I'm heading from here to Vancouver and then when I return to the yard, I'm taking some time off to enjoy my life. When I get home, I'll wait for Kevin to get back and then we have a flight scheduled to Nashville. I want to go to the Grand Ole Opry. If I was older, I'd retire, but I have quite a few years to go yet."

"Why not get something local? Where you're home every night."

"You're one to talk. You get out of trucking only to end up writing a blog while travelling coast to coast in a van."

"Okay, point taken. We both like the freedom of the road. Did you get the wasp and hornet spray I suggested?"

"Yes, I picked up a can. It's in the cubby in the driver's door."

"That makes me feel better."

The server arrived with their food and they turned their attention to their meals, digging in to enjoy while hot.

When they'd finished and paid their bill, Maggie and Tammy went to the driver's lounge to continue chatting for a little longer. This was one of the rare truck stops that had a large driver's lounge with plenty of comfortable seating. Soon Maggie begged off, explaining to Tammy that she needed to check on Edison. Tammy agreed it was time to call it a night because she wanted to get a shower before turning in. They made plans to meet for breakfast the next morning.

57

Before heading to bed, Maggie took Edison out for another walk. He'd been cooped up in the van while she visited with Tammy and had some pent-up energy. The wind had died down, and the air felt warm against her skin. Edison vibrated with excitement at all the fresh scents. He kept his nose to the ground, in-between bouts where he pranced and showed off his form. She marvelled at what a character he was and couldn't help but smile. He'd brought joy back into her life, filling the void left by Liam's death and her inability to have a child.

On her way back to the van, she noticed the interior light on in Tammy's rig. She'd get Edison settled and if it was still on, she'd check on Tammy. Maggie looked at the time on her phone and thought, *'Tammy should have finished her shower long ago and been settled for the night.'* Her walk with Edison took over an hour, so Tammy had plenty of time.

After Edison lay down in his sleeping crate, she stepped back outside and locked the van. From this angle, she couldn't tell if the light was still on or not. The only way to be certain was to check. Maggie touched the knife at her hip and walked across the lot.

The amber glow from one of the interior lights indicated Tammy was still up. Maggie couldn't see her through the windshield and she felt a chill run down her spine. She paused, Un-holstered her knife and debated whether to go back for her gun, but she felt silly because the light could be on while Tammy sat out of view doing paperwork, housekeeping, or for another reason. Continuing to scold herself for her paranoia, until she was only a few feet away. Noticing the driver's door ajar, her heart pounded in her chest as she crouched down, scanned the area, and approached the driver's side of Tammy's truck with caution.

Maggie hesitated before calling out. "Tammy? Are you okay?"

Inside the cab, she heard some garbled sounds. She swung open the door and saw blood on the driver's seat. Without thinking, she climbed up inside and onto the seat, smearing her pants with blood. She looked in the back and saw Tammy stretched on the bunk, blood pulsing from her slashed throat. Maggie's guts clenched as Tammy's tear-filled eyes turned towards her. She slid her knife back into its sheath and climbed over the seat, tripping in her haste.

"Oh, my god! You're alive!" Pulling the air horn cord, hoping to signal for help.

She used her hand to staunch the flow of blood from Tammy's throat, and tried pinching the edges of the wound together.

"Oh Tammy, I'm so sorry. Who did this?" She asked, tears trickling down her cheeks.

Tammy's mouth opened and closed, but no words came out. Blood frothed in her throat and bubbled through her open lips; panic filled Tammy's eyes as they flicked to the back of the driver's seat. Maggie fumbled with her cell phone, putting it on speaker before she called 911.

"911, what's your emergency?"

"I'm at the Flying J in Headingley. Blue Volvo in the back row back corner. A woman has been attacked, her throats been slashed, but she's still alive. Please hurry."

"Help is on the way."

The operator stayed on the line and instructed Maggie while she tended to Tammy's wounds. A chill ran up Maggie's body as Tammy's eyes roll back. The blood flow slowed and with a slow release of air, she was gone.

Maggie sagged to the floor of the cab, sobbing, and for the first time noticed the rose petals scattered on the bunk beside Tammy and her stomach heaved. She turned to see what Tammy was looking at on the back of the driver's seat and found a note pinned there.

You're running out of friends. As a killer, you're weak. Come get me before I get you.

Maggie tore the piece of paper from the seat, crumpled the note and dropped it to the floor of the cab as tears streaked her face. She looked back at Tammy and felt a pain deep inside her chest as a sob escaped her lips. It wasn't until she heard the sirens in the distance that she realized the police couldn't find the note. Blood from her hands smeared the paper, and it held an incriminating message. She stuffed it in her pocket. Then looked down at Tammy's blood on her hands and clothing. She panicked and wiped her hands on her pants, trying to remove the blood.

Her eyes blurred with tears as she looked down at Tammy's now vacant ones. "I'm sorry Tammy. This is all my fault." She whispered as she kissed Tammy's forehead and closed her eyes.

Soon, flashing blue and red lights surrounded the truck. Maggie took a deep breath, stood up, and made her way to the driver's seat, preparing to climb out of the truck.

"Hands where I can see them." A cop bellowed to her. She

turned and saw him standing at the front of the cab with his weapon drawn.

She paused and raised her blood-smeared hands. "I'm the one who called 911."

"Step out of the vehicle."

"I'm going to need my hands to do that, sir."

"Okay, but no sudden movements."

As soon as her feet hit the pavement, the cop spun her around, grabbed her hands behind her back, pushed her face into the side of Tammy's rig, and cuffed her.

"My friend's inside. Someone slashed her throat. She was still alive when I called 911, but she bled out before you got here."

"You're the one covered in blood."

"Because I tried to stop the bleeding!" Maggie yelled in exasperation.

The officer pulled her to one side as the EMTs entered the cab to check on Tammy. One came to the window and shook his head, indicating it was too late.

The officer patted Maggie down and took her knife out of the sheath.

"What's this? Looks like you had the means to do the crime."

Unable to control the emotions that bubble up within her, Maggie spat out, "Are you a total moron? Look at my blade. There's no blood on it or on the handle. If I killed my friend with that knife, there'd be blood! Look at my hands and clothes! I'm covered in blood from trying to stop the bleeding." Her chest rose and fell as she seethed in mix emotions, both anger and grief, and looked at the gathering crowd.

The officer pushed her towards his cruiser as several other police cars pulled in. Maggie couldn't believe he'd cuffed her without talking to her. She looked up at his youthful face and thought, *'he's fresh out of the academy and has something to prove'.*

The officer opened the back door, put his hand on the top of her head, guided her in, and closed it. Then joined the other officers.

Rage seethed within Maggie as she searched the faces in the crowd. Her guts told her the killer was out there watching. She scanned each face until her gaze landed on a man who was staring back at her. She calculated his height and build, and her eyes widened. It was him. When he saw the recognition in her eyes, he smiled at her and nodded.

She began yelling and banging her body into the door, shaking the cruiser to get the police to notice her. One cop turned towards her, his face puzzled, as he walked to the car. Maggie turned back to where the killer stood and noticed he'd faded back into the crowd. The air left her lungs with her last scream of frustration. Her stomach sunk, knowing he'd escaped.

58

Maggie endured hours of interrogation before being released. Her head pounded with a constant thrum. She rubbed at her temples on the ride back to the Flying J, trying to ease the pain. She blinked through bleary eyes at the bright entrance as she stepped out of the cruiser and went inside to wash Tammy's now dried blood from her hands. The look of horror on the face of the poor girl working behind the counter told Maggie how bad she looked as she entered the washroom.

She stood at the sink, staring at her reflection in the mirror. There was a smear of blood on her left check. Her eyes looked sunken and haunted. She grabbed some paper towels, wet them and scrubbed at the spot of blood, scrubbing so hard her cheek remained red long after the blood was gone.

She leaned forward with her hands on the edge of the sink and looked at the eyes staring back at her without recognition. Over the years, she'd killed many deserving men, but watching a friend die and not be able to help tore at her. She blinked back the tears, slammed her fist on the edge of the sink and winced in pain.

This was her fault. She knew agreeing to meet Tammy was

wrong. If she hadn't, Tammy would still be alive. Somewhere deep down, Maggie knew this wasn't true. The killer knew too much about her life and who her friends were. He would have gone after Tammy, anyway. But tonight, she saw him. To anyone else, he was just another gawker in the crowd, but she saw his true nature as he gloated over the pain he inflicted on her and the position she was in. Now she'd recognize him. He'd let her see him, which meant the game he was playing was ending.

Maggie splashed some water on her face and took a deep breath. She had to get back to the van and Edison. When she went to check on Tammy, she expected to return in a few minutes and instead he'd been alone for hours. She knew he wouldn't settle by himself.

Maggie could hear Edison whining as she approached the van. Relief washed over her. She hadn't realized how worried she was that the killer would go after Edison until just now. When she opened the door, Edison's head was low until he started wriggling with excitement. She sat on the floor, unzipped his crate and allowed him to jump up, paws on either shoulder as he licked her ears. She reached out and wrapped her arms around him and accepted the comfort he offered, feeling the vibrations as his body wiggled.

With slow, leaden movements, she got up and removed her bloody clothing. She wouldn't even try to wash them. Instead, she rolled them up and stuffed them in a garbage bag. While tying the bag closed, she remembered the note, and let out a deep breath that the police hadn't discovered it. She retrieved the stiff, now rust coloured piece of paper from her pocket.

Bloody fingerprints marred the surface, but no one else was going to see it and she dropped it in the sink. She'd add it to the other notes later. Maggie looked down at Edison, who was leaning up against her, and took him out again. She was too wired to sleep right now and wanted to drop the bloody clothing in the trash.

There was a dumpster around the back of the building. Lifting the lid, she deposited the bag inside. Then Maggie glanced up at the rows of trucks and the one in the corner wrapped in yellow crime scene tape and walked through the parking lot to see if any trucks looked familiar. She wanted a sign to let her know if he was still here or not. But in her heart, she knew he was long gone.

59

The sky was still dark when Maggie awoke from a short, restless sleep, her body slick with sweat. She'd tossed and turned with repeated dreams of Tammy's murder, her face blurring and changing to those of her own victims. Each one accusing her through the gaping wounds in their necks. Rubbing the sleep from her eyes, she picked up her cell to check the time. 5 am. Edison whimpered from his crate. He sat up with his head poking over the top, and in the darkness, all she could see was his white blaze.

"Hold on a minute, boy." She called out and swung her legs over the edge of the bed. She grabbed a pair of yoga pants and a long sleeve t-shirt to wear. It had only been a couple of hours since she went to bed, but she knew she wouldn't go back to sleep.

Maggie glanced at the coffeepot and couldn't remember if she loaded it yesterday and reached out to check. A slow, sad smile crept into one corner of her mouth when she saw the grounds and pushed start. The coffee would be ready when she and Edison returned. She'd pour herself a cup and decided what her agenda was before she went anywhere today. One thing she needed to do was call the people she cared about, and for his own safety, she'd start with Ryan.

Edison now crunched away at his kibble after his walk. Maggie settled into the driver's seat and stared out at the rising sun. She took a tentative sip of the scalding liquid and sagged back into her seat. Her emotions were raw, and she needed time to think. It was too early to call Ryan, so she considered her next move while she waited until the sun was high in the sky and she could make her calls. Her swollen eyes were red rimmed and a heaviness spread through her soul as a fresh sob escaped her lips.

Ryan answered his phone. "Hey Maggie, Krissy and I were just talking about you. She's been following your trip by reading your blog."

"Hi Ryan. I hope she's enjoying it." Maggie replied, trying to sound normal.

"Yes, she is. You have a special spot in her heart. It's because of you I'm an owner/operator and the money I'd have spent on truck payments went into an education fund. That's how we can afford to send Daniel to McMaster. In two years, Jessica will be off at university. God, I'm old."

"I hate to tell you this, Ryan, but you've always been old." Maggie teased.

"Ouch. That hurts."

"I'm only kidding. Are you home now?"

"No, I'm in Saskatchewan. I have a load heading to Vancouver. Why are you in the area?"

"I will be. Listen Ryan, you know I told you about the guy killing truckers?"

"Ya, everyone's talking about it. Don't go saying anything to Krissy, though. She worries enough."

"Ryan, he killed Tammy last night." Maggie whispered through strangled tears.

"Tammy? The name sounds familiar. How do I know her?"

"She was my friend; you met her the last time we were in Chilliwack together."

"Oh ya, both she and her husband were truckers. Someone killed her last night. Shhiiittt. I'm sorry Maggie. How'd you find out?"

"I was the one that found her." A sob escaped as tears sprang to her eyes.

"Oh Maggie, oh shit, I'm so sorry. Do you want to talk about it?"

Maggie took a deep breath and told Ryan everything that had happened the night before, including the fact that she saw the killer. When she finished, she blew her nose and wiped the tears from her eyes. Edison, who sensed her despair, had placed his head on her lap. Absently, she rubbed his ears, finding the action calmed her.

"Where did you say you were?"

"At the Flying J in Headingley."

"Which way do you think the killer is going?"

"If I had to hazard a guess, I'd say west. This is the second time on my trip he's killed someone. I know it's the same person because he leaves rose petals at the scene. I don't know what that symbolizes, but it's his calling card."

"Maggie, you could be in danger too? You're stopping at truck stops. He saw you last night. Have you considered he's watching you?"

"Yes, I've considered that. But I also stay at hotels, Walmart parking lots and other non-truck places. So, it could be just a coincidence that I've been at two truck stops where he's killed. Just promise me you'll be extra diligent. Don't make me call Krissy and warn her about what's going on."

"Ouch. Don't do that, I'll take precautions."

"Oh, and Ryan, today I am writing about what happened in my blog. I think it will be therapeutic. I'm only going up the road a bit until I find a hotel. Then I'm getting out of the van and off the road for a few days to think. My next calls are to my family. I just wanted to give you a heads up and to prepare you for Krissy's call after she reads the blog."

"Okay Maggie, keep me posted where you are. Maybe we can grab a bite if we end up in the same area."

"Sure thing. Be safe Ryan."

Maggie disconnected the call. She had no intention of connecting with Ryan. Doing so would put his life at risk. Tammy's murder proved she was a danger to everyone she knows and loves. Even those she knows casually.

60

Maggie had just ended her call with Ryan when her screen lit up, alerting her to an incoming call from Colby.

"Hel..."

"Maggie! What the hell? I thought you were going to stay away from the truck stops."

Maggie rolled her eyes. *That didn't take long.* She shifted uncomfortably, not wanting to have this conversation now.

"I guess you heard."

"Heard? Heard that you were in a truck next to a body and hand-cuffed in the back of a cruiser? Yah, I heard."

"I'm fine, thanks for asking." She snapped, her tone sounding harsher than she intended.

"Oh Maggie, I'm sorry. Since the report came in linking it to the serial killer, I've been worried sick. You don't understand how much restraint it took for me to hold off calling you until now. I had to remind myself of the time difference."

"Tammy was my friend," Maggie said, her voice barely a whisper.

"What?"

"She was my friend. She was the one I told you I was having supper with. After dinner she went to shower, and I took Edison out for a walk. On my way back, I noticed her interior light was on, so I put Edison back in the van and went to check on her."

"Of course you did."

"If you want me to tell you what happened, keep those comments to yourself." She retorted. Anger cutting through the line on the edge of her voice.

Colby swallowed. "I'm sorry. If I didn't love you, I wouldn't be so worried. Please tell me what happened."

Maggie's heart warmed at hearing him say he loved her, but that was part of the problem. If she didn't catch this man, who knows how far he'd go to hurt her once he'd killed off all of her friends? Her relationship with Colby put him and Evelyn in danger.

"I understand. I love you too. It's been a rough 24 hours." Maggie paused before continuing. "When I got close to her truck, I noticed that the driver's door was ajar. So, I pulled out my hunting knife. And yes, I know I don't hunt: it just makes me feel safer to have it." She waiting for Colby to comment. When he didn't, she continued. "I climbed up into the cab and saw Tammy. I put my knife away as I went over to the driver's seat to get to her. She was still alive. I put my hands to her neck, trying to hold the wound closed, hoping to stop the blood as I called 911."

"Okay, before you go further, I want you to tell me what you saw."

Maggie expelled a long breath of air. "Tammy was on the bed bleeding from a neck wound. Her eyes begged me to help her. She opened and closed her mouth, but no sound came out. Tears leaked from the corners of her eyes. The cab smelt like blood and roses. And a hint of tobacco, but Tammy didn't smoke."

"Smelled like roses?"

"Yes, from the rose petals scattered all over her body. She died while I was on the phone with 911, just before the paramedics arrived. The cop that cuffed me was first on the scene. As soon as he saw me, he drew his weapon and aimed it at me. He wouldn't listen to me when I tried to tell him Tammy was a friend, or that I found her and called 911. I think he was a rookie. When his superior spoked to me, and got my statement, they released me."

"I'm sorry Maggie, seeing a friend die like that is traumatic. Why don't you head home? Or take a different direction. It's like you're driving the same route as the killer. If I didn't know better, I'd think you were the killer." He teased, but then the flash of long red hair on a motorcycle broke into his memory and he cursed under his breath.

"If I was a killer, I wouldn't kill my friends." Maggie snapped.

"No, I guess not." Colby replied. "I'm glad you're ok. Do me a favour and try to stay out of harm's way."

"I'll do my best. I was just about to call you, anyway. You should know, I'll be writing about what happened in my blog. And don't worry, I won't say anything about the rose petals. I didn't think you'd find out about it so fast, and I didn't want you to read about it without hearing it from me first."

"I appreciate that. Now, if you can, please stay away from the truck stops."

"I'll do my best. Give Evelyn a squeeze from me."

<h1 style="text-align:center">61</h1>

aggie's next call was to her aunt. Julie's gruffness was predictable. She didn't mince words. She told Maggie she was sorry to hear about Tammy, but was happy Maggie was okay. After promising to be careful, Maggie disconnected her call and made her next call to Audrey.

"Hey Maggie. How are things?"

"That's why I called."

"What happened?"

"He killed another one of my friends." Maggie wept.

"Oh, Maggie, I'm so sorry."

"It's worse than that. I found her."

"Nooo. Are you okay?"

"I need to tell you what happened."

Maggie reiterated the same story she told to Colby. But this time, she held nothing back. She went into detail about the petals, Tammy still being alive and the note the killer left for her on the back of the driver's seat.

"He knew you'd find her."

"He left the door ajar so the interior light remained on. Somehow,

241

he must have known I was outside walking Edison and would notice it."

"Maggie, this is serious. He knows where you are, he's learning your routine. I'm guessing he plans to go after you next."

"But Audrey, this time I saw him. From the back of the cruiser, I found him in the crowd. He knows I did. I'd recognize him if I ran into him again. Now I just have to find him."

"Maggie, why don't you just tell the police what you know? Give them a description and let them go after him?"

"If they'd even believe me. They treated me like a criminal. I was grieving and in shock and they didn't care. I have to do this myself. You know me better than to think I'd let this go. I'd hoped the cops would have more information than I have by now, but they don't and I can't afford to lose any more friends. This is personal, Audrey. He's trying to ruin my life."

"But you saw him. Call Colby and give him a description."

"I already spoke to Colby, but I didn't mention seeing the killer. He found out about Tammy and the cops placing me in cuffs at the back of the cruiser. He was worried about me, but his biggest concern was where I planned to park each night."

"I'm sure it's because he has feelings for you."

"Yes, he's told me he loves me."

"Oh Maggie, that's wonderful, and I know you love him."

"Yes. But what does that change? I can't move forward until the killer is dead. If I don't take care of him, he could go after Colby or even Evelyn!"

Maggie heard Audrey gasp. "He wouldn't!"

"He would and he could. Think about what he did at your place and at my aunts. You were both lucky, but that won't continue. If I came back now, he'd just follow me."

"So, what's the plan? Do you want me to fly out and help you?"

Maggie laughed, and the soft sound filled the line. "You're the best! But no, this time I need to take care of things myself."

"I understand. But Maggie, please be careful and continue

checking in with me every day. If I don't hear from you, I'm going to call the police and send out a search party."

"I'll message you like I have been, twice a day. Listen, I'd better get going. I've taken my time here so I could make the calls, but I still have to write my blog before I leave."

"Okay Maggie, please just keep in touch, and if you're struggling, call me anytime."

62

Maggie sat rooted in place as she continued to stare out the window. Lost in the thoughts that whirled through her mind after putting down the phone. She knew Julie would call uncle Bobby, and fill him in, which was one less call for her. She stood up and went to the back to pull out her laptop. It was time to write about what happened last night while it was still fresh in her mind. Hoping it would be therapeutic as well.

The curser flashed on the screen as she sat staring at the blank page, struggling to find the words to express her feelings. This was the most personal blog she'd write to date. Then the words came to her with a flash of emotion. She began with the trip to Headingley and her dinner with Tammy. A tear formed in the corner of her eye as she remembered the look in Tammy's eyes when she found her. Her breath hitched as she paused, unable to control the shaking that ebbed over her body. Fingers clicking on the keyboard as she relived the sense of helplessness she felt last night. Edison came over and laid his chin on her lap. His soulful eyes looking up at her.

She reached down and stroked his head, his fur velvety smooth across his brow. Distracting herself from the emotions that swirled within her as she reviewed what she'd written so far. Then she began again. This time, the words flowed with ease. She told the entire story, only leaving out the rose petals, seeing the killer and the note he left for her.

'...loss is a shadow that envelops us, wrapping around with a strangling hold on our hearts. I've suffered many losses over my life, both of my parents, my husband and unborn child, but this was different. No matter how hard I tried, I couldn't save my friend, and that will haunt me forever...'

Maggie continued reading and editing until it felt right, before clicking send. With a whoosh, it went off to Ripley. Then she remembered she needed to warn him.

"Shit," she said out loud. "I'd better call and let him know what's coming."

"Ripley."

"Hi Ripley, it's Maggie."

"Ah Maggie, I see your latest blog just came through. I haven't reviewed it yet."

"That's why I'm calling."

"Oh," he paused, "did something happen?"

"You know me too well. It's best that you hear it from me first. Last night, someone murdered a friend of mine. I found the body and ended up handcuffed in the back of a cruiser."

"What the fuck?"

"Let me explain."

Once again, Maggie repeated the story about the previous night, with each telling the pain in her heart eased. But nothing could stop the overwhelming guilt that riddled her soul, leaving her feeling raw and exposed. She'd lost four friends to this monster and some poor sap whose only crime was speaking to her.

The tears didn't come during her conversation with Ripley. She'd already cried enough for one day. She knew she owed Kevin a call, but the police asked for time to notify him first. When they did, she'd call him and tell him about Tammy's last night.

Maggie looked around the parking lot. Tammy's truck still sat in the back, surrounded by the crime scene tape. As much as she didn't feel like driving, the idea of staying put was more repulsive. The truck and tape drew her eyes to it every time she looked up. There were flashes of Tammy's last moments playing in her memory. Her mouth opening and closing as she tried to speak, the look of horror in her eyes and Maggie's feeble attempt to stop the flow of blood.

There was no way she was going to stay at another truck stop tonight. Nor would she pick one of the small towns or roadside stops along the way. She figured it was best to push through until she got to Regina and stay put a couple of nights in the city while she regrouped. Maggie decided it was in her best interest to stay at a hotel again. It would allow her to use the gym to work out some of her frustrations and give her some space while she debated her next move.

She pulled out her phone and searched for pet friendly hotels that met all of her requirements. In the end, she decided on the Best Western and picked a king room with a sofa and made her reservation. If she was going to stay for a couple of days, she might as well make herself comfortable.

Her hand quivered as she put the van in gear and left the parking lot, refusing to look at the back corner.

63

Her phone rang, and she looked at the caller display. It was Kevin. Her heart sank. She wasn't ready for his call, but couldn't ignore it. When she answered, his hostility took her off guard.

He must have called her as soon as he got off the phone with the police and discovered she was with Tammy when she died. He begged her for information, and she tried to be cautious as she repeated the events of the previous evening. In his grief, he cursed her and asked why she hadn't called him herself. She feebly explained that the police told her to wait for them to notify him. He let out a long line of expletives.

Maggie's eyes welled when she heard his strangled sobs as he asked her to repeat everything several more times, not grasping how this could have happened to his wife. Her heart ached every time she heard him sob before asking for more details. Hearing the pain in Kevin's voice caused Maggie's eyes to blur with tears, forcing her to pull over for the rest of the phone call. The events of the last 24 hours left her raw. She'd planned to call him tomorrow morning from the hotel, but didn't know the police would track him down so fast. If she had, she'd have called him while still at the Flying J.

Her body was shaking when she disconnected the call. Thoughts of having the same call with Krissy swirled in her mind like wintered leaves, curled and brown. There was no way she was going to let that happen. She had to protect Ryan at all costs. He was the only friend she had left on the road, and their connection was more than friendship. For the time being, she wasn't worried about her uncle. He was stateside for the next couple of weeks, and she knew the killer was following or waiting for her as she made her way west.

It was well past suppertime when Maggie pulled into the hotel parking lot. Her body ached and her eyes drooped. Taking a deep breath and releasing the air from her lungs helped ease the sensations ebbing through her. She needed to take Edison out for a walk, check in, and get settled.

The range of emotions twirling inside of her were overwhelming, and she noticed a slight shake in her hands. She wanted a drink to calm her nerves, so she stuck a bottle of wine in her overnight bag and slung it over her shoulder. In the morning, she'd come back to the van for anything else she forgot, but for now, she had everything she and Edison needed.

The bag pulled on her shoulder and Maggie had to adjust it as Edison searched for a spot to relieve himself. The weight of it pulled on her and she yanked on his lead to redirect him. Tension built in her jaw, and with it a pain that radiated up the back of her skull. *'Hurry up dammit.'* She thought, dragging at the leash. Edison's paws dug in and he turned his head, looking back at her. The bag slipped off her shoulder and she cursed. Bending over to pick it up loosened her grip and Edison could back up finishing his business. Maggie lowered her gaze from Edison's upturned face and sighed as she scooped up the mess. Tears prickled her eyes as she led Edison to the trash and the hotel lobby, feeling guilty at her impatience with him.

Maggie's shoulders sagged as she entered her room and took Edison out of his harness. He looked back at her, jumped on the bed, and curled up in the middle. Maggie glanced towards him and gave a small, weak smile.

"This is getting to be a habit. Pick one side or the other."

Looking at his upturned face and sad expression, she crossed the room and plopped down on the bed beside him. Gently rubbing his ears, she looked into his eyes, trying to gain his forgiveness. He rolled over, exposing his tummy, which she rubbed as his paws crossed over her hands in play, and she knew all was well.

Maggie slipped from the bed and placed her overnight bag on the dresser, pulled out Edison's bowls and filled them, then uncorked the wine to allow it to breathe while she showered.

She stepped into the large walk-in shower, turned the water to as hot as she could stand, and allowed the steam and jets to rinse away the events of the last two days. Maggie placed her hands on the back wall and leaned over, stretching out the tension that built up in her back and neck. She remained like that until the water cooled, then she turned off the shower and stepped out.

After slipping into PJ's, she poured herself a glass of wine, texted everyone where she was, turned on the tv and stared blankly at the screen, lost in thought. It wasn't long before exhaustion took over and Maggie drifted off to sleep.

The next morning, Maggie awoke to find herself pushed to the edge of the bed, with Edison curled up beside her in the crook of her legs. She reached out and stroked his back at the same time stretching her legs out and dislodging him from his position.

"What do you say, boy? Should we go for a run?" Maggie asked, throwing back the covers. Edison just cocked his head and yawned.

She dragged out her running gear and headed to the washroom to brush her teeth and tame her hair. When she looked into the mirror, the first thing she noticed was the dark circles under her eyes and knew her decision to stay in the hotel for a couple of nights was the right one. She may even extend it another day, depending on how she felt the next morning.

When Maggie was ready, she and Edison set off at a light jog to explore the area. Edison's high-level energy made him the perfect jogging partner, and he seemed to enjoying going with her. She set off to the right on E Quance Gate and almost stumbled when she realized how close she was to the Husky truck stop. Her guts rolled, but she pushed on. She thought about the proximity of the hotel to the truck stop and considered parking her van around the back, but decided against it. With the tracking device still attached, he'd find her, anyway.

Maggie pulled out her phone and took some shots of the trucks parked there. She'd look at them when she got back to her room and compare them to the ones she took at the Flying J.

Before putting her phone away, she checked the time. Her stomach growled, reminding her she hadn't eaten dinner and if she timed it right, she'd make it back before they stopped serving breakfast.

64

After eating and showering, Maggie rethought her decision not to move the van and pulled it around to the back parking lot. While there, she checked both cameras, ensuring they'd record if anyone neared or disturbed her van. She closed the blinds and the curtains at the front to hide the interior from prying eyes and grabbed her laundry before heading back inside to the on-site laundry room to wash her clothes and bedding.

Over the last 24 hours, she'd had plenty of time to think about the killer and his MO, and knew Ryan was the next logical victim. But the killer would want her close at hand when he went after Ryan and had already demonstrated patience. He would wait until they were all somewhere on the West Coast. If she deviated from her planned route, the killer would still go after Ryan, but if she was in the area, maybe she could prevent it from happening by killing him first.

What she couldn't understand was why her? This killer murdered people important to her, but why? What had she done to him? At least now she knew what he looked like; and knew she'd never met him—not when she searched for Carter, or when she went after the Dark Enders. What put her on his radar? The unknown irked her, causing her hand to ball into a fist. Allowing her anger to surface, she punched the washing machine, bruising her knuckles. Cursing, she paced the hall and waited for the machines to stop.

After folding and putting away her laundry, she checked on Edison. He looked content, lying on the bed watching TV. Maggie laughed at him and took him out for a mini walk so he could relieve himself. After getting Edison settled, Maggie changed into her workout gear and headed to the gym to get rid of her frustrations. She'd break her knuckles if she hit another unrelenting surface. While she rode down the elevator, she thought of the jacuzzi tub in her room and planned to soak in it when she returned.

Maggie entered the small facility and decided not to bother with the treadmill. If she was going for a run, it would be with Edison. Instead, she focused on the free weights. She wished the gym had a punching bag, because it would help get rid of the pent-up energy that coursed through her veins. Maggie pushed herself until her body glistened with sweat before deciding she'd had enough.

When she returned to the room, she soaked in the tub to ease her sore muscles. Tonight, she planned to do something she couldn't do in the van, order in a pizza for dinner. The rest of her night, she'd snuggle up on the bed with Edison and watch some TV, but only after she wrote today's blog.

Early the following morning, Maggie awoke feeling refreshed, although sore from her workout. The time out of the van and off the road was just what she needed. It gave her time to think and formulate a plan on how to catch the killer. Ripley wouldn't like it, but she'd head straight to Chilliwack. Ryan had texted his eta, and she wanted to be there before him. Arriving early was the only chance she had to protect him. Stopping to do the touristy things would delay her and it might be too late.

Maggie got Edison settled in the van before checking the cameras, then went inside to check-out. The desk clerk smiled at her when she handed in the key and requested a printed receipt, which Maggie folded up and put in her pocket. As she turned to leave, the desk clerk called her back.

"Ms. Murphy?"

"Yes?"

"I forgot to give you this," she said, handing Maggie an envelope.

Maggie took it in her hands and turned it over. The front displayed her name in neat block letters.

"What is it?" Maggie asked.

"I don't know. Someone left it for you last night."

Maggie felt the familiar lump forming in the pit of her stomach as she spun around the lobby looking for HIM.

She hesitated before asking, "Was it a guest?"

"No. The night clerk told me he came in from outside and requested we give this to you when you checked out. Is there something wrong?"

"No." Maggie muttered, "Thank you." She turned and walked away, feeling the churning in her stomach. Each leaden step marked her unease as she returned to the van. The envelope crushed in her hand.

A breeze kicked up, and she noticed something skipping across the parking lot. She paused, and her eyes widened at the single rose petal. Her heart palpitated, and there was a tingling in her chest. "Edison!" She screamed and ran.

Her muscles weakened as she got close enough to see Edison sitting with pride in the driver's seat, watching her. She reached out and touched the window by his face, her chest heaving as he licked the glass. Her legs felt weak as she circled her van, checking that he didn't tamper with it.

The tires looked ok, the locks on the doors held, so far, so good. Then she remembered the tracking device and wondered if he'd removed it or added another. First, she checked the engine compartment. If he was going to mess with her van, this was the place to start. She let out a breath and whispered a silent thank you to her aunt for teaching her so much about engines when she closed the hood and stood back. The idea of a second tracking device made the most sense, so she slid under the van and searched.

She was about to give up when she found it. This time, he did a better job of hiding it. She removed it and attached it to the large metal trash bin and brushed herself off. She couldn't find the original device and figured it must have dislodged at some point, which explained why he'd put on a new one. She would no longe make finding her easy. Let him think she stayed another night.

65

Satisfied he hadn't tampered with the mechanics of the van, Maggie sagged into the driver's seat and pulled out the note. She smoothed the crumpled envelope across the steering wheel before opening it. Inside was a single sheet of paper and some petals from a black rose. She opened the door and dumped the rose petals out onto the pavement. The scent of roses engaged her gag reflex, and she rolled down the window for fresh air. She'd forever associate the sweet aroma of roses with the killer and death.

Maggie took a deep breath before she unfolded the page to read what he'd written. Her jaw sagged when she saw he hadn't written his typical one line to her, but wrote much more.

Her eyes blurred with tears and her body tensed as she read what the note said.

Hello Maggie,

I will always know where you are. You can't hide from me. I know you saw me the other night. I'd introduce myself, but then you'd chicken out and call the cops. Maybe even your boyfriend?

We can't have that now, can we? You see, I know who you are. You're the Trans-Canada Killer. Pleased to meet you. You don't know me, but you can call me Vern. That's not my real name, but I know you want to call me something.

I'm sure you're wondering why you? Quiet, simply, you pissed me off. You created notoriety with your killings, whereas I kept to the sidelines. I've been at this a long time. It satisfies a deep urge inside of me, one you're probably familiar with.

How do I know who you are? Because I saw you in Chilliwack. Then I followed you and saw you frame that other trucker. Although he wasn't innocent, but we both know he wasn't the Trans-Canada Killer. I always planned to come for you, and then you disappeared.

Imagine my surprise when I saw your picture in the papers. Then finding you was easy. Let's see if you can stop me before I kill everyone you love.

I'm coming for you.

Maggie crumpled the note and tossed it to the floor of the van and slammed her fist onto the steering wheel. How had she been so careless? The cover of darkness always served her well, but she got cocky and now her friends paid the price. She turned and looked at Edison and resolved to put an end to this.

"We have to keep moving today, boy, maybe only one or two quick stops. I want to get to Golden by nightfall. That would put us in Chilliwack tomorrow. A full day ahead of Ryan." Edison stared at her, his ears twitching. She brushed away the last of her tears and tried to smile at him, but her heart wasn't in it as she left the hotel and made her way back to the highway.

Darkness blanketed the sky when Maggie pulled into the Visitors Centre in Golden. Under different circumstances she would have gone a little further to the Husky, but she was trying to avoid truck stops for the time being. The note, which she'd folded up and put in her pocket the first time she stopped, filled her with rage and uncertainty. This combination of feelings was something she wasn't used to, and she needed more time to process them.

She took care of Edison's needs first, then she washed and changed into her PJs. When she took him out next, it would only be for a quick pee. Maggie thought about calling Audrey, but when she checked the time, she realized it was too late. She'd call her from the road tomorrow. She wanted to get her advice on the letter. Maybe she should have called Audrey today, but there was too much on her mind.

For dinner, she opted for a simple salad. She didn't have the energy to cook, pulling out the one she'd made up before leaving the hotel. Then she opened her laptop and wrote her blog. Maggie hesitated about including where she'd parked for the night, but then decided all she needed to say was Golden. She didn't have to say where in Golden.

If she was a betting woman, she'd wager 'Vern' was also heading straight to Chilliwack to finish this. So, he didn't need to know where she was. This had to end.

66

The sky was dark and angry with flashes of lightning when Maggie awoke the next morning. She checked her weather app and discovered thunderstorms were in the forecast for the rest of the day. Maggie debated staying put, but decided against it. She needed to get to Chilliwack well ahead of Ryan. No matter what, she would guard him with her life. She owed him that. He was the reason she was alive today. Maggie knew if Ryan hadn't found her when he did, she'd have died. There was no way she'd let this 'Vern' person kill him and make Krissy a widow. Even if she died in the process.

Ryan was a good man. Kind, gentle, and caring. There was no comparison between them. Her past was darker. She knew she belonged in prison for the crimes she'd committed, even if her victims deserved what they got. But not Ryan. He was nothing like her or Vern.

The highway ran beside the Visitors Centre, giving her easy access as she merged into the flow of traffic and called Audrey while she still had a cell signal.

"Good morning, Maggie. How's the drive?"

"The drive's good. I'm just leaving Golden. I'll be in Chilliwack this afternoon."

"I saw you were in Golden when your blog came out. How are *you* doing? I felt so bad for you when you told me Tammy's husband called you. Maggie, I can't believe the police gave him your name."

"I was going to call him, anyway. You knew that. His call caught me off guard, that's all, and was more difficult than I imagined it would be. It's even worse because I know she died because she was my friend."

"You can't think like that, Maggie. She died because that man is a monster."

"Speaking of him," Maggie paused, swallowing. "He left me a note when I was in Regina."

"A note! In Regina? And you're just telling me now! What did it say? How did he know where you were?"

Maggie took a breath and told Audrey what the note said. She recited it word for word, having read it so many times she'd memorized it. When she finished, Audrey remained silent.

"Audrey? Are you still there?"

"I'm here. You realize he's playing cat and mouse with you, don't you?"

"Of course, I know that. That's why I stayed at the Visitor Centre. But Audrey, he didn't leave the note on my van, he left it at the front desk of the hotel I was staying at. My view of him has changed. He can't be driving a rig, because he's keeping his own schedule following me around. A trucker couldn't do half of what he's done since I left the Rock. Not if he was driving a semi. He has to be in a four-wheeler like me. My guess would be some sort of van so he can sleep in it or a pickup with a cap on back for the same reason."

"I agree, but that also makes him more dangerous. When we

thought he was a trucker, he'd have restrictions, now he could be anywhere."

"Maybe he was a driver at some point. Those first few bouquets didn't come at regular intervals. Their arrival was sporadic and unplanned. If I was to hazard a guess, I'd say he changed his plans when he learned about my trip through my blog. That's when I'm guessing he parked his truck and started following me."

"But how are you going to find him? It's what you're planning, and don't deny it. I know you too well."

"I have to find him before he kills everyone I care about. But knowing he's not in a rig is a good thing. It would be harder to find him in a rig. But a van or pickup? That makes my job easier. If one shows up where I'm parked, I'll know. To put your mind at ease, I'm not staying at the truck stop tonight, but once Ryan is there, I will."

"Maggie, let me fly out there. If something bad happens, my medical training will come in handy."

"NO! Don't you dare come out here! I'll have enough to worry about protecting Ryan. I can't be worried about you as well."

Audrey mumbled something under her breath, which Maggie didn't catch.

"Audrey!"

"Yes?"

"Promise me."

"Ok, I promise I won't get the next flight out."

"Good! Now that we've got that settled, I'm hanging up. I'm going to lose you in the mountains. Bye Audrey."

"Stay safe Maggie."

After disconnecting the call, Maggie thought about Audrey's promise. She'd said, 'the next flight', not that she wouldn't come at all. When she stopped, she'd send Audrey a text clarifying 'No Flights'.

<h1 style="text-align:center">67</h1>

Maggie's shoulders slumped when she turned off the highway onto the exit for Chilliwack. The thunderstorm raged the whole way and every time a clap of thunder sounded, Edison shook on the floor beside her. She tried to keep the radio volume loud enough to drown it out, but he still heard it.

There was plenty of time before Ryan arrived, so she went to the Sani Dump to get rid of her waste and refill her water tank. After tonight, she'd hunt 'Vern'. In her heart, she knew he was here somewhere. Wondering how she'd protect Ryan, and for that matter, Edison without knowing what he drove. Would he park at the mall, like she planned?

She couldn't forget she still had a job to do and needed to add something new to her blog. There was a White Spot restaurant in the area. She'd go there for dinner, describe the interior and menu, and that might satisfy Ripley.

Maggie glanced out the window while getting Edison ready for a walk as the sky cleared. She let out a deep sigh. She couldn't leave him alone in the van if the storm still raged outside. No longer having to fight the rain meant they could go for a nice, long walk to wear him out. Then she wouldn't have to worry about him while she ate.

Maggie left the restaurant after dinner and drove to the Husky to check the parking lot. Her eyes scanned the area for a van or pickup, but there was no sign of one parked there. She circled the lot several times, also keeping an eye out for Big Red, her old truck, in case Ryan arrived early.

She pulled off to the edge of the lot and took some more of Noelle's ashes from the box. Noelle spent her life working this truck stop. A part of her would always belong here. The rest she'd take home and put in a small urn to protect her, something she failed to do while Noelle was alive.

Maggie picked an area by the back fence and dug a hole. She lifted the sod, loosened the soil, and dumped the ashes in the opening. Finally, replacing the piece of grass to cover it up. It didn't take long to tamp down the ground. She placed a rock overtop as a marker.

"I brought you home," Maggie whispered to the night air.

She brushed her hands off on her jeans and went back to the van for one more look around the lot for Ryan or Vern. Satisfied that neither was there, she headed back to the mall to park for the night.

The sky was a dingy grey when she got up, but rain wasn't in the forecast. Maggie headed to the laundromat to wash her clothes before it got busy. She had very little to wash, but with the limited space inside the van, she carried little with her. Edison's bedding also needed to be washed, so she'd use the big washer and throw his bed in. That way, if it didn't dry, it could air dry before he'd need it that night.

As her laundry spun in the dryer, she messaged Ryan to find out when he expected to arrive. She didn't want to be too far away in case 'Vern' was lurking, but she didn't want him to surprise her either. If she timed things right, she'd arrive at the Husky around the same time as Ryan.

<h1 style="text-align:center">68</h1>

When Audrey hung up the phone, the first thing she did was to check for a flight to Vancouver. She'd keep her promise to Maggie and didn't book the first flight out, but only because she needed time to make her travel arrangements. Audrey found a flight that left later in the afternoon and booked a rental car and a hotel. With the time difference, she'd arrive, pick up the car and head to the motel at check-in. Then she had to get to Chilliwack. Her gut told her Maggie needed her.

She couldn't tell Maggie she was coming. Maggie was stubborn and would tell her not to, but she was stubborn too, and nothing could stop her. She packed a bag and put the cats into their carriers and loaded everything into her car. She packed some cat food and their clean litter box and headed to Julie's.

Audrey knew Julie would take the cats without question. Julie did so the last time she'd gone to Maggie's rescue: the time Maggie got shot, when she was chasing down the Dark Enders. Of course, Julie now knew the truth about her trip to Nova Scotia, but it didn't matter. In the long run, she'd saved Maggie's life, and she'd do it again. Julie would assume it had something to do with Maggie, but wouldn't ask questions.

On her way to Julie's, Audrey made a side stop at the pharmacy to restock her first aid kit. She hoped she wouldn't need her medical knowledge, but this was Maggie. Nothing would stop her until 'Vern' was dead.

Audrey pulled into the compound at Julie's garage and noticed there was a new security gate and a man sitting by the trailer parked by the entrance. She wondered if it had anything to do with the killer hunting Maggie. She thought of her own extra security measures and remembered Julie telling her about someone who messed with the trucks.

Julie was walking out of the garage wiping her hands on a rag, and noticed Audrey step out of her vehicle. Julie raised her hand in greeting.

"Hi Julie. Impressive new security set up." Audrey called out.

"Ya. I had to put it in. If you remember some jackass messed with a few of the rigs. There was a time we didn't have to worry about that shit. Not here in Cobden anyway."

"Times are changing. Remember why Maggie insisted we install cameras at my place? I'm sure it was a prank, but I'm pretty remote out there, so I decided not to take any chances."

Julie nodded as she stuffed the rag into the back pocket of her coveralls. "So, what brings you out here?"

"I was chatting with Maggie today and I'm flying out to meet up with her. She seemed a little lonely." Audrey embellished. "I know where she's going to be for the next couple of days, so I booked a flight and a rental car."

"And you want me to look after Ash and Blue?"

"If you don't mind."

"You know I don't mind. Give that niece of mine a hug for me. Something's been weighing on me, but I'm not sure why. I'm getting the feeling she's in trouble. Every time I talk to her, she's found or is near a body."

"I know what you mean. That's why I'm joining her for a while. She seems to attract trouble and I'm hoping with me tagging along, she'll pick different places to hang out."

"You might be right." Julie reached into her pocket and pulled out a key ring. "Go let yourself in and get the cats situated. Not long ago, I wouldn't have locked the door to the house, especially when I'm right here." Julie finished with a shrug.

Audrey took the keys from Julie. "Thank you so much. I'll get the cats all set up, put out their food and water and beds. Do you want me to put the litter box in the same spot as last time?"

"Yes, that works. Any idea how long you're gonna be?"

"My ticket is one way. I'll see how she's doing and then book my return, or I may drop off the rental car and catch a ride back with her."

"No worries, just keep me posted."

Julie turned and went back to the shop, leaving Audrey alone to head up to the house. She let herself in and began setting up for the cats. When she'd settled them, she left the house and noticed Julie had installed a doorbell camera. She tsked to herself at how much this 'Vern' person had changed all of their lives.

69

Colby turned on the computer in his home office and waited for it to start up. A short while ago, he'd tucked Evelyn into bed and she was now sound asleep. He entered his password into the system, allowing him to access his current caseload and pulled up everything they had on what the department was now calling the Rose Petal Killer.

A detective from the last crime scene where Maggie's friend Tammy died took a picture of Maggie in the back seat of the cruiser. His guts rolled every time he looked at it. She was lucky. If she arrived at the scene a few minutes earlier, he'd be investigating her murder, too.

He'd concluded that either she was unlucky to draw so much chaos to herself or she sought it out. Colby opened the files on the other victims. JD, Tom and Josh, who all drove for the same company as Maggie had. She'd also told him she'd met the victim from Edmundston, Tucker, before he died and now her friend Tammy. Maggie either was the killer or someone was trying to hurt her by killing people she knew. In his heart, Colby knew she wasn't the killer, but based on the evidence, so far, it had to be one or the other. If someone was killing to hurt Maggie, he'd eventually come for her.

Colby thought back to the Trans-Canada Killer case. He'd been working on it the first time he met Maggie. He'd interviewed her and noticed how attractive she was, but his wife was still alive, so she was a blip in his investigation. Colby remembered being surprised when he learned she was a trucker. Her tiny stature didn't scream truck driver.

It wasn't until after The Dark Ender's murdered her husband, and he was investigating the case that he remembered her. It didn't take long before all the principal members of the gang they assumed ordered the hit died. There was nothing too unusual about that. Gang members die, but the figure fleeing one of the crime scenes looked a lot like Maggie.

Something bothered him. He couldn't quite put his finger on it, but it was a feeling. He opened all the files on all four cases. And then, on a hunch, he pulled up the case file from her attack as a child. He needed another pair of eyes on this, but he didn't want to raise suspicion with his partner.

Tomorrow he'd bring home all the print files from the cases and start at the beginning. He knew he was missing something. Somehow, they were all interconnected.

With the next few days off, Colby brought home the files to review and arranged for Evelyn to stay with his mom. Normally, he spent his off time with Evelyn, but something bothered him about the cases and their connection. Evelyn couldn't be in the house while he mapped out crime scene photographs, and he didn't want his partner looking over his shoulder.

Colby pulled out his marker board to create a timeline to see if there were any links between the cases. He started with the case of

Maggie's assault and her father's murder. It tore him apart looking at the pictures of a young, vulnerable Maggie. The injuries she sustained were horrific. His breath hitched as he read and reread the reports and made some notes on his board. He read the name of the trucker who found her, Ryan Walker. There was something about him that rang a bell. He made some more notes.

Then he opened the files for the Trans-Canada Killer case. He noticed the method of kill was the same for all the victims. The trademark hair barrette left at each crime scene. The barrette was why they'd thought it was a vigilante killer. They'd learned during the investigation that every victim had an unnatural interest in children. Discovering Frank Carter's body with all the tools of the Trans-Canada Killer in the ditch near his truck, was what lead them to believe they'd found their killer. But when he checked his notes, he found he'd interviewed Carter. His opinion that day was Carter felt more like a potential victim of the Trans-Canada Killer than the killer.

But there was Ryan Walker's name again. He remembered him. Tall and thin, a family man. He also remembered Maggie telling him she gave her truck to him. Who does that? Did she know he was the one who saved her life all those years ago? Was that why she gave him her truck? Or was there another reason?

Something about the barrettes niggled at the back of his mind. He pulled up the files of Maggie's assault. There it was. Her attacker took one of her barrettes. He made some more notes.

He was more convinced than ever that there was a connection between the two. Could it be someone who knew Maggie? Knew what happened to her and was seeking retribution? There were only two people from Maggie's life who would have the means and desire to kill pedophiles. One was Maggie's uncle, and the other was Ryan Walker. Both were truckers.

On a hunch, Colby pulled up the database and searched for crimes involving hair barrettes. The screen came alive with cases. The most recent was the Trans-Canada Killer. But then he saw a pattern form. Cases of abducted and murdered children. The connection between them was the missing hair clips. The cases were similar to Maggie's, except she survived. Of course, the man who attacked Maggie attacked others. There was no way Maggie was his only victim. Monsters like that don't stop until they're caught. Colby went to his white board and added notes regarding missing hair clips from the cold cases.

His eyes were bleary as he stared up at the board. Lines connected the mess of notes and when he ran out of room to write on the board, he began sticking sticky notes on the surrounding wall. He rubbed at his eyes and went in search of some more coffee before he continued.

Colby moved on to the shooting in Halifax that claimed Liam's life. This one was 100% bad timing and mistaken identity. There was nothing that linked it to the first two crimes other than Maggie, and he'd seen the devastation in her eyes at her loss. He moved the file aside and started on the files of the dead members of the Dark Enders. Maggie had a reason to want each of them dead, and she could have contracted a hit, but there was no way she could infiltrate a gang to seek her own redemption.

He thought some more and remembered the injury to her arm. She'd said it was from shrapnel off the road, but it looked very much like a bullet graze. Then he had a thought and flipped to the file on the warehouse shootout. The blood they found on the second floor had belonged to an unknown female. Could it be? The timeline matched, but his heart said no. Still, he could find out if there was a sample of Maggie's blood on file from her shooting and compare the two. But then what?

He flipped over the picture of the rider fleeing the scene of Butch's murder. The more he looked at it, the clearer it became. The rider was definitely a woman. It was the same make and model of motorcycle Maggie owned. He felt his palms moisten as he let the picture drop back onto the table.

Colby pulled up the pictures of the alley where they'd found Quinton Mars' body. According to the evidence, he'd been in a brutal fight. He felt Maggie was incapable of fighting Quinn. Mars outweighed her by 80 pounds. Then he remembered the call he got the next day telling him she was in the hospital. He flinched when he remembered how she looked, broken and bruised. She was a mess. Someone had given her a severe beating, too much for a mugging. It seemed personal.

He hated himself for what he was thinking. But it was where the evidence was pointing. Maggie, Ryan or Bobbie was the Trans-Canada Killer and Maggie was the one who killed the members of the Dark Enders. He'd have to send the blood samples off to the lab anonymously and see if they came back as a match. Sample A and sample B. If they matched, he'd have his answer. He prayed he was wrong. Colby shook his head with his lips pressed together as he rubbed his chin.

He felt a roll deep in his stomach. If his suspicions were correct, could he arrest the woman he loved? He'd always played by the rules, upholding the letter of the law, but this was Maggie? Should he just close the files and stop looking? He knew he still needed the answers to his questions. Colby wasn't sure what he'd do with the information, but the investigator in him couldn't leave it alone.

He was sure of one thing: she wasn't the Rose Petal Killer. She wouldn't kill her friends and they'd been together when some drivers died. If she was a killer, she was a vigilante, but that still made her a killer. The evidence suggested the Rose Killer killed his victims for sport. His hand shook when he pulled up the lab reports and saw that the blood samples from the warehouse shooting and Maggie's blood type matched. Both were AB+. Now to wait for the DNA.

<h1 style="text-align:center">70</h1>

Ryan wheeled his rig into the Husky and searched for a place to park. Immediately, he noticed how much had changed since the last time he was here with Maggie and her crew. The owners were now renting out parking spots, so truckers left their personal vehicles in the spots they paid for, limiting the spots available for drivers like him who were transient, needing a place to park for a night or two while delivering to Vancouver and the surrounding area. He understood why the owners did it, but it was still frustrating knowing how limited parking was in the area.

He spied a spot in the far back corner and reversed in. Over the last few days, Maggie had been on his mind a lot. Her call about this new killer hunting truckers bothered him. He couldn't imagine how she felt after discovering Tammy's body.

Krissy knew nothing about the serial killer which nagged at his soul. They told each other everything, but this would worry her. When he got home, he'd tell her about Maggie and the killer. He knew she read Maggie's blog, but it mentioned nothing about a serial killer, for which he was thankful.

He was in the back of his cab gathering his garbage to drop in the dumpster when a vehicle pulled up and parked in front of his truck. The headlights were on, blinding him so he couldn't make out the driver. He instinctively locked the doors and waited until the driver turned off the engine and killed the lights. At least then, he'd be able to see who it was. It bothered him knowing he didn't feel comfortable on the road anymore.

The lights went out, and he watched as the driver opened the door, setting off the interior light and allowing him to see Maggie inside. A smile split his face as he opened his door and climbed out of the cab.

"Well, you're a sight for sore eyes!" Ryan exclaimed, wrapping Maggie into a bear hug and lifting her feet off the ground.

Maggie returned the embrace. "You don't know how good it is to see you." She replied, stopping herself from adding 'alive' to her greeting.

"I was just heading up to drop my trash. Do you want to get a coffee?"

"Sure, but first I have to take Edison for a walk. Why don't you come with me?"

"Edison, eh? So, I finally get to meet your new boyfriend." Ryan teased with a nudge to her shoulder.

"When you meet him, you'll see why."

Ryan followed her around to the side of the van. He wanted to meet Edison and get a look inside to see how she'd set it up.

Maggie slid open the door and Ryan leaned forward to look, but paused when he heard the growl. He stopped dead and looked into Edison's eyes. Who stood firm, guarding the van, muscles rippling.

"Uh Maggie?"

"Edison down." Maggie commanded, and Edison immediately laid down on the floor, but kept his eyes glued to Ryan. "It's okay Edison, this is Ryan." She turned to Ryan. "Put your hand out for him to smell. You're the first male stranger he's met who's tried to get in the van."

"He won't bite?"

"No, although if he senses you mean me harm, there are no guar-antees." She laughed.

With his fingers curled down, Ryan reached his hand out to greet Edison. Edison crept closer and sniffed Ryan's hand. His tail wagged, snapping against the cabinets with a clang. Then Edison jumped up and licked Ryan's hand.

"Well, I guess he thinks you're okay. Come here, boy, let's go for a walk." Maggie held up the harness while Edison put his head through the opening and waited for her to fasten it.

"Holy cow. He just puts himself in the harness. Wow, I've never seen a dog do that before. He's a fine-looking dog, Maggie."

"Thank you. The way he greeted you put my mind at ease. Now I know he won't let a stranger inside the van or near me."

"This killer really has you worried."

"Let's take Edison for a walk. When we drop him back off at the van, then we can go grab a coffee. I have a lot to tell you."

71

The restaurant was empty when they entered, so they chose a table in the back corner. Maggie couldn't help but remember the last time she was in here. She sat at the same table, being interviewed by Colby after her last kill as the Trans-Canada Killer. So much had changed since then. Maggie positioned herself across from Ryan with her back against the bank of windows for two reasons: one, she could monitor the entrance and two, she could watch the customer parking lot in case a van or pickup truck pulled in.

With nervous energy, she told Ryan everything she knew about the killer. She started by divulging the killer was following her, leaving notes, and about him killing people she knew. Maggie watched as shock flashed across Ryan's face. She even described the blood-soaked stuffed cat at Audrey's. The only thing she left out was that she was the original Trans-Canada Killer and somehow 'Vern' knew that.

She watched the expressions crossing Ryan's face as she finished telling him what she knew. She saw how he struggled to find the words he was looking for before responding to her.

He swallowed a large gulp of coffee and then spoke.

"So, this guy is stalking you and killing people you know or interact with. Did my meeting up with you just put me in danger?"

"You were already in danger. He knows too much about my trucking days. There is no way he doesn't know you're driving, Big Red."

"Fuck Maggie. What am I supposed to do?"

"I've seen him Ryan, I know what he looks like. I figured I'd travel with you to your drops and follow you back to Ontario. My knowing what he looks like will help, and I can protect you."

"Protect me? Jesus Maggie, you're a girl, and a tiny one at that. How are you going to protect me?"

Maggie unzipped her jacket and opened it just enough for Ryan to see the butt of her gun.

"What the hell Maggie! Do you even know how to use that?"

"Shh, keep your voice down. Yes, I know how to use it. I learned after that biker gang killed Liam. I was living on my own after a vicious gun attack. It was one of the first things I did, that and learn how to fight."

Ryan ran his hand over his face. His eyes were wide. "Oh, my god. I'm shocked. What am I supposed to tell Krissy?"

"Nothing for now. This person is after me, too. I thought we could use the buddy system until you get home. We stand a better chance if there are two of us."

"And your guard dog."

"Yes, and Edison."

"I agree that there's safety in numbers, Maggie, but what's stopping this guy from killing both of us?"

"Hopefully me."

Ryan sighed as he leaned back in his chair. "What about the police? I'm sure you gave them a description and told them he was heading this way."

"Of course I did!" Maggie lied. "I just don't have faith in their abilities. Even if I'm dating one."

"All right Maggie, you win. We'll stick together. But you have to tell me what this guy looks like."

Maggie reached across the table, offering her hand for them to shake on it. Ryan took her hand.

"Okay. He's 5' 10". Average build. He appears fit, so no pot belly. The last time I saw him, he was clean shaven, but that could have changed. He has brown hair that he keeps short and he wears a ball cap."

"Maggie, that describes so many people."

"Well, if you get close enough, which I hope you don't, his eyes will give him away. They are almost yellow with gold flecks. His eyelashes are very dark, making it look like he's wearing eyeliner."

"Oh geez, so now to identify him, I'll have to get close enough to see his eyes without him killing me." Ryan threw up his hands in frustration.

"I know it's a lot for you to process. But at least you have a chance. Something Tammy, JD, and the rest didn't."

72

It was late in the day when Audrey's flight touched down in Vancouver. She was thankful she'd thought to book a room at a nearby hotel. The idea of travelling unfamiliar highways at night didn't bode well with her. There was a time, not too long ago, that it wouldn't have bothered her, but her eyesight wasn't what it used to be.

Audrey grabbed her luggage and picked up her rental car before making her way to the hotel. Check-in was easy, so she entered her room, locked the door, kicked off her shoes just as a wave of exhaustion washed over her and she collapsed onto the chair in the corner of her room.

The threat of a migraine pulsed at her temples, which she rubbed with slow, circular movements. She looked at her medical bag and searched for her medication before the headache took hold and left her writhing in pain. She rummaged around until she found the bottle.

Audrey padded in her stocking feet to the minibar and pulled out a bottle of icy cold water. She swallowed two pills and placed the cold bottle at the nape of her neck while she took long, deep breaths. She'd lay down and close her eyes for just a minute until it passed.

Audrey awoke to the sun streaking through the open window. She rubbed the sleep from her eyes, still wearing yesterday's clothing. Lying prone, the ache in her neck force her to roll it from side to side, hearing an audible crack as the vertebra aligned themselves. Putting her wrist to her eyes to check the time made them widen to discover it was a quarter to ten.

It was late, and she had to hurry to shower and be ready before checkout. She swung her legs off the bed and got moving. The suitcase was still by the door where she left it, so she put it up on the bed, pulled out her shower stuff before stripping out of her soiled clothing and folding them into her laundry bag.

Looking down while standing under the hot water allowed the jets to soothe her sore neck. Twisting and turning as the heat loosened her muscles, allowing the tension that built up over the last few days to ebb away. At least the migraine was gone. Standing in front of the mirror after drying off, she noticed the dark circles under her eyes. It could be a side effect from the migraine, but it could also be the overwhelming exhaustion that hung over her like a damp blanket. Without a sleeping pill, there were too many restless nights to count. She thought getting closure for all of Carter's victims would allow her to sleep again, but it didn't. The fear of losing Maggie was what kept her up at night.

She slipped into a pair of slacks and a blouse before drying her hair and tied to conceal the dark circles. Unfortunately, the soft lines around her eyes made her efforts collect in the folds and she ended up washing her face again and adding a good moisturizer instead.

She slid her feet into a comfortable pair of loafers and headed down to the front desk to check out. She'd missed both supper and breakfast, so she asked them to recommend somewhere she could still get breakfast. They suggested the iHop, and gave her the address, which she assured them she could find using her phone's GPS.

Audrey took her time over breakfast and searched on her phone for a hotel in Chilliwack. In the end she decided on the Hampton. It was both pet friendly and close to the truck stop. She knew Maggie would be somewhere nearby, and hoped by booking a pet friendly room with two beds, Maggie would join her and be out of this 'Vern's' range.

After she paid for her meal, Audrey went back to her rental car, got on the highway and headed to Chilliwack. When she booked her room, she'd arranged for an early check-in, because she'd arrive in Chilliwack before 2.

As she pulled off the highway, she saw the Husky and at the last minute checked the parking lot for Maggie's van. When she didn't see it, she headed straight to the hotel. She needed to organize her medical bag, so it would be easier to locate items if she needed them.

Once organized, she stared at the two scalpels she'd packed. Her friend, one who didn't ask questions, got some emergency items from the hospital for her. The suture kit, injectable numbing and antibiotics were a god send, but she wasn't sure if she needed the scalpels.

The more she thought about it, the clearer it became. If Maggie got shot, she'd need a scalpel to remove the bullet, so she'd need at least one. The other would come in handy as a weapon. It didn't occur to her to pack a knife. The scalpel wouldn't make a deep stab, but it would slice through flesh like butter. She slipped one into her jacket pocket and took the medical bag back to her car and locked it in the trunk.

With some time on her hands, Audrey pulled up the Facebook page she and Maggie created. The last time she spoke with Maggie, she said she'd mailed the final package out and the family should have it by now. Knowing the family received it would bring closure, and she wanted to check if they'd been in contact or posted anything.

The red indicator dot showing there was a private message was up at the top of the page. Both she and Maggie had access to these messages as joint administrators, so she knew Maggie hadn't been on recently. She clicked the dot and read the message from Debra.

'I want to thank you for helping my family bring closure to our loss. Wanda's death overshadowed our lives and now we know the monster responsible paid the price. You truly are angels.'

Audrey's chest swelled with the pride she felt. "It's over." She said to the air, "We found the families of all the known victims." She couldn't wait to share this news with Maggie and tried texting her again, but there was still no response, and she wrinkled her brow. Audrey would make another run through the Husky parking lot before supper and then again afterwards if she still hadn't heard from Maggie. It was unusual for her not to reply.

73

The next day, Maggie followed Ryan while he did his deliveries. He suggested she ride with him, but she wouldn't leave Edison in the van or get him up inside the truck. It felt good to make herself useful. She helped Ryan unstrap his load and strap up the return one. They chatted about a variety of things while they worked, except for the one thing that hung over both of their heads. 'Vern', or whatever his real name was. No one followed them, but she'd kept a vigilant eye out just in case.

Maggie thought long and hard about who this killer was while driving and wondered if he was a relative of one of her victims. It would explain why he was making his revenge so personal. But what she couldn't figure out was how he found her or knew of her existence. Her mind rolled with varying possibilities as she drove the highway behind Ryan. Yes, she realized he said he saw her in Chilliwack and in the paper, but that didn't give him access to her personal data. She was at a loss.

Dusk had settled around them with its hidden shadows as they pulled into the parking lot at the Husky. Ryan was lucky to get the same spot in the back corner and Maggie pulled her van up close to

282

the front bumper of his rig and as far over as possible to be out of the way of trucks as they maneuvered the lot.

The first thing she did was take Edison out for a quick pee, and then she and Ryan would to go inside the restaurant for supper. So far, there were no vehicles like what she expected 'Vern' to be driving, and allowed herself to relax as she made her way up the street with Edison.

When she returned, she saw Ryan wave to her from inside the restaurant and she cursed to herself. He was supposed to wait in the truck. She didn't worry about him because he said he would call Krissy while he waited. She slipped into a light jog and got Edison settled so she could go back and join Ryan. He was underestimating the danger they were in.

Ryan waved in greeting as Maggie entered the restaurant. His lopsided grin washed away her anger. *'One more night,'* she thought. *'Then we'll be on our way back to Ontario and I can get him home to safety.'*

"I thought you were going to wait for me?" She scolded, her face stern.

"Aw, come on Maggie. If it's safe enough for you to go out walking Edison by yourself, I think I'm okay to walk up to the restaurant."

"Do I need to remind you I'm the one with the gun?" she said, flipping her jacket open to reveal the holstered weapon.

"Sheesh Maggie, put that away. You're having a gun still freaks me out. Do you really think you'd be able to pull the trigger and kill someone?"

"If I was defending you, Edison, or myself, I'd do it in a heartbeat."

Ryan's eyes narrowed. "You've changed."

"You, of all people, know what I've been through in my life. It's hard not to change. Especially since this killer is after those closest to me. I don't have many friends left and I know the cops are looking for him, because Colby has kept up-to-date. But he's still out there and a danger to both of us."

Ryan raised his hands in the air in mock surrender. "Okay Maggie, I won't go wandering around by myself again. It's a good thing we're heading back tomorrow. The idea of you offering me protection is a blow to my ego and manhood."

Maggie leaned back and laughed. "And if you get yourself hurt, Krissy is going to do more than injure your ego." She paused and added, "Or your manhood."

Ryan rolled his eyes. "That's for sure."

Under the bright overhead lights, Maggie felt herself relax as they continued chatting while they waited for their food. Maggie heard her phone go off, and she checked the screen. It was another text from Audrey. She turned the phone over. Audrey could wait.

"Who was that?"

"Audrey."

"Okay, now I'm worried. Why are you ignoring Audrey's texts?"

"She knows what's going on and she's worried. I just don't want to talk to her right now."

"If she's worried, that's all the more reason for you to respond to her."

"Oh okay." Maggie replied in exasperation.

Maggie picked up the phone and fired off a quick text to Audrey.

> Hey sorry. I was out helping Ryan deliver today. We plan to head east in the morning. I figured if we stay together, we'll be safer.

> Ok as long as you're safe. I've been worried.

Ya, we're going to get something to eat and stick close together. I've even parked near him.

Maggie, we had a deal that you'd keep me in the loop. If I get radio silence again, I'll call the cops.

Ok, I get it. Sorry.

"Everything okay?" Ryan asked when he saw the expression on Maggie's face.

"Yup, like I said, she was just worried."

74

After supper, Ryan and Maggie returned to their respective vehicles. Maggie waited until the lights went out inside Ryan's cab before harnessing Edison to take him for a walk. She'd take her time walking along the rows of trucks, looking for 'Vern' until she felt satisfied, he wasn't there. She patted her holstered gun, unsnapped the restraining strap for easy access, and fastened her knife to her leg. Then she slipped out of her van into the night, the crescent moon high in the sky. Watching the shadows, she held Edison's leash with her left hand to keep her right hand free.

Inside his darkened cab, Ryan watched Maggie leave with Edison. She was up to something, but he didn't know what. He'd sensed something as they walked back to their vehicles. A trucker couldn't carry a weapon, but he had a sharp carving knife, which he stuck in his pocket, then climbed out of his truck and followed Maggie.

286

Meanwhile, at the Hampton, Audrey checked her watch and assumed Ryan and Maggie would be back in their vehicles. Not telling Maggie she was in Chilliwack, had served her well, but it was time to rectify that.

Audrey got into her rental and drove the short distance to the truck stop. She didn't tell Maggie she was in the area by text, figuring it was too late for Maggie to do anything if she just showed up. Maggie would be furious, but she couldn't worry about that.

Maggie took her time walking up and down the rows of trucks with Edison's lead wrapped around her wrist and her grip tight. He tugged her along, sniffing the ground. She didn't see 'Vern' or what she assumed he'd be driving, but that didn't mean he wasn't nearby. If she was 'Vern', she'd park in a neighbouring parking lot and walk over. It was easy to blend into a crowd if someone found a body.

She could tell that Edison was getting tired. She'd already made two passes through the parking lot, but something didn't feel right. Her stomach clenched as she paused and looked up along the line of trucks, deciding to make one more pass before settling in for the night. The last thing she'd do was check that Ryan locked his doors. It was the only way she'd get any sleep.

The hairs on the back of her neck prickled with the cool wind that blew against her. Edison stopped and let out a low growl. Maggie crouched down beside him, stroking his ears, and whispered, "What's wrong, boy?"

A commotion behind her drew her attention, and she spun around towards the sound. Edison lurched forward, yanking on her arm. It took everything ounce of strength to hold him. Her eyes narrowed as she struggled to determine what made the sound, then she noticed two people in the distance. Edison pulled and pulled until she had no recourse but to follow, stumbling behind him, hoping not to trip. If she let go of his leash, he'd run at full speed towards the two figures, but then he'd be in danger of being hit. She hadn't trained him to be off the leash.

When she got closer, the long and lean outline of one figure, compared to the other of average build, caused her pulse to race. She heard the tone of their angry voices, but not what they said. She pressed her lips together, holding tight to Edison's leash, unable to shake the sensations that crept up her spine. There was something about the taller man she couldn't put her finger on. A curse rang out. Followed by a struggle. Maggie saw the flash of steel as a blade swung through the air. Then the pieces fell into place as she screamed, "Ryan!" Her feet pounded against the pavement as she raced forward.

<h1 style="text-align:center">75</h1>

Ryan lost sight of Maggie. He couldn't believe how quickly she moved in the dark, even with a dog. He listened for her, but the idling engines and echoes of traffic from the highway drowned out any sound she made. She must be in another row.

The gun was a problem for him. He felt it gave her a false sense of security. Even with a gun, too many bad things could happen. They'd made a deal to stick together, and she'd broken that deal. Now he'd do what he could to look out for her. The image of her as a broken, abused child shadowed him his whole life and now the knowledge that she was that child solidified her importance to him. He'd give his life for her, but he hoped it wouldn't come to that.

Ryan listened for her footsteps, but couldn't hear anything over the rumbling of the truck engines. She was here somewhere. He just had to find her. He saw a movement across the lot and thought he saw Edison. Ryan turned to investigate, but felt a searing pain spread through his left side.

Ryan spun around just as the knife came down again, slicing across his raised forearm. He yelped in pain. His attacker raised the knife once more. This time, Ryan caught the man's wrist. The man used his free hand to dig his fingers into the wound on Ryan's side.

Ryan felt his stomach roll with the blinding pain and his knees weakened. The man sneered at him; the light catching his yellow eyes. "You can thank her for this," he said as he hooked his leg behind Ryan's and pushed him with surprising strength. Ryan stumbled backwards before losing his footing. His skull connected with the pavement with a sickening thud, his eyes rolled back as blood oozed like a halo around his head.

The killer raised his knife and paused when he heard 'Ryan!' screamed through the air. He turned and saw her running towards him. Tonight, he'd finish her. He looked at Ryan's unconscious body and the blood that seeped from the wound in his head, and decided he was as good as dead. If he wasn't, he'd finish him after he killed Maggie. As much as he'd enjoyed the hunt, it was time to end things.

Maggie's feet pounded the pavement, with Edison at her side running at full speed. Her stomach clenched when she saw Ryan go down and heard the gut-wrenching thud of his head hitting the ground. She was going to stop 'Vern' if it was the last thing she did.

She pushed forward as he turned towards her; his knife ready. Maggie fumbled with the clasp on her holster as she tried to bring out her gun. She couldn't stop. He ran towards her, instead she grabbed her knife. The old friend that had helped her right the wrongs and injustices in the world and wrapped her fist around it. Edison growled and barked at the fast-approaching man.

76

"You bastard!" Maggie screamed; her knife poised to attack. "Killer to killer. Did you see it ending this way?" He mocked.

Her throat dried as her body vibrated. Maggie pushed forward to close the distance, swinging her knife, only catching air as he stepped out of the way.

He brought his knife down, and the hand attached to Edison's leash shot up and grabbed his wrist, holding tight. He tried to shake her off. "You bitch." He hissed.

Edison broke free of Maggie's grasp and lunged at the man. Who kicked Edison, connecting with his shoulder. Edison yelped as he went over and skidded away across the pavement.

"Edison!" Maggie cried, momentarily distracted.

Her heart pounded as she swung her knife. 'Vern's' free hand took his knife from the hand Maggie restrained, and swung blindly, nicking the flesh at the swell of her breast. Blood bloomed. She cursed and kicked out at him, connecting with his shin. She swung her blade again, and this time felt it sink into his stomach.

Maggie grinned. Vern broke his hand free and his fist connected with her nose. She heard the snap as it broke. Blood trickled down her throat. Her head swung back and her vision blurred. Edison leapt at the attacker, teeth bared, snarling and barking.

The man cursed as he lost balance from Edison's sudden attack. He swung his knife, and Maggie heard Edison cry out, followed by the most pitiful howl. She swung her head to see Edison laying on the ground, blood seeped from a wound in his hip. She seethed, blood filled the back of her mouth and she spat a wad to the ground.

"Let's finish this," he said.

Maggie jabbed her knife towards him as he swung his down, sinking it in her chest. The air hissed from her punctured lung as she struggled to breathe. A look of surprise crossed her face as her knees buckled.

He pulled his knife out and pushed her to the ground with his foot. "Hey what's going on there?" Someone called out.

'Vern' looked at both bodies he'd left on the ground and knew he had to leave. Before he left, he looked down at Maggie, her mouth opened and closed as she gasped for breath, and spat on her. Then ran clutching his abdomen.

Edison whimpered and dragged himself to Maggie. He draped his body over hers, offering his protection. His head lay on her chest as he whined and barked. Maggie, through strangled breaths, brought her hand up, touched his head and choked out the words, "I'm sorry, boy."

77

Audrey pulled into the parking lot and saw Maggie's van, so she parked her car behind it. She recognized the truck in front and knew it belonged to Ryan. After getting out of the car, she tried the door to the van. Finding it locked, she banged on it.

"Maggie! It's Audrey, open up!"

Failing to get a response, an uneasy feeling trickled her spine, so she knocked on Ryan's door. There wasn't an answer there either. Whispering a silent prayer that they were together somewhere safe; she went to find them. The sound of a dog barking in the distance alerted her, and she followed it, hoping it was Edison.

A man approached her, hunched over and lurching side to side. His hands clutched his stomach. Her eyes narrowed, and she backed away. Something wasn't right. She slid her hand into her pocket and felt the scalpel. When he was closer, she called out, "Are you ok?"

The man looked up, startled, and said, "Some crazy person just attacked me and that other guy." He said, jerking his head back the way he came and continued walking. "I think I need a doctor."

293

"I'm a doctor."

Audrey paused and followed his gaze. Noticing for the first time, the two human lumps on the pavement. She squinted and made out the shape of a dog laying across one of them. Her mouth went dry and her heart pounded. Maggie! She turned back to the man.

"Why would she attack *you*?"

He paused. "Who the fuck knows? She's crazy." His eyes narrowed. "Wait, who said it was a she?"

The light caught his eyes with a glint of yellow. Audrey's jaw dropped as recognition registered. The killer had yellow eyes. Her fist tightened around the handle of the scalpel, and before she knew it, she'd pulled her hand out of her pocket, surprising him, and sliced it across his throat, feeling the splatter of warm blood as it hit her face. His eyes grew wide as both hands grasped his neck to staunch the flow of blood.

Audrey ran a hand across her face, smearing the blood as she glared at the man. Watching him drop to his knees, a look of surprise registering across his face. "Just die already!" She seethed as she turned and ran towards the two bodies on the ground.

Audrey saw one figure roll onto his knees, attempting to get to his feet. He wobbled and sank down. His focus was on the prone woman with the dog across her chest and croaked, "Maggie!" He gasped, repeated her name again, and crawled toward her.

A man ran out between two trucks and stopped dead. "Holy shit!" Several cabs lit up as truckers dragged themselves from slumber at the sound of the commotion.

Audrey got to Maggie first. Edison whimpered and looked up at Audrey with soulful eyes. She swore she could see tears in them. Audrey struggle against Edison as she tried to push him away and access Maggie's injuries, but he wouldn't budge. She turned to the man who crawled up beside her, realizing it was Ryan.

"Oh, my God Ryan? Are you hurt?"

"Yes, but take care of Maggie. I think she's worse."

"I need you to get Edison off her. He's protecting her, but I can't see the wound. There's a lot of blood. Too much."

Ryan dragged Edison off Maggie by using the harness to lift him free. Edison yelped in pain, growled and bared his teeth. Ryan looked down at the dog and noticed the knife wound on his hip. "Oh shit, that bastard got him, too." Before, he sank to the ground beside the dog.

"Keep him calm and hold him tight. We'll get help for him too."

Audrey turned to Maggie as she wheezed. A bubble of blood burst from her chest and a trickle seeped from the corner of her mouth.

"Maggie, can you hear me?"

Maggie's eyes fluttered. "It hurts!" She croaked.

"I know, honey. It's Audrey. I'm going to take care of you."

"Ryan? Edison?" Maggie rasped.

"Ryan has Edison. They'll be ok."

Maggie struggled to get up. "The killer." She wheezed.

"He's dead." Audrey replied, putting pressure on Maggie's chest.

"I'm...done...Audrey...no...more...killers." Maggie gasped for breath between each word before her eyes rolled back.

"Stay with me Maggie!"

Audrey yelled, "Help, somebody help! Call 911!" Several more bunk lights went on as a crowd formed.

"I already called. They're on their way." A man said. "What can I do?"

"Hey, there's another guy on the ground over there." Someone called out.

"Leave him." Audrey hissed. "He's the one that did this."

"Can't you help her, Audrey?" Ryan pleaded.

"It's bad Ryan, she needs a surgeon." Audrey replied, her hands pressed to Maggie's chest. "Can someone call an emergency vet? When Maggie gets better, she'll want Edison alive."

"If she survives." Someone muttered. Audrey turned and scowled at him.

In the distance, they heard the sirens. Audrey glimpsed the gun under Maggie's jacket and removed it. There was no way to get the holster off without disturbing her. Audrey looked over at Ryan, their eyes locked as she shoved the weapon into the inside pocket of her jacket. Neither was sure if the EMTs would get there in time, but they couldn't find the weapon. Audrey felt the rise and fall of Maggie's chest slow as the first responders arrived on scene. They immediately started working on Maggie as Audrey stepped back and stood beside Ryan. Shaking as the adrenalin left her body. Audrey sobbed. She looked at her bloody hands, a mixture of the killers and Maggie's, and frantically wiped them off on her trousers. Edison howled as they loaded Maggie onto the stretcher and into the back of the ambulance before it sped away.

Someone from the crowd called an emergency vet, who arrived on the scene to take care of Edison. At first, he resisted the vet, growling and snapping as she inserted a needle with a sedative, but settled as soon as the sedative took effect. One bystander helped to get him in the vet's van, and all Audrey could do was stare as it drove off.

A second set of EMTs treated Ryan before loading him into another ambulance. He had a head wound that needed stitches. It was pure luck that the stab to his side wasn't deep. But because he lost consciousness, the EMTs said he needed a head CT and be put under observation.

The police turned to Audrey and asked about Vern, who still lay on the pavement, now covered by a tarp.

"I killed him." Audrey stated.

"We all did," Ryan interjected before they closed the back of the ambulance. "He attacked us and tried to kill us. That's the guy who's been killing truck drivers."

Audrey looked up at Ryan, tears streaked the blood on her face, "Yes, we all killed him, before he could kill us." Her legs wobbled and her body shook. Audrey reached out to support herself, finding nothing close by, sank to the ground. A police officer was quick to assist her and called out to the paramedics. "This one needs the hospital, too."

78

TWO YEARS LATER

Colby rolled over and looked at the sleeping form in bed beside him. He swept an errant strand of hair from her face and placed a kiss on her brow. The television sprang to life in the living room and he realized Evelyn was awake. He wondered if he should go make her breakfast, but wrapped his arms around the waist of the woman he loved and hoped to one day marry.

She pushed back into his embrace and smiled, revealing her wakeful state.

"Playing possum?" Colby teased, kissing her behind the ear.

"No," she purred, "just looking for a few more minutes before the Saturday morning cartoons."

Colby propped himself up on one arm and looked into her emerald green eyes. His fingers made lazy circles around the scar on her chest, feeling the puckered flesh.

Her hand slid up to the nape of his neck and her fingers wove into his thick, greying hair before she pulled him to her, capturing his lips in hers, finishing with a playful nip to his bottom lip. A deep growl escaped from between his lips.

"You're starting something we don't have time to finish. If we're not careful, Evelyn will come bounding in here looking for breakfast."

The bedroom door creaked as it cracked opened, and Evelyn bounced into the room, jumped up on the bed, and positioned herself between them. Behind her, with a burst of energy, Edison followed, his wound long healed, as he went to Maggie's side of the bed and placed his paw up on the edge, indicating he wanted to go out.

"Okay you two, let us get dressed and we'll be there in a minute." Maggie mumbled. "Evelyn, can you open the back door and let Edison out, please?"

"Okay Maggie. Come on dad, I want pancakes this morning."

"I told you there wasn't time for shenanigans this morning, Mr. Tate."

"Okay, okay, let's get up before they come back." He smiled, playfully smacking her bottom.

After the attack in Chilliwack, it was a miracle that everyone survived. The police investigated and concluded they'd killed the man who called himself 'Vern' in self-defence. The investigation revealed that his real name was Marcus Carter, and he was a distant relative of Frank Carter's. In his vehicle, which was a pickup with a cap on the back, they found enough evidence to link him to the murders of the truck drivers.

At the scene, Audrey had collapsed in exhaustion, but as soon as she recovered, she divided her time between the bedsides of both Ryan and Maggie. At least, until Krissy showed up to be with Ryan.

Krissy flew in as soon as she heard what happened, against Ryan's wishes, but her being there was the tonic that helped him regain his strength. The knife wound to his side wasn't deep, but still needed ten stitches to close up and a few more to the slice on his arm. His head wound was another matter. He had a small brain bleed, and the doctors thought the best course was to drill a borehole and attach a drainage bag until it cleared. Krissy stayed until the hospital felt he was fit for travel. She chose not to fly home, but to travel back with Ryan in the truck. Big Red was still in the parking lot in Chilliwack. At Krissy's insistence, he took his time heading east and home.

Edison had some scrapes and bruising which were minor and the vet sutured the wound on his hip. When the vet was sure the risk of infection had passed, she called Audrey to say he could go home. She picked him up and brought him back to the hotel to recover under her care while they waited for Maggie to be released. During this time, Audrey returned the rental car and drove Maggie's sprinter van. Having it, allowed her to take Edison with her to the hospital, knowing he was safe in the climate-controlled van in his familiar surroundings, plus she wasn't far away when he needed to go out on his walks. He was a handful, and she felt happy that she still had the strength to handle him.

Maggie suffered the worst injuries. She underwent immediate surgery to repair the damage inflicted by Marcus Carter. The injuries were life threatening, and it was touch and go for a while, but Maggie was a fighter and pulled through. Audrey believed the turning point was when she snuck Edison in to see Maggie, because it wasn't long after that she improved.

When the hospital released Maggie, she and Audrey drove back to Cobden with Maggie as a passenger. Because Maggie had the front passenger seat removed to make room for Edison's crate, Maggie had to sit in the dinette using the seatbelts she'd installed for Edison.

Maggie remained in Cobden until she was well enough to make the drive back to Nova Scotia on her own. She continued writing her blog, posting when she was well enough, describing the events that led to her hospital stay and her recovery. Writing about the attack was difficult. It was personal and left her feeling exposed.

She spoke with Ripley and told him she was coming off the road. It had proven too dangerous. For the time being, she could write stories for her blog about her trucking days, but she planned to finish the novel she started. They would reevaluate her work when she fully recovered.

During her convalescence, Colby called daily to check on her. When she finally returned, Colby noticed a unique energy about her and felt elated over her choice to give up her life on the road to write a book. The experience blurred the tough edges that surrounded her. He guessed almost dying one too many times might have something to do with it. Colby wanted to talk to her about what he learned during his investigation, but changed his mind. He knew if he asked her about it, she'd be honest, and he really didn't want to hear the truth from her lips.

It wasn't long before Colby asked her to move in and she accepted, even listing the house she'd shared with Liam. Eventually, they'd sell his house too and find a place that would be theirs, but for now, they didn't want to upset Evelyn's life more than necessary.

On the night Maggie agreed to move in with him, Colby went

home and removed some files from his desk. He took them out to the backyard and dumped them inside a metal garbage can. Then poured lighter fluid on top of the pages to ensure they'd burn and held up the DNA match and lit the pages before dropping them into the can, watching it erupt in flames.

After Colby left the room, Maggie sat on the edge of the bed as the aroma of pancakes drifted through the air. Colby was busy making breakfast and she could hear him talking to Evelyn. She slid the bottom draw of her bedside table out and removed her belongings. Her eyes never left the door. Once the drawer was empty, she found the clasp for the false bottom she'd installed. Hidden beneath it was her gun safe.

She ran her fingers over the safe containing her gun and hunting knife before putting the false bottom back in place and returning everything to the drawer. The urge to look for trouble left her in the parking lot in Chilliwack, but if trouble came looking for her, she'd be waiting.

Acknowledgments

Like all authors, I spend a lot of time alone in my head. I dream in colour and often come up with solutions for my characters while I sleep. Noelle's death in book two happened because of a dream.

Although writing is a solitary pursuit, I don't do it alone. I have a wonderful network of family and friends that I can lean upon when I'm struggling with a concept or an idea.

My husband Steve, for example, is my biggest supporter. We spend hours talking about my characters, ideas and thoughts and he offers feedback on book titles, cover blurbs and a variety of other topics. He hasn't complained so far. I'll just keep my fingers crossed.

My mother is another member of my support system. She is the first person to read my manuscripts. The teacher in her automatically pulls out the red pen to mark punctuation and glaring typos. Of course, when she reads it, it's only a first draft. I go back to the book many times and continue to fill in plot holes and overused expressions and words. I try to let her reread the final draft.

My beta readers have been a big help in completing my novels. Beta readers are the next step in my finished novel. A beta reader notices things I can no longer see, such as a character wearing a dress in one scene and jeans in the next, without a reason to change. But I have been lucky with my beta readers, especially Laima, who read Restitution. She pointed out errors and overused words, and made suggestions by telling me how the characters made her feel. This helped me make my story more engaging for the reader.

I also get a lot of support from my writing group, Author's Ink. I rarely read from my manuscript during our meetings, but I discuss areas I'm having trouble with, and I will read things I want feedback on. One thing this group offers me is the solidarity, which I get by being surrounded by like-minded people who are creative and talented. I come out of our meetings inspired.

I dedicated this book to my children. They have grown into wonderful adults that I'm very proud of. Raising them was pure joy.

About the Author

J. E. Friend is an author of crime thrillers. She lives in the beautiful Annapolis Valley, Nova Scotia, with her husband Steve and their dog, Hartley. There she enjoys the peace and solitude offered in order to immerse herself in her writing, whether she chooses to write in her writing room or out on the deck in their little piece of paradise. She has a Bachelor's Degree from Waterloo, where her field of study was psychology. This enables her to delve into the mindset of her killers.

She is a member of Author's Ink, a writing group in Nova Scotia, consisting of published and non-published authors, and for the past few years, she has also been The Municipal Liaison for NaNoWriMo (National Novel Writing Month) for her geographical area. NaNoWriMo promotes writers with an annual challenge to write 50,000 words in November, which she has won each year since 2017. She is an active member of the Writer's Federation of Nova Scotia, where she has reviewed and short-listed emerging authors in several competitions.

Design of Deception was her debut novel, released in 2020. Her second book, Redemption, the first in the Trans-Canada Killer Series, released in 2022. Retribution was the second in the series and was released in 2023. Restitution is the final book in the series. She is currently working on her next book, a stand alone.

You can find her books under J.E. Friend on Amazon for print and kindle, Barnes & Noble for nook and print copies. On Indigo/Chapters for print and kobo, by typing in the name of the book and J E Friend.

This is our boy Hartley, who is the inspiration for Edison.

Design of Deception is my first novel, published in 2020 as a stand alone.

*Redemption is Book 1 in the Trans-Canada Killer Series,
published in 2022.*

Retribution is book 2 in the Trans-Canada Killer Series, published in 2023.